hunt me darling

Maree Rose

hunt me darling

by Maree Rose

First Edition: August 2023

Published by Maree Rose

Cover Art by Temptation Creations

Blurb

FBI forensic profiler Agent Alexandra Darling is known for her unsettling affinity for murderers and their victims.

As she joins a task force assigned to capture a notorious duo of killers, her forbidden fascination with the twisted motivations behind their crimes takes a dangerous turn.

Delving deep into the darkness, she finds herself entangled in a dangerous game that blurs the lines between hunter and hunted, love and obsession. One that would forever redefine her understanding of desire, and the depths of her own soul.

She quickly learns nothing is what it seems. Alexandra's journey will test the limits of her sanity at the same time as it challenges her perceptions of justice.

Will she be just another victim? Or do they have something different in mind for their little Darling?

Foreword

Hello readers!

Thank you so much for choosing up my book!

Please be aware that this book is a MFM romance, meaning our leading lady Alex will not have to choose between her men, because #whychoose.

Warning, this book is a dark contemporary romance. It contains very explicit 18+ dark, sexual content, and straight-up smut.

The male leads are not prince charming, they are the opposite with psycho tendencies and therefore there is stalking, obsessive and possessive behavior, unaliving people, and lots of dark and twisted content. All the characters are 18+

Proceed at your own risk, if you dare

Thank you and I hope that you enjoy hunt me darling.

Content Warnings

If you don't have any triggers and feel like taking a gamble on the content then just skip the next page completely.

For those who do need to check the warnings then they are listed on the next page for your reference.

Warnings

I know we all love a shopping list of warnings so here is the one for hunt me darling:

- Mask Play
- Knife Play
- Blood Play
- Primal Play
- Stalking
- Bondage
- Dubcon
- Violence
- BC Tampering
- Somnophilia
- Sexual Asphyxiation
- Serial Unalivers
- Mentions of past child neglect
- Mentions of past drug use (not main characters)
- Detailed on page murder
- Detailed on page death of a parent

Apologies if I missed any, please reach out to me on social media if that is the case.

Playlist

I know how much you all love a
good playlist to set the mood…

For your listening pleasure:

https://tinyurl.com/huntmedarling

PLAYLIST

"Every Breath You Take" – Chase Holfelder
"Villains Aren't Born (They're Made)" – PEGGY
"Middle Of The Night" – Elley Duhé
"Bad Dreams – Stripped" – Faouzia
"Monsters" – Ruelle
"Kiss or Kill" – Stela Cole
"I'm Gonna Show You Crazy" – Bebe Rexha
"Do It Like A Girl" – Morgan St. Jean
"Ghost" – Natasha Blume
"Find You" – Ruelle
"Crazy" – ADONA, Seibold

"Wicked as They Come" – CRMNL
"Deep End" – Ruelle
"RABBIT HOLE" – AViVA
"My Heart's Grave" – Faouzia
"How Villains Are Made" – Madalen Duke
"Into the Woods" – PHILDEL
"Down" – Simon, Trella
"Who Are You" – SVRCINA
"Can't Help Falling In Love – Dark" – Tommee Profitt
"Man or a Monster" – Sam Tinnesz, Zayde Wolf
"Look What You Made Me Do" – Kurt Hugo Schneider, Kirsten Collins
"I'm Not Afraid" – Tommee Profitt, Wondra
"Never Surrender" – Liv Ash
"The Devil Within" – Digital Daggers
"Vendetta" – UNSECRET, Krigaré
"Good to Be Bad" – CRMNL
"Villain" – CRMNL
"Paint It, Black" – Ciara
"MONSTER" – Chandler Leighton
"Cruel" – The EverLove
"Smother Me" – Kelaska
"I Get Off" – Halestorm
"Hide and Seek" – Klergy, Mindy Jones

For those who grew up wanting to play all the dirty games...
Well, how about the dirtiest game of Truth or Dare you hopefully won't regret...

Prologue

The dimly lit room envelops me as I stand in silence, surrounded by the haunting echoes of my thoughts. The photographs of crime scenes, the sketches of disturbed minds, and the meticulous case files line the walls, forming a macabre tapestry of human darkness. This is my sanctuary, the place where I can surrender to my most forbidden fascinations.

I am Agent Alexandra Darling, an FBI forensic profiler with an unsettling affinity for murderers and their victims. It's a predilection that sets me apart from my colleagues, an illicit fascination that courses through my veins. While others shy away from the horrors that plague our society, I find myself inexplicably drawn to the twisted motivations that drive individuals to commit unspeakable acts.

News of my unconventional skills had spread throughout the Bureau, leading me to this moment. I am on the verge of joining an established FBI team assigned to track down a notorious duo of murderers, who have been terrorizing women in the city. The brutality of their crimes sent shockwaves through the media, their actions leaving behind shattered lives and unanswered questions. And I, with my peculiar desires, feel an exhilarating anticipation at the prospect of joining the hunt.

As I delve into the evidence, examining each crime scene with meticulous detail, a thrill courses through me. The victims had been stalked, their lives invaded before being ruthlessly extinguished. And it is with this realization that an unexpected allure begins to take hold of me. The thought of being stalked myself, of being intimately observed by someone consumed by obsession, stirs a strange arousal deep within.

While my colleagues see the victims as tragic figures, I can't help but see them as something more—a tapestry of vulnerability and power. They became muses, their suffering igniting a fire within me, propelling me to unravel the twisted minds of their killers and to unmask the hidden truths of their desires. It is a dangerous dance between empathy and attraction, a blurred line that I walk like a high wire.

Within the confines of my office, the walls bear witness to my fixation. Photographs of the dead adorn the space, their faces etched into my mind, their voices haunting my dreams. It is a shrine of sorts, a testament to my commitment to their memory. But it is also a reflection of the darkness that dances within me, the magnetic pull that draws me towards these murderers and their chilling artistry.

Little did I know, as I prepared to join the team in pursuit of these serial killers, that this assignment would test the limits of my forbidden desires. The seductive allure of their actions would entwine itself around my very being, unraveling the threads of my sanity and challenging my perceptions of justice and love.

In the heart of the darkness, where the line between hunter and hunted becomes blurred, I would find myself entangled in a perilous dance—one that would forever redefine my understanding of desire, fulfillment, and the depths of my own soul.

Chapter 1

Alex

The morning sun casts a golden glow through the dense forest as I step out of the car, the crunch of leaves beneath my boots. The scene before me is both familiar and alien, a paradox that seems to accompany every investigation. Police officers and forensic technicians swarm the area like insects moving over flesh that is already decaying. But I knew it wouldn't be, the murderers never let it go undiscovered for long.

The few media personnel who already heard about the case and appeared like scavengers are being held back by hastily erected barricades and a few uniformed police.

The lifeless form lay at the center of the chaos, a new addition to the gallery of horrors I had come to know so well. Her body, posed and marked, bears the unmistakable signature of the murderers I had been called upon to hunt. I observe from a distance, taking in the movement of investigators, the variety of emotions painted across their faces—a cocktail of shock, disgust, and grim determination.

I arrived on the scene unannounced, a phantom observer amidst the commotion. The team members, easily identified in their plain clothes, move around with a sense of purpose, their focused gazes dissecting the crime scene. But one man catches my attention—an impeccably dressed attractive figure, exuding an aura of confidence amidst the chaos.

He stands near the body, studying it with a furrowed brow, his piercing blue eyes betraying the weight of the horrors he has witnessed. His straight black hair is cut close to the sides of his head, but the top is left long enough to allow it to fall across his forehead as he looks down at the victim on the ground. His sharp jawline is covered in black stubble that only frames his handsome face. As I approach, his gaze meets mine, and a hint of intrigue flickers in his eyes.

He moves to intercept me, striding towards me with a confidence that speaks to his reputation. I know who he is, I had only recently studied his photograph and all the information I could find on him. The same as I did for the rest of the team I am joining. Agent Derek Matthews. I watch as his sharp blue eyes travel down the length of my body and back up as he approaches, a small smirk pulling at his lips. "And you are?" he inquires, his voice laced with a subtle curiosity.

"Unimpressed," I reply, my tone indifferent. But inwardly, I can't deny the flicker of admiration and attraction within me. Derek is already known as an exceptional FBI agent, his track record marked by a series of high-profile cases that earned him both accolades and a legion of admirers. The fact that he is extremely good looking just adds to his qualities.

In truth, the depths of my fascination with the darkness that plagues our society led me to delve into the records of the Bureau's most notorious cases in recent years, where Derek's name surfaced time and time again. I am aware of the aura that surrounds him, the whispered stories of his unwavering resolve and innate ability to understand the minds of those he pursued. It was a reputation that left an undeniable impression.

As Derek takes a step closer, his eyes narrow slightly, studying me intently. "You must be the new addition to our team," he remarks, a hint of amusement touching his words. "Agent Alexandra Darling, the profiler with a penchant for the macabre."

I raise an eyebrow, impressed by his knowledge. "You've done your homework, Agent Matthews."

He offers a half-smile, the corners of his mouth curling in a way that sends an unexpected shiver down my spine. "Only the essentials," he replies, his voice tinged with a magnetic charm. "But I have a feeling there's more to you than what's written in the reports."

I allow a ghost of a smile to grace my lips, relishing in the subtle play of veiled truths we are beginning to play. "The same could be said for you, Agent Matthews. Rumor has it that you possess an uncanny ability to understand the minds of murderers."

Derek's gaze locks with mine, the intensity of his scrutiny revealing a hint of the darkness he has faced. "Sometimes the darkness calls to us," he murmurs, his voice carrying a weight that resonated within me. "And it takes a certain kind of person to answer."

The words hang in the air, full of unspoken understanding. In that moment, I realize that Derek and I share a similarity beyond our chosen profession. We were both drawn to the abyss, the forbidden allure of the human psyche.

Moments later Special Agent in Charge James Bennett emerges from the shadowy outskirts of the crime scene and approaches us. I trained under his guidance at Quantico, and his arrival brings a sense of comfort amid the unknown. His short wavy hair and beard had become more salt and pepper since last I saw him and his brown eyes more hardened.

"Alexandra, glad you could make it," James says with a nod, his voice resonating with the commanding authority that had earned him his position.

"Thank you, sir," I reply, offering a small smile. "I'm ready to assist in any way I can."

He regards me for a moment, his gaze assessing. "I have no doubt about that, Agent Darling. Your reputation precedes you nowadays. But I must warn you, this case will test even the strongest of minds. Are you prepared for what lies ahead?"

A flicker of anticipation ignites as I reply, "As you know, I've spent my life preparing for a case like this, sir."

James' expression softens, a glimmer of understanding reflected in his eyes. "Then welcome to the team, Alex. Let's bring these culprits to justice and find some solace for the souls they've taken."

James turns his attention to the rest of the team. "Listen up, everyone," he calls out, his voice cutting through the background noise. He waits for the last two members of the team to join us and huddle closer before continuing. "This is Agent Alexandra Darling, our newest profiler. She brings a unique perspective and expertise to the table. I expect all of you to extend to her the same level of respect and cooperation you would to any other member of our team."

They nod in acknowledgement, their focus shifting towards me. I can see a mixture of curiosity and anticipation on their faces, as if they are eager to see how I would fit into the dynamics of the group. I already know who each of them are from studying their files and images when I was requested for the team. They are good agents and I know we would work well together.

James continues, "Each of you has been handpicked for this task force because of your exceptional skills and dedication to justice.

Together, we will solve this case and put an end to the reign of these serial killers. We won't let them claim any more victims."

The weight of James' words hang in the air, reminding us of the grave responsibility we carry. We were tasked with bringing justice to those who had fallen victim to unspeakable crimes, and we were determined to see it through.

His eyes scan each member of the team with a sharp gaze. "We've seen the work of these murderers before," he begins. "They're methodical, calculating, and leave behind a trail of psychological torment. But we won't let them continue."

With a renewed sense of purpose, the team members gather closer, their eyes fixed on James as he outlines the preliminary plan. I listen intently, absorbing the details of the case and the strategy we would employ to catch the killers.

"Emma, I want you to gather every piece of evidence from this scene. We need to examine it meticulously for any trace that could lead us to the perpetrators," James instructs, turning to our forensic expert.

Agent Emma Richards nods, her focus unwavering. She looks exactly like the file image of her: short straight dark blond hair cut in a sharp angle to frame her face and her brown eyes looked like they had seen too much death. "Understood, sir. I'll make sure to document every detail and process the evidence as soon as possible."

James then turns his attention to Agent Michael Peters. "Michael, I want you to dig deep into the local community, talk to witnesses, and follow any leads that could provide valuable information. We need to understand the context and potential motives behind these killings."

Michael's blue eyes sparkle with determination. His brown hair is military short, but I know that was because he spent years in the Army before joining the Bureau and some habits were hard to change. His army photo did not do him justice. "Consider it done, sir. I'll gather every bit of intel I can find and start building a comprehensive picture of what we're dealing with."

Finally, James turns his gaze towards Derek and me. "Derek, I want you to work closely with Alex. Use her profiling skills to our advantage. Together, I expect you to penetrate the minds of these psychos and uncover their darkest secrets. Begin constructing the profiles of them based on the evidence and the patterns we've seen so far. We need to understand their psychological makeup and anticipate their next move."

Derek and I exchange a knowing glance, a silent agreement that we would push each other to unravel the twisted labyrinth of the murderers minds. "We'll get to the bottom of it, sir," Derek affirms confidently.

James looks at me, his eyes filled with a blend of expectation and concern. "Alex, you've earned a reputation as one of the best profilers in the field. I need you to dive deep, trust your instincts, and uncover the truth."

A surge of determination courses through me as I meet James' gaze. "I won't let you down, sir. I'm prepared for the challenge, and I'll give everything I have to bring justice to the victims."

James nods, a flicker of pride crossing his features. "I know you will, Alex," he says before turning and walking away.

As the team disperses to their respective tasks, Derek lingers by my side.

"I've heard about your uncanny ability to unravel the darkest recesses of a killer's mind," I admit, genuine curiosity evident in my voice. "Care to share any insights on this case?"

Derek looks back at the body with a frown. "We're dealing with a pair of highly organized and meticulous killers. The only reason we even know there are two of them is because of a few minor details on the stalking reports," he explains, his voice tinged with somberness. "The reports indicate a pattern of control and manipulation, as if they derive pleasure from exerting power over their victims. We'll need to delve deep into their psyche to understand their motivations."

I nod, absorbing his words. It is clear that this case will require us to dig beneath the surface, to uncover the twisted minds behind these heinous acts. I feel a surge of excitement, eager to contribute my own insights.

As Derek and I continue our conversation, we begin to exchange theories and observations about the case. It becomes apparent that our perspectives align in many ways, as if we are two pieces of a puzzle that fit together seamlessly.

"There's a calculated precision to their actions," I note, my voice laden with a mix of intrigue and concern. "It's as if they're playing a deadly game with their victims, leaving behind clues and symbols for us to decipher."

Derek nods, his gaze fixed on the crime scene. "Exactly. They want to taunt us, to challenge our abilities. It's a power play—a sick display of their dominance and intelligence."

I considered his words. "But why? What drives them to commit these acts? Is it a thirst for power, or a need for control?"

Derek's eyes darken slightly, his voice tinged with melancholy. "It could be a multitude of factors—past traumas, a desire for notoriety, or even a distorted sense of morality. To truly understand, we'll have to delve into their histories, their past experiences. But to do that we would need to know who they are."

Derek's words hang in the air, emphasizing the crucial missing piece of the puzzle—the identity of the murderers. Without knowing who they are, understanding their motivations and unraveling their histories would prove to be a formidable challenge.

I turn my gaze toward the lifeless body, a chilling reminder of the victims who had already fallen prey to them. The crime scene holds the key to unlocking the secrets that lay hidden within the minds of the killers. It's up to us to interpret the cryptic messages they left behind.

Chapter 2

Alex

There are crime scene photographs now covering a new murder board. Though technically it's meant to be called an evidence board, its true focus is undeniably the murder.

Most of the team returned to the office after concluding our work in the field, eager to dive into the extensive collection of evidence. Setting up the new board became our priority upon arrival, seamlessly joining the seven other boards that adorn the room. Each one is meticulously covered with photographs and intimate details of the previous victims. As I observe the array of boards, it faintly reminds me of the sanctuary I hastily established in my rental house the day before, though devoid of the fresh crime scene that now consumes my attention.

I'm not sure if it was pure fate or coincidence that landed a fresh body in our laps the morning after I moved here to join the investigation.

Contemplating the photographs that cover the new board, it strikes me as a macabre work of art, a piece to be both admired and analyzed. My gaze hungrily devours every tiny detail, trying to absorb the essence of the crime captured within the frames. Lost in my study of the images, I am completely unaware of Derek's presence until he speaks, his voice cutting through my concentration.

"What do you see when you look at those?" Derek's tone holds a mixture of fascination and intrigue, leaving me uncertain whether it is directed at me or the crime scene itself.

Glancing at him out of the corner of my eye, I realize his attention is not fixed on the photographs but rather on me. I take a moment to collect my thoughts before responding. "I don't see the full picture," I admit, my words laced with a tinge of frustration at the elusive nature of the truth.

Derek shakes his head slightly, indicating his disappointment with my answer. "That wasn't what I asked," he says firmly, his gaze unwavering. His thirst for understanding urges me to delve deeper, to uncover the hidden layers of the crime scene that lay beneath the surface.

I concentrate back on the images, the scene, the body, the marks and cuts decorating it like it is a piece of art. "They didn't spend as much time with this one."

He tilts his head, his attention going between me and the board. "I'm assuming you're not just basing that on the time between kills?"

My head also tilts in contemplation, thoughts going through my mind as I take a longer look at the images. "No."

He huffs quietly and I drag my attention back away from the images and glance at him. His attention is completely on me with a raised brow. I feel my lips twitch in response to the annoyance I see on his face. I'm not being obtuse, it is just fun to play with him.

Looking back to the images, I reach out and softly slide my finger down one of the images of the victim's body. I can see him following the movement out of the corner of my eye. "They didn't mark her as much, and the healing had barely begun. They killed her pretty quickly."

His focus is now back on the crime scene images with a frown and narrowed eyes. Maybe he hadn't noticed that before.

I let my fingers slide back off the photograph and step back, looking around at the other murder boards around the room. I had already studied all of these images in my sanctuary, I knew every little detail of every scene.

"There is no set time frame or schedule for them, they kill randomly. You can see by looking closely at the bodies that the amount of time varies a lot across all the victims. They spent a lot of time with some of them but about half of them were killed after only a matter of days," I muse as I focus on each victim. "So why were those ones different? Why did they kill them quicker?"

Derek's eyes narrow as he absorbs my observations, I could see his mind working on the puzzle laid out in front of him. He looks a bit frustrated, like he is trying to connect the dots.

"Right," he murmurs, his voice filled with curiosity. "There's gotta be a reason why they varied the time between kills. Maybe it's related to their state of mind or something about the women themselves."

I continue studying the photographs, searching for any other patterns or clues that might help us understand the motives. Each victim holds a piece of the puzzle, and I am determined to find it.

His words send a chill down my spine. "So you think they have some specific reason for choosing their victims? Or for when they kill them?"

He gives a shrug as he returns his attention to the latest victim, his own fingers following the path that mine had taken on one of the images. "Maybe they choose them thinking they can provide something for them or fill a role in their lives. Then their time frame depends on when they realize she won't provide that. It could be a reflection of their disappointment."

I nod, captivated by Derek's theory. It makes sense in a twisted way, the idea that they had expectations or desires from their victims, and when those expectations were shattered, they swiftly ended their lives.

"But how do they determine if a victim can fulfill their expectations?" I muse aloud, my eyes scanning the photographs once again, searching for any clues that might shed light on their selection process.

Derek's gaze lingers on the images, his brow furrowed in deep contemplation. "Perhaps there are subtle signs, details in their lives or behaviors that they pick up on. They might be looking for specific traits or qualities that indicate a potential match."

His words spark a realization within me. "It could explain why some victims receive more attention and time. They become more invested, hoping they've finally found someone who meets their criteria. And when they realize the victim doesn't fulfill their expectations, they discard them quickly."

He blinks rapidly and looks at me as though just waking from a trance. "Exactly," he murmurs almost absentmindedly. "They're searching for a connection, a bond that they believe will bring them fulfillment. And when that bond doesn't materialize, they move on, searching for the next potential match."

The realization sends a shiver down my spine, the psychology behind the killers' motives becoming clearer with each passing moment. It is a chilling reminder of the darkness that lurked within the human psyche, the depths of which we were now tasked with exploring.

As Derek and I stand there, surrounded by the haunting images of the victims, my mind races with possibilities. I know that understanding the motives behind the varying timeframes and victim selection would be key to catching them. But it is a complex puzzle, one that requires careful analysis and a deep dive into the darkest recesses of the human mind.

"We need to look beyond the surface," I say, breaking the silence that had settled between us. "There must be something that ties these victims together, something they see in them that we haven't yet discovered."

Derek nods, his eyes still focused on the photographs. "Let's revisit the backgrounds of each victim, their personal lives, their relationships. There might be a common thread, a hidden connection that they are fixated on."

I turn my attention back to the boards, the photographs staring back at me with solemn faces. Each victim had a story, a life cut short, and I felt a deep sense of responsibility to uncover the truth and bring justice to their memories.

"We also need to consider the psychology of the murderers," I suggest, my voice filled with conviction. "What drives them to seek this twisted fulfillment? What void are they trying to fill through their victims?"

Derek's gaze meets mine, his blue eyes holding emotions I can't decipher. "We can't forget that behind every act, there's a person. A person whose mind we need to understand."

I nod in agreement, we can't afford to lose sight of the fact that our investigation is not just about solving a puzzle, but also about unraveling the motives and intricate workings of the minds behind the murders.

"Exactly," I reply.

Derek's gaze holds mine for a moment longer before his lips pull into a slight smile. "We make a good team," he says.

I return the smile, appreciating the partnership that had formed between us in such a short time. "We do," I agree. "Together, we'll find the answers we're searching for and put an end to this."

"Oh, I'm positive we will," Derek replies, his smile widening. There is determination in his eyes, like a shared resolve that we would not rest until we unraveled the twisted motives behind these killings and brought the perpetrators to justice. We were ready to embark on this dark journey together, drawing strength from each other as we delved deeper into the darkness that lay before us.

I look around at the boards again, taking in the various images of the different crime scenes. "Let's have a look at each of the victims again, see if we can find out why they spent more time with some and not with others."

Derek and I began the meticulous process of revisiting each victim's background, their personal lives, and their relationships. We examine every available piece of information, from their social media accounts to their past interactions with others. We sought to uncover any hidden connections or patterns that might shed light on the killers' motives.

As we delve into the victims' lives, I see a disturbing pattern start to emerge. The victims who had been killed quickly, without much investment of time, had one thing in common: they had confided in close friends about being stalked. The chilling realization sends a shiver down my spine.

"It seems that the victims who reported being stalked were disposed of more swiftly," I point out to Derek, my voice filled with concern. "On the other hand, the victims who lived longer never disclosed their experiences of being stalked to anyone. The only reason we even know about it is that there were subtle clues in the evidence."

Derek's brow furrows as he processes the information. "So, reporting the stalking seems to be a trigger for them. They eliminate those who have reached out for help or sought protection?"

I nod, the pieces of the puzzle starting to fit together. "It's as if the murderers see reporting the stalking as a betrayal or a threat to their power and control. They want their victims to remain isolated and helpless, without any external support."

Derek leans over the table we are working at, studying the photographs of the victims. "But how do they know which victims have reported the stalking? Is there some way they're able to track this information?"

My mind races, searching for possible explanations. "It could be that they have a way of keeping an eye on their communications. Perhaps they're technologically skilled or have access to personal information that allows them to identify those who have spoken out about the stalking."

Derek's eyes remain thoughtful as he contemplates the possibility. "They may have some sort of surveillance or access to the victims' personal devices or accounts. It would explain how they stay one step ahead."

After hours of intense brainstorming and investigation, we decide to focus on the technology angle. Maybe they are tech-savvy or have access to some surveillance techniques to keep tabs on their victims. We reach out to our tech experts within the team and ask them to dig through the victims' digital footprints for any signs of unauthorized access or out of the ordinary monitoring.

At the same time, we dive deeper into the backgrounds of each victim, searching for potential connections beyond the stalking aspect. We look into their workplaces, social circles, and any common events they might have attended. We even analyze their habits, hoping to spot patterns that could give us a clue about how the killers are selecting their targets.

But exhaustion is starting to take its toll, and Derek glances at his watch. "Hey, it's almost midnight," he says, sounding concerned. "You've been at it since early morning, and you seriously need some rest. We'll pick this up fresh in the morning."

Suppressing a yawn, I realize just how tired I am. "You're right. I won't be any good if I'm running on empty," I admit reluctantly. "But we can't afford to waste time. They may already be looking at their next victim."

He hums in response. "But you won't solve anything if you miss important details because you're too tired. You'll be more effective after some shut-eye," he assures me.

I can't argue with his logic, even though the urgency of the case weighs heavily on my mind. "Alright," I finally relent with a nod. "But promise me we'll hit the ground running tomorrow. There's so much more to uncover."

Derek smiles almost affectionately. "Absolutely. We'll pick up where we left off and keep pushing forward. We're on the right track, and I have a feeling we're getting closer to understanding them."

Chapter 3
Alex

I gratefully accept an offer from Derek to walk me to my car. "Do you find it strange that I joined the investigative team and then immediately got a fresh case?" I inquire curiously as we stand in the elevator to go to the parking garage.

Derek chuckles, his shoulders relaxing a bit and a smile tugging at his lips. "Well, it's not every day we have a new team member arrive and immediately get a front-row seat to a new body. It's almost like they were giving you a welcome present."

I smile, appreciating his sense of humor amidst the gravity of our situation. "I guess fate has a way of putting us exactly where we need to be, even if it seems coincidental."

He nods, his expression thoughtful. "It does make you wonder, though. Sometimes life has a funny way of intertwining paths and bringing people together at just the right moment."

I lean against the wall of the elevator. "I've always believed that everything happens for a reason, even if we can't always see it right away. Maybe my arrival here was meant to be. Maybe I was always destined to be the one that connected with these killers."

Derek's intense eyes meet mine. "I believe that too," he says earnestly. "We were brought together for a reason."

Our moment of reflection is interrupted as the elevator reaches the basement, and we step out into the cool night air. As we take a few steps away from the elevator, I notice a man leaning against a nearby wall, seemingly waiting for us. Tall, slender, and with auburn-toned, wavy hair, he exudes a certain charm. A mischievous smirk plays on his lips, accompanied by a crinkle in the corner of his green eyes.

“Good evening, agents,” he says cheerfully, as though it isn’t almost the middle of the night.

Derek huffs beside me, clearly annoyed by the newcomer's presence, and I could tell from his reaction that he already knows who this person is. “What are you doing lurking here? Isn’t it past your bedtime, Winters? I mean this with the utmost disrespect, but fuck off,” he growls, surprising me with his vehemence.

The newcomer disregards Derek's remarks and turns his attention to me, extending his hand. "Tristan Winters," he introduces himself, his voice laced with confidence.

I go to shake his hand, but Derek's firm grip on my shoulder halts my movement. "Careful, Alex, snakes bite," he warns, his tone protective.

Tristan simply laughs, as though he finds Derek to be the funniest person alive, and makes a placating gesture with both hands. But behind the façade, I notice a hint of anger in his eyes as he looks at us. “So, I gather I’m not going to get a comment from you on the body you found this morning?”

Realization dawns on me, and I almost want to take a step back. “You’re a reporter?”

Tristan's smirk widens, confirming my suspicion. "You catch on quick. I'm an investigative journalist, always on the lookout for a juicy story. And it seems like I stumbled upon one right here," he says, eyeing both Derek and I with an intensity that makes me slightly uncomfortable.

Derek's eyes narrow at him, and his grip on my shoulder tightens protectively. "You're not getting any information from us. This is an ongoing investigation."

Tristan raises an eyebrow, seemingly undeterred by Derek's defensive stance. "Oh, come on. A little scoop won't hurt anyone. Help a journalist out, and I might even make you both look good in my article."

Maintaining a polite demeanor, I interject, trying to diffuse the tension between Derek and Tristan. "We appreciate your interest, Mr. Winters, but as Derek mentioned, this is an ongoing investigation, and we are not at liberty to disclose any information at this time."

Tristan's eyes flicker with an emotion I can't identify, "Derek, huh?" he glances at Derek before returning his attention to me. "Look, I understand your position, but you must admit, a collaboration between law enforcement and the media could shed light on the case and potentially lead to valuable insights."

Derek's annoyance remains unwavering. "We have our own methods and protocols. We don't need the interference of a journalist."

Tristan's smile turns slightly more genuine, his voice tinged with persuasion, but I could hear the undertone of annoyance. "Oh, I assure you, Agent Derek, I'm here to help your work, not disrupt it. I'm genuinely intrigued by the case and the opportunity to get to the truth behind these deaths. We could work together, with mutual respect and shared goals, and all that."

Derek crosses his arms, his expression unyielding. "I've dealt with people like you before, and they always have their own agenda. We don't need any distractions or leaks jeopardizing the investigation."

Tristan's charm doesn't waver, but another flicker of frustration flashes in his eyes. "I understand your concerns, Agent, but not everyone is cut from the same cloth. I assure you, my goal is simply to help you get what you want."

The tension in the air is palpable as Derek and Tristan continue to face off, their personalities clashing like two opposing forces. I found myself caught in the middle, torn between the curiosity that Tristan's proposition stirred within me and Derek's protective instincts, which warned me to be cautious.

Tristan's smile remains persistent, though I could see exasperation in his eyes. "Agent, I'm not your enemy here. I understand your reservations, but I assure you, my intentions are genuine. I want to uncover the truth behind these deaths as much as you do."

Derek's jaw clenches, and he gives Tristan a stern look. "We'll handle this investigation our way, and we won't be sharing confidential information with anyone outside of our team. You can report on whatever public information is available, but that's it."

Tristan sighs, accepting Derek's stance for the time being. "Alright, I'll respect your wishes for now. But consider this," he says, maintaining eye contact with Derek, "if you ever find yourself in need of an extra set of eyes or a different perspective, you know where to find me."

"I highly doubt that'll ever happen," Derek retorts, unyielding.

Tristan chuckles lightly. "You never know. Cases have a way of taking unexpected turns. I'll be around, lurking in the shadows, waiting for that moment when you might change your mind." With a slight nod to both of us, he turns and starts to walk away.

As we watch Tristan disappear into the darkness, I can't help but feel conflicted. On one hand, I understand Derek's caution and the importance of keeping the investigation confidential. On the other hand, Tristan's offer had a certain appeal, as he seemed genuinely passionate about helping us through his journalism.

Derek's voice breaks my train of thought. "We need to be careful, Alex. Trusting outsiders can be risky. They have their own agendas, and we can't afford to have anything jeopardize our efforts."

"I know, Derek," I reply, feeling torn. "But there might come a point where we need all the help we can get. I don't want to shut out a potential resource if it could aid the case."

Derek sighs, understanding my perspective but remaining steadfast in his stance. "We'll see how things progress. Let's focus on our investigation for now and gather as much information as we can. We'll consult with our superiors about this later, but for now, we keep things to ourselves."

I nod, acknowledging Derek's decision. "Agreed. Our priority is solving this case and finding these killers."

With that, we make our way to my car, both of us deep in thought. The night air feels heavy with the weight of the ongoing investigation, and I couldn't shake the feeling that the road ahead is filled with uncertainty and challenges.

After Derek wishes me a good night to start fresh in the morning I drive back to my rental property. The encounter with Tristan and Derek's adamant stance replays in my mind. The tension between them lingered, and I can't help but wonder if there is a way to bridge the gap between their opposing perspectives.

Arriving at my temporary home, I park the car and step out, the night air enveloping me. The street is quiet, with only a few dimly lit street lights casting long shadows. The encounter with Tristan left me with mixed feelings, and I couldn't shake the curiosity he sparked within me.

Entering the house, I close the door behind me, leaning against it for a moment to gather my thoughts. Derek's words echo in my mind, reminding me of the importance of staying focused and cautious. Trusting outsiders, especially journalists, is a risk, but what if Tristan's intentions are genuine? What if he could provide valuable insights or uncover leads that we hadn't considered?

I pace around the living room, contemplating the pros and cons of involving Tristan in the investigation. On one hand, his perspective as an investigative journalist could shed light on aspects we might have overlooked. On the other hand, I understood Derek's concerns about leaks and distractions that could compromise our progress.

As I mull over the possibilities, my eyes land on the door leading to my sanctuary. I know beyond that door the victims' faces would stare back at me, their lives cut short by faceless killers. I couldn't ignore the weight of the responsibility on my shoulders. If there is a chance that Tristan's involvement could aid us, I couldn't dismiss it outright.

Feeling physically and mentally drained, I decide it is best to get some rest before diving back into the investigation. The encounters with both Derek and Tristan left me with a whirlwind of emotions, and I need time to process everything that happened.

I make my way to the bedroom, undress, and slip into my pajamas. The soft fabric provides a comforting sensation against my skin as I climb into bed. Despite the exhaustion, my mind continues to buzz with thoughts of Derek and Tristan. Their presence, their attractiveness, and the conflicting dynamics between them had stirred something within me.

As I lay in bed, my thoughts wander, and I find myself replaying their interaction in my mind. Images of Derek's intense eyes and Tristan's mischievous smile flash before me. The attraction I feel toward both of them, though unexpected, is undeniable.

My body, despite the fatigue, hums with energy. I couldn't help but let my hand travel down into my pajama bottoms, unashamedly using the images of Derek and Tristan that fill my imagination as fuel for my growing desire. The combination of exhaustion and arousal creates a heady mix.

The room is bathed in the soft glow of moonlight filtering through the gaps in the curtains. In the quiet semi darkness, my mind continues to replay the encounter with Derek and Tristan, their voices echoing in my head. I could vividly recall the way Derek's voice growled with protectiveness. And then there was Tristan, with his confident charm and persistent smile, his voice full of intrigue.

The images of their faces intertwine with my fantasies, fueling my arousal. I could visualize Derek's strong physique, his muscular shoulders and arms, his blue eyes filled with intensity. And Tristan, his slightly slimmer yet toned frame and mischievous green gaze, exuding a magnetic energy that drew me in.

As I replay the moments in my mind, my hand moves instinctively, my fingers tracing delicate patterns along my inner thighs. I allow my fingertips to venture further, teasingly grazing over the sensitive skin, as I succumb to the intoxicating sensations that envelope me. The warmth between my legs grows with each of my touches, a delicious ache that demands attention.

My mind becomes a canvas for vivid scenarios, a play where Derek and Tristan take center stage. I imagine their strong hands exploring every inch of my body with a hunger that mirrors my own. I could almost feel their touch, their fingers leaving a trail of electric sparks in their wake.

I let out a quiet gasp as I allow my fingers to slide along my wet pussy then up to circle my throbbing clit. I moan as the touch of my fingertips ignites a surge of pleasure that radiates from within. The anticipation grows with each caress, the rhythm of my hand mirroring the heated tempo of my thoughts.

In the quiet of the room, the only sound is my own breathing, slightly labored with each stroke of my fingers. In my mind, Derek's hands squeeze at my breasts, his thumbs moving over my hard nipples before he closes his mouth around one, his tongue flicking at it while the fingers of his other hand twist and pinch at my other nipple. My own hand comes up to mirror the images in my mind, the sharp pain from my fingers shooting straight to my clit.

My hand on my pussy moves faster, guided by the fervor of my imagination and the primal yearning that surges through me. The pleasure intensifies with each stroke, each flicker of sensation pushing me closer to the edge.

The room fills with the symphony of my own gasps and moans as I circle my clit harder before plunging my fingers inside myself. I whimper to myself as I press the heel of my palm against my clit, moving it in rhythm with my fingers as I fuck myself on them. The sounds of my pleasure mingle with the soft rustle of the bedsheets as I writhe on the bed. Shadows dance on the walls, their undulating forms mirroring the waves of ecstasy that wash over me.

As I near the peak of pleasure, my breaths grow shallow and erratic, my body quivering with anticipation as my pussy tightens on my fingers. The world around me dissolves into a haze of sensation, the boundaries between reality and fantasy blurred. My fingers curl inside myself as I press my hand harder against my clit, the tremble in my body only adding to the stimulation.

I imagine Tristan behind me, his hand reaching around my body to thrust his fingers inside my pussy, curling and pumping in and out of me in time with my movements. His other thumb presses hard against my clit, rubbing and circling it and making me moan.

In the darkness of the room, I surrender to the intoxicating sensations, my hand moving with increasing urgency, fueled by the maddening desire that courses through my veins and my own fantasies. Each movement of my hand brings me closer to that cliff, the orgasm building within me like a dormant volcano ready to erupt.

And then, as if on cue, the dam of pleasure breaks, sending shockwaves of bliss pulsating through my body. I cry out, the pleasure escaping my lips as my climax washes over me, leaving me trembling and breathless in its wake.

Afterwards, as I lay there catching my breath, a sense of calm washes over me. The orgasm had provided a temporary escape from the complexities of the investigation and the conflicting emotions within me. It was a reminder that amidst the chaos, I'm still a woman with desires and needs.

The weight of the day's events seem momentarily distant, replaced by a sense of clarity and tranquility.

With a contented sigh, I pull my hand away, my body now calm and at peace. Slowly, I adjust the covers, settling into a comfortable position. The fatigue that initially weighed heavily on me now felt like a comforting embrace, guiding me towards much-needed sleep.

As my eyelids grow heavy and my breathing steadies, I let go of the lingering thoughts of Derek and Tristan, allowing my mind to drift into a deep slumber. Tomorrow would bring new challenges, but for now, in the quiet of my bedroom, I succumb to the oblivion of rest. Hoping that I wake up refreshed and ready to face whatever lay ahead.

Chapter 4

Alex

There is no food in my rental house as I still haven't had the chance to go grocery shopping. I had prioritized setting up my sanctuary at the house and then the fresh case landed in our laps. So I grab a drive through coffee and bagel on the way to the office the next morning.

James is standing next to the main table when I enter and raises an eyebrow at me as I walk in. "That looks like a healthy breakfast, Alex."

I cringe in response. "I haven't had the chance to get groceries yet."

He chuckles and shakes his head as he looks at the table covered in photographs and crime scene reports left there last night. "Yes, I saw that you and Derek have made some progress. Walk me through what you have come up with."

I nod, taking a sip of my coffee to fortify myself before launching into a summary of our findings. "We are taking a deeper look at all the victims, trying to identify why the killers spent longer on some of them over the others. There appears to be a direct correlation between those who reported being stalked to those who were killed sooner. We are also trying to identify what it is about the victims that makes them a target," I take a breath before continuing with confidence. "As you know all the women are different, there is no specific type that they are targeting. They are all attractive women, but we have blondes, brunettes, redheads, different body types, a range of ages from mid twenties to mid thirties. There is no way of predicting who they would even target next. But we know that something about them makes them a target."

James nods along with me before rubbing a hand along his jaw in contemplation. He looks past me briefly. "Do you have anything else to add?"

Glancing behind me I see that Derek has entered the room.

His lip twitches as he glances at me before returning his focus to James. "Nothing yet, we are still going through all the details of each woman to piece together their lives before they were killed. We are hoping to get more information from Michael and Emma on yesterday's victim to find out if that helps paint a clearer picture."

James nods again, his expression thoughtful. "Good. Keep digging into their backgrounds. We need to find any common threads or connections among them. And make sure you stay in close contact with Michael and Emma. Their insights could be invaluable in unraveling this case."

"Absolutely, sir. We're also going to review any previous reports of stalking or harassment in the area. It's possible that some of the victims might not have reported incidents directly to the police but might have confided in friends or family. We'll reach out to their acquaintances as well, see if there's any information they can provide," Derek agrees.

James rubs his temples, clearly feeling the weight of the case on his shoulders. "This is a tough one, no doubt about it. But I have confidence in both of you. Keep working together, share your findings, and let's catch these murderers before they strike again. We can't afford to lose any more innocent lives."

Derek and I exchange glances. I understand the gravity of the situation and the urgency to solve the case before more lives are lost.

As James leaves the room, we turn our attention back to the task at hand. The table is scattered with photographs, crime scene reports, and victim profiles. It's a puzzle waiting to be solved, and we are determined to find the missing pieces.

"Derek," I say, "let's start by reviewing the stalking reports filed by the victims. We need to understand the extent of their experiences, the conversations they had when they sought help, and if there are any commonalities in the patterns of stalking."

Derek nods in agreement. "Absolutely. We also need to explore their social circles, talk to friends, family, and co-workers again. Someone might have noticed something that could help us piece together the puzzle."

As we begin to delve into the reports, we divide the workload, each taking a set of victims to investigate further. We scour through their backgrounds, searching for any connections or recurring themes that might shed light on the motivations behind the killings.

Hours pass as we pore over the details, analyzing every piece of information we have. It's a meticulous and painstaking process, but we know that even the smallest detail could be the key to cracking the case wide open.

As the hours stretch on, I feel the fatigue starting to weigh me down. The lack of proper sleep and nourishment begins to take its toll. I find it harder to focus on the reports, my eyes growing heavy and my mind becoming foggy.

Derek notices my struggling state and places a hand on my shoulder. Concern is evident in his voice as he says, "Alex, you've been working non-stop. It's clear that you need a break. Why don't we step out for a bit and grab some lunch? There's a local sandwich place nearby that makes the best sandwiches. It'll give us a chance to clear our minds and recharge."

I hesitate for a moment, knowing that time is of the essence in this investigation. But I also recognize the importance of taking care of myself to maintain the clarity needed to solve the case. I finally relent and nod in agreement. "You're right. I could use a break. Let's go grab those sandwiches."

Leaving the files behind momentarily, we step out of the office and head towards the sandwich place. The fresh air rejuvenates my senses, and the thought of a delicious meal brings a faint smile to my face. It's a brief respite from the intensity of the case, a chance to temporarily set aside the weight on our shoulders.

As we enter the sandwich place, the aroma of freshly baked bread and savory ingredients fills the air. Derek places our order, and we find a quiet corner to sit and enjoy our meal. The first bite of the sandwich is a burst of flavors that momentarily distract me from the grim realities we're facing.

Over lunch, we briefly discuss our findings so far, bouncing ideas off each other and sharing new insights. The break allows us to approach the case with a fresh perspective, giving our minds a much-needed breather. We make mental notes of our conversation, ready to dive back into the investigation with renewed energy once we return to the office.

Finishing our meal, we pay the bill and make our way back. My head feels clearer and I have a renewed sense of determination.

Just before we go into the building Derek stops and offers to get us coffee as my phone buzzes in my pocket. Moving to the side of the entrance, I wait for Derek while checking the notification.

You look very pretty today, Little Darling.

I frown down at the phone, not knowing what to make of the message. Glancing around I can't see anyone focussed on me. A sinking feeling hits me as I look at the message again.

Who is this?

You know who it is...

My heart thuds in my chest, I look at Derek. I should tell him that the serial killers we are hunting are sending me text messages. But before I can do more than open my mouth to call out to him, my phone buzzes in my hand again.

I would keep this just between us if I were you...

Why should I do that?

We will know if you even hint at this to anyone, and the moment you do, we are gone. You will never find us.

I frown to myself. I don't want them to disappear. I want to find them. I need to stop them from killing more women.

So what happens if I do keep this to myself?

Hmmmm... how about we get to know each other?

And how would we do that? I don't imagine you would sit down in an interrogation room with me.

You're funny, Little Darling... How about we play a game...

Glancing toward Derek I see he's now at the front of the line for coffee.

What game?

Truth or Dare...

Is it just me playing this game or are you playing too?

Please say yes, it would be the perfect opportunity to help give me more details to track them with.

Hmmm... I'll play along, no dares to turn ourselves in or tell you our names or things that could give us away though, that would be cheating. ;)

Fuck. Well I could still try.

Fine, agreed.

Truth or Dare, Little Darling?

Truth

Did you like the present we left you?

Present?

She wasn't as pretty as you, but there was a certain beauty with how we gave her to you.

They thought giving me a fresh body was a present? I can see Derek glancing in my direction as he waits for our coffee and I hope the flush that I feel creeping up my neck isn't obvious to him.

I'm sure her family would be happier if she was alive.

That's not your truth, Little Darling.

My heart races as I try to think of a response that won't give too much away but would also satisfy their question.

I'm an FBI agent, my job is to find the truth and bring justice to those who have been wronged. I can't say I 'liked' the present you left, but I am going to find you and stop you from hurting anyone else.

The reply comes quickly.

Ooh, feisty. We like that. But be careful, Little Darling, too much feistiness might get you into trouble.

The ominous message sends shivers down my spine.

Is it my turn then? Truth or dare?

Truth, Little Darling.

Do you already have your next woman picked out?

Yes, we do.

Just then, Derek returns with the coffees, handing me mine with a curious look on his face. "Everything okay?" he asks.

I force a smile, not wanting to involve him in this just yet. "Yeah, just an old friend. Nothing to worry about."

Derek seems unconvinced but doesn't press further. We walk back into the office, and I can't help but feel the burden of the truth or dare game lingering in the back of my mind as we wait for the elevator.

Stepping inside to head back up, my phone buzzes again in my hand.

Want to know what is even prettier than you are today?

I frown at the message, a little unsure I want to know where this is going.

Sure.

Your beautiful face as you came
all over your fingers last night.

Fuck. I think I just stopped breathing. My head feels light and dizzy. I focus back on the phone again as another message comes through.

Happy hunting, Little Darling.

My heart pounds in my chest, and a sense of dread washes over me. They were watching me?

Chapter 5

Alex

I take a deep breath, trying to regain my composure. I couldn't let it show how this affected me. Derek is still beside me, and I can't risk him seeing these messages. I quickly pocket my phone and pretend nothing is wrong.

Internally, however, I am having a panic attack.

I try to push the rising panic down, reminding myself to stay composed and focused. Derek glances at me with a concerned expression, but I quickly force a smile, hoping he wouldn't pick up on my distress.

As we enter the office, I excuse myself, claiming that I need to make a quick phone call. Hurrying down a hall and into an empty room, I close the door behind me and take a few deep breaths, attempting to steady my racing heart.

Once I feel somewhat more collected, I retrieve my phone from my pocket and examine the messages again. The unsettling words echo in my mind

I am torn between fear and arousal that they watched me during such an intimate act. That they had somehow been in my personal space without me knowing and seen me pleasuring myself.

I know I can't let those emotions cloud my judgment. I have to remain focused on the task at hand. Taking a deep breath, I compose myself and prepare to respond.

I type a reply, keeping my words as neutral as possible:

> I'm not one to be intimidated easily. Your actions only strengthen my resolve to catch you.

The response comes almost immediately:

> Oh, we're counting on it, Little Darling. We love a challenge. But be careful what you wish for.

I know I have to tread carefully. These murderers are testing me, pushing my limits, and toying with my emotions. But I can't let them see how much their messages affect me. I have to maintain control.

Playing along is my best option for the moment. I do not want them to disappear.

The phone buzzes again.

> Better get back to your partner... wouldn't want him catching us first...

That dizzy feeling is back again. They could see me even now?

I suddenly feel like I am drowning. They really would know if I told anyone. They would disappear at the first hint of me going against their wishes. I close my eyes and take a moment to breathe and slow my racing heart. They were right; I do need to get back out to the main room so as to not draw more attention.

It is a dangerous game I am about to play.

As I step out of the room in order to rejoin Derek, I keep my phone close, ready to respond if they send another message. I can't afford to let my guard down. The case just took a personal turn, and I need to stay vigilant.

Michael and Emma are in the hallway talking quietly between themselves. Their voices come to a stop as soon as they see me and Emma sends a forced smile in my direction as Michael walks away.

“Hey Alex, we just left our updated reports on the latest victim with Derek,” she says simply before following after Michael and disappearing.

Entering the main office Derek glances at me, concern evident in his eyes. "Is everything okay, Alex? You seem a bit off."

I give him a reassuring smile, trying to mask the turmoil inside me. "Just a personal matter. I'll be fine. Let's get back to work."

Derek nods, accepting my response for now. We resume our investigation, poring over the reports, as well as the new information from Michael and Emma, and looking for any leads that could help us track down the killers. The messages from the unknown sender linger in the back of my mind, but I push them aside, channeling my energy into the task at hand.

The information that Michael and Emma gathered is sparse with nothing helpful that we didn’t already know, so Derek and I delve deeper into the stalking reports filed by some of the victims. We carefully analyze each account, looking for patterns, similarities, or any information that could lead us to the murderers. It is a painstaking process, but we know it is crucial in understanding each woman’s experiences and potentially uncovering valuable clues.

Simultaneously, we start reaching out to the families and friends of the victims. We want to gather more information about their lives, relationships, and any potential conflicts or individuals who might have posed a threat to them. It is essential to cast a wide net and explore every possible avenue that could provide insights into the motives and identities of the murderers.

With each conversation, we discover more about the women's personalities, their aspirations, their habits, hobbies and the challenges they faced in their daily lives. While some had reported instances of stalking or harassment, others had mentioned in passing to loved ones about feeling uneasy or being watched, while some gave no indication at all of anything out of the ordinary. These details add to the complexity of the case, as there is no clear-cut profile of the victims or a single evident link connecting them.

The hours pass, and the afternoon turns into evening. Derek and I continue our relentless pursuit of any leads or connections. We discuss theories, analyze evidence, and try to make sense of the puzzle before us.

All the while, my phone remains by my side, its screen dark and silent. Part of me dreads another message from the killers, yet another part of me wants to know more about them, to understand their twisted minds and motivations.

As the night wears on, frustration settles in. We had gathered an extensive web of information about each victim, but nothing seemed to intersect. The murderers are disturbingly adept at selecting women who had no common connections, making it challenging to identify any potential links or motives behind their actions.

"Derek," I say, breaking the silence that had settled between us as we continued our investigation. "This is maddening. It's like they deliberately chose victims with no apparent connection to one another. We're hitting dead ends everywhere."

Derek nods, his face mirroring my frustration. "I know, Alex. It's as if they planned this meticulously to keep us from finding any solid leads. But we can't let it deter us. Let's make it an earlier night tonight, so we can start fresh and sharp tomorrow."

He is right. Fatigue is beginning to take its toll on both of us, and we need a clear head to approach the case. As much as I want to stay up all night and keep digging, I know it wouldn't be productive in the long run.

"Alright," I agree reluctantly. "Let's call it a night. We can meet here in the morning and we'll hit the field, retrace the victims' steps, and talk to anyone they came into contact with. Maybe we'll find something that the previous canvas and reports haven't revealed."

Derek nods, relieved that I agreed. We pack up our belongings and lock the office door behind us. The parking garage is quiet, with only a few stragglers making their way home. The weight of the case presses heavily on my shoulders as we walk towards our respective cars.

As I sit in my car, I can't shake off the feeling of being watched. It is a paranoia that has settled deep within me since receiving those messages. I check the rearview mirror, scanning the almost empty garage for any signs of danger, but there is nothing that seems out of the ordinary. Taking a deep breath, I remind myself to stay vigilant and not let fear consume me.

Driving home, my mind fills with thoughts of the case. The images of the victims, the cryptic messages, and the unknown culprits dance in my head. I know I have to find a way to gather more information, to uncover a lead that would break open the case. But at the same time, I can't help but feel trapped in their twisted game.

Arriving home, I step into the comfort of my rental house. Locking the door behind me, I double-check the windows before finally allowing myself to relax.

I sink into the couch, still fully dressed, my mind racing with possibilities and unanswered questions. The silence of the house is unsettling, and I can't help but feel like someone is lurking in the shadows. Shaking off the feeling, I remind myself that it is just my imagination running wild.

With a weary sigh, I decide to take a hot shower to wash away the day's stress. The water cascades over me, soothing my tense muscles and momentarily providing a respite from the darkness of the case. But even in the solitude of the bathroom, I can't escape the haunting words of the text messages.

Finishing my shower, I wrap myself in a towel and enter the bedroom. I turn on a small bedside lamp, casting a soft glow in the room. As I prepare to change into my pajamas, a chill runs down my spine, causing me to freeze in place.

On the bedside table, illuminated by the gentle light, is a rose. Stuck to one of its thorns is a small torn piece of paper.

Stepping closer, I could see there are typed words on the lined paper, each side is torn as though to frame the black ink on it.

My heart races as I pick up the rose and the piece of paper, trying to steady my trembling hands. As I examine the rose, I notice a faint scent emanating from it. It is subtle, almost imperceptible, but there is a hint of something familiar. I can't quite place it, but it triggers a memory buried deep within my mind.

Looking at the paper up close, I am able to make out the words.

Simple and beautiful
like you,
Little Darling.
If I press myself to
your thorns, will you
make me bleed?

My mind races, trying to process the implications of finding the rose and the cryptic message. The chilling words send shivers down my spine, mingling fear with a strange sense of fascination. It is clear that the psychos are toying with me, escalating their game to new levels.

A mixture of emotions floods over me, the adrenaline from the investigation mingling with a dangerous curiosity and a slight shiver of arousal. I can't deny the affect their twisted messages have on me.

I take a deep breath, trying to steady my racing heart. This is another test, another attempt to unnerve me, to get beneath my guard. But I can't let them win. I have to find the strength within me to confront this darkness head-on.

Setting the rose and the piece of paper aside, I quickly check the rest of the house to ensure that I am alone. Every creak and shadow seems ominous, but I find no signs of them. It is clear that they were here, but they are long gone.

I know without even asking that, just like the phone messages, I wouldn't be able to tell anyone about their gift. Or about them being in my personal space. They would disappear like they promised. I feel caught between my duty and my need to confront these murderers on my own terms. Telling anyone about the rose or the messages isn't an option. I can't risk losing their trail. At the same time, I can't shake off the unsettling feeling that they are always one step ahead, watching my every move.

In a way, their sick game is working. The more I tried to stay composed and in control, the more I found myself tangled in their web. I need to regain my focus, channel my emotions, and turn their psychological warfare against them.

The rose and the cryptic message shook me, blurring the lines between fear and fascination. But I couldn't let those emotions cloud my judgment or compromise the investigation. The words on the paper hint at their fascination with me, and I have to use that to my advantage.

Taking a deep breath, I make a decision. I would play their game, but on my own terms. I need to gain their trust, to keep them engaged, and to extract any information that could help us catch them. It is a dangerous path, but I am willing to take the risk.

I carefully pick up the rose and the torn piece of paper, placing them in a plastic bag to preserve any potential evidence. Then, I quickly change into my pajamas and return to the living room, my mind racing with the possibilities.

Sitting on the couch, I retrieve my phone and open the messaging app, preparing to respond to their latest message. I want to show them that I am not easily intimidated and that their actions only fueled my determination.

With a steady hand, I type a message.

> You're trying to get a reaction out of me, but you won't succeed. Keep watching. I'm not afraid of your games.

Sending the message, I hold my breath, waiting for their response. The seconds feel like an eternity as I stare at the screen, my heart pounding in my chest.

Finally, a new message comes through.

> Brave words, we shall see how long you can keep up this facade. We have only just begun. Sweet dreams, Little Darling.

Chapter 6

Alex

After receiving their gift and that last message, it is a struggle to find any sleep. When I eventually drift into an exhausted, restless sleep in the early hours of the morning, my dreams are haunted by masked men and strong hands moving intimately on my body. Touching me and whispering to me about games of Truth or Dare and the things they wanted to do to me that had nothing to do with killing.

I wake up with a start, drenched in sweat, my heart pounding loudly in my chest. The killers seem to have taken over my subconscious mind, blending my reality and my erotic dreams into a disturbing mixture. The image of those masked men and the feeling of their hands on me lingers like an echo and my body throbs with need in a way that should feel wrong but somehow doesn't.

Feeling a mix of guilt and confusion, I push aside the conflicting emotions that surge through me. I can't let myself be consumed by desire or be distracted from the task at hand. It is crucial to maintain my focus on solving the case and bringing these murderers to justice.

It is still mostly dark outside, only the first hints of light peeking through the blinds on my bedroom window. Determined to regain control, I force myself out of bed and make my way to the bathroom.

Another shower seems necessary to wash away the sweat and the remnants of the unsettling dreams that plagued my sleep.

Stepping under the hot water, I let it wash over me, hoping it would cleanse not only my body but also my mind. I close my eyes, trying to find a sense of calm amid the chaos that surrounds me. The water soaks my hair, cascading down my face, and down my body, soothing the tension in my muscles.

I reach for the shower gel and lather it onto my skin, letting my hands glide over my body, the warm water enhancing every sensation. My whole body pulses as I let my fingers brush against my throbbing clit. As much as I try to push away the disturbing images and dreams that still linger in my mind, it is as though my subconscious wants to keep playing them on repeat to fuel the desire coursing through my body.

As the pleasure intensifies, I couldn't help but give in to my body's demands, even though it feels like a betrayal to myself and the victims. The conflicting emotions surge within me, but in that moment, the allure of escape and temporary relief overwhelm any rational thought.

I lean against the tiled wall of the shower, my breathing becoming heavy and erratic. The hot water continues to pour over me, amplifying the sensations that electrify every nerve ending. My fingers dance across my pussy, tracing circles and teasing touches, succumbing to the overpowering need that consumes me.

My mind brings forward images of gloved hands dragging down the front of my body, pinching at my nipples. It conjures another body pressed to my back, one of their gloved hands wrapping around my throat from behind and squeezing hard as their other gloved hand moves between my legs.

In my mind it is their hands moving over me as my fingers plunge into my wet pussy and touch my clit. With each stroke, the images from my dreams intertwine with my reality, blurring the line of right and wrong. My mind becomes a battleground of desire and guilt, but the hunger for release grows more insatiable with every passing second.

As my body trembles, getting closer to the edge while I move my fingers on my clit, I could almost hear their whispers echoing in my ears, fueling the fire that burned deep within. I surrender to the raw intensity of the moment, allowing myself to momentarily forget the horrors of the case, losing myself in a world of primal desires.

The tension builds, coiling tightly within me until it becomes unbearable. My body is poised on the edge of the cliff as my fingers continue their movements, thrusting deep inside my pussy before moving to circle my clit, pressing against it with a trembling hand.

"God, yes," the cry escapes my lips as my back arches against the wall and a wave of ecstasy crashes over me. Washing away the torment and uncertainty, at least for a fleeting moment. But as the pleasure subsides, reality crashes back in, reminding me of the unresolved murders that await my attention.

Regret washes over me as I turn off the water, the remnants of desire slowly fading away. I step out of the shower, feeling a mix of shame and relief. While the experience granted me a reprieve, I know it was only a temporary escape.

With renewed state of mind, I dry myself off and dress, ready to face the day ahead. I resolve to compartmentalize my desires and focus solely on the investigation, ensuring that justice would prevail and the victims would find peace.

After dressing for the day, I leave the rental house and head to the nearest drive-through coffee shop. The familiar aroma of freshly brewed coffee greets me as I order my usual strong black coffee and a bagel to go. The caffeine would help keep me alert and focused during the long hours ahead.

With the hot cup of coffee nestled in the cup holder and the bagel resting on the passenger seat, I drive towards the office. The streets were still quiet in the early morning, offering a sense of solitude that allowed me to gather my thoughts.

When I walk into the office, carrying my breakfast and feeling a little exhausted, I am surprised to find two unfamiliar men standing inside the room, their attention fixed on the murder boards.

One of them is standing near the board displaying information about our newest victim, his eyes glued to the images of her body, while the other is sitting at the table where Derek and I usually work, nonchalantly cutting an apple with a sharp knife. Their presence unnerves me, especially considering the sensitive nature of the case.

They glance in my direction as I walk in. The one near the murder board gives me a curt nod, his hazel eyes assessing me with an intensity that made me uneasy. The way he has his light brown hair slicked back to his head makes his look even more intense.

The other, with his feet propped up on the table, continues to casually slice through the apple as if he were in his own domain. A strand of his dark brown hair falls forward with the tilt of his head.

They are both attractive men, and I can see their muscles filling out the black suits they wear. But that still doesn't explain what they were doing in our space.

"Who are you, and what are you doing here?" I ask, trying to maintain a composed demeanor despite the unease creeping in.

The man with the knife looks up at me, his piercing brown eyes meeting mine. "Just fellow agents, interesting case you have here," he replies curtly, his voice steady and devoid of any emotion.

Something doesn’t feel right about these two men. Their demeanor and casual intrusion raises suspicion within me. They didn't introduce themselves voluntarily, so I decide to take the initiative.

"Let’s try that again, I'm Agent Darling," I state firmly, taking a step closer to the man with the knife. "And you are?"

The man smirks, his gaze shifting back to the apple he is effortlessly slicing. "Agent Thomas Decker," he replies, his voice dripping with a smugness that only intensifies my suspicion.

"And I'm Agent Darius Travis," the other man near the murder board chimes in, his tone devoid of any warmth. He doesn’t bother looking away from the photographs and evidence spread out before him.

I couldn't shake off the feeling that these two are not here to genuinely assist with the case. Their behavior and lack of professionalism signals a different motive—one that seems focused on prying into our investigation rather than aiding it.

"What brings you here, Agents Decker and Travis?" I ask, narrowing my eyes at them.

Agent Decker puts down the knife, his gaze finally meeting mine with a calculated intensity. "Oh, we're just curious," he replies with a smirk. "Word spreads fast about high-profile cases like this one. We thought we'd come and have a look for ourselves."

His nonchalance grates on my nerves, and I couldn't help but feel that they were encroaching on our territory. The investigation had become deeply personal to me, and I didn't appreciate their intrusion or their dismissive attitude.

"This is an ongoing investigation," I assert firmly, my voice filled with authority. "If you're not here to provide meaningful assistance, I suggest you leave. We have no time for distractions."

Agent Travis finally tears his gaze away from the murder board, his eyes narrowing at me. "You should watch your tone, Agent Darling," he retorts coldly.

I stand my ground, refusing to back down in the face of their intimidating presence. "I'll watch my tone when I'm dealing with professionals who are genuinely interested in solving this case," I shoot back, my voice laced with defiance.

Agent Decker chuckles, his smirk widening. "You've got some fire in you, Agent Darling. I like that," he says, leaning back in the chair with a casual arrogance. "But don't worry, we won't get in your way. We're just here to observe."

Their words do little to alleviate my concerns. I have no reason to trust them, especially with their vague explanations and unknown intentions. Their presence feels like a threat, an unwelcome intrusion into a case that demanded the utmost focus and dedication.

"Well, your observation skills won't be needed here," I reply icily. "This investigation is under my jurisdiction, and I won't tolerate any interference. If you're not here to assist, then I suggest you leave immediately."

Agent Travis' cold gaze bore into mine, his eyes filled with a mix of disdain and curiosity. "We'll be watching," he states, his voice carrying a warning. "You might find our observations more valuable than you think."

I don't have time for their mind games or veiled threats. I need to protect the integrity of the investigation and the well-being of the victims. It is clear that dealing with these two would require careful navigation.

"I appreciate your concern, but I assure you, I have everything under control," I reply, my tone firm and unwavering. "If you have any relevant information or resources to offer, feel free to share.

Otherwise, I expect you to respect the boundaries of this investigation."

Agent Decker pushes himself off the chair, his eyes gleaming with a mixture of amusement and challenge. "We'll see how long that control lasts," he remarks cryptically before heading towards the exit. Agent Travis follows suit, his gaze lingering on me for a moment longer before he turns away.

As the door closes behind them, I couldn't shake off the unsettling feeling that their presence is a harbinger of more complications to come. I know I have to stay focused, not only on the case itself but also on protecting myself from any potential threats lurking in the shadows.

Taking a deep breath I put my breakfast on the table along with my phone and turn towards the murder board of our recent victim. I need to make sure everything is still intact and that Agents Decker and Travis hadn't messed with the board before I arrived.

Running my eyes over it I can tell that nothing changed, everything is where it should be. I let out a sigh of relief. Then my phone buzzes behind me.

My heart races as I cautiously approach the table, fearing what I might find. Picking up the phone, I unlock it and see a new message notification.

I swallow hard, my hands trembling slightly as I open the message. It is from them, and this time the message is accompanied by a photo. I hesitate for a moment before opening the photo, bracing myself for what I might see.

The image that greets me makes me sit heavily in the chair. It is a photo of me, naked, in my shower only this morning, taken from inside the house. It was taken at the exact moment my orgasm crashed over me. My head was tilted back with my eyes closed and my mouth was open as I had cried out. There is no mistaking the look of pleasure or the sight of my fingers on my own pussy.

My whole body flushes hot and my stomach drops as I realize that they watched me again, invading my most private moments. How had they managed to get so close without me noticing?

With a trembling hand I close the photo and look at the accompanying message.

God wasn't there, but we were... Next time you cum it is only to be our names on your lips, Little Darling.

Holy. Fuck.

My mind races, a mixture of anger, fear, and a strange sense of exhilaration flooding over me. The audacity of these murderers is beyond comprehension. But there is no denying the effect their twisted actions had on me, stirring a dangerous concoction of emotions within.

With a deep breath, I compose myself and decide to respond to their message. I need to let them know that I wouldn't cower from their tactics, even as their intrusion cuts through my defenses.

With still-trembling fingers, I type a response, carefully choosing my words.

If that's so, what names exactly should I have on my lips?

Their response is almost instant and chillingly straightforward.

You'll find out soon enough, Little Darling. We have plans for you.

Chapter 7

Alex

I feel a surge of conflicting emotions after seeing the photo and reading their twisted messages. Part of me is furious at their audacity, their violation of my privacy, and their attempts to control and manipulate me. But another part of me couldn't deny the strange sense of exhilaration that their actions awakened within me, blurring the lines between fear and desire.

I know I couldn't let their sick games consume me. I have to stay focused on the investigation and not let them succeed in their attempts to unnerve me. But I also couldn't ignore the feelings that they are creating within me. These killers are not just cold-blooded murderers; they are psychopathic manipulators who seem to derive pleasure from tormenting me. And I am starting to enjoy the feelings it gives me.

Putting my phone back down on the table, I rub my hands over my face before pressing them to my weary eyes. Hearing movement behind me I turn to see Derek standing just inside the room with a frown on his face directed at me.

"Morning, Alex," Derek greets me, his voice laced with concern. "Did you get any sleep? You look exhausted."

I offer him a weary smile. "Just a restless night, Derek. You know how it goes with cases like this. It's hard to turn off your mind."

He nods, understanding the pressure of our work. "Well, let's try to make some progress today. I have an appointment this evening so we will make sure you get an early night. You look like you desperately need some sleep."

I can't share the full extent of what transpired. The last thing I want is to burden him with the disturbing presence of Agents Decker and Travis, or the way the murderers are now focused on me. Not only that, I know that if I mention the messages or other disturbing things that were interrupting my sleep, the murderers would simply vanish and we would never close the case.

"Thanks," I reply, mustering a smile. "Let's focus on the case for now. We've got a lot of ground to cover, and I want to get ahead of these killers."

Derek nods in agreement, "Absolutely. We'll get to the bottom of this. But don't forget to take care of yourself along the way. We're in this together."

I nod, grateful. We turn our attention back to the murder board, discussing potential leads, connections, and patterns we uncovered so far.

As we set out on our investigation for the day, I make a conscious effort to push aside the unsettling feelings that are stirring within me. I have to compartmentalize the disturbing messages and focus on the task at hand. We needed to gather as much information as possible, reconstructing the victims' movements and interactions prior to their deaths.

Derek and I visit the places where the victims were known to frequent. We speak with their coworkers and retrace their steps, visiting bars, gyms and even the corner store that one victim visited the day she disappeared, trying to piece together a clearer picture of their lives and identify any potential new suspects. Each conversation brings us closer to understanding the victims' relationships, motivations, and potential threats.

As we interview witnesses and collect information, I couldn't help but feel a lingering sense of unease. The murderers are taunting me, watching my every move. It is as if they revel in the knowledge that they invaded my privacy and left me unsettled.

If Derek notices my distraction he doesn't show it, his presence a grounding force in the midst of the chaos. He maintains his professionalism and never tries to pry into my personal struggles.

It is still early evening when we make our way back to the office. We only made a small dent in the list of people that we wanted to talk to. Stepping out of the elevator we almost collide with a very upset looking Emma.

Emma's face is flushed, and her eyes are filled with distress. She quickly composes herself as she notices Derek and me standing there, but it is evident that something has deeply affected her.

"Emma, are you okay?" I ask, concerned about her well-being.

She hesitates for a moment before responding, "I... I can't talk about it right now. It's personal. Just some family issues. I'll be fine."

Derek looks at her with genuine concern, "If you need to talk or take some time off, we understand. Family comes first."

She manages a faint smile, appreciating our support, but she shakes her head. "No, I need to keep my mind occupied. The case is important, and I want to help stop these monsters."

"We're here for you, Emma," I assure her, placing a hand on her shoulder. "If there's anything you need, don't hesitate to let us know."

She nods gratefully and then takes a deep breath, trying to compose herself. “Thank you, I’m sorry but I need to go, I’ll see you tomorrow." With those parting words she gets into the open elevator and disappears behind its closing doors.

Derek and I exchange worried looks as we turn to make our way into our office, only to stop again at the sight of Michael engaged in a heated conversation with another man. The stranger, dressed in a CSI uniform, has a strong presence, with sharp features and piercing eyes that seemed to take in every detail of his surroundings. His neatly combed hair and serious expression give him an air of authority.

Michael looks startled when he notices us and almost reluctantly waves us over. "Alex, Derek, this is Mark Thompson," he introduces, gesturing towards the man. "He's our lead Crime Scene Technician and has been assisting us in the case."

Mark extends a hand towards us, and we shake it in turn, his grip firm. "Pleasure to meet you both," he says, his voice deep and commanding. "I specialize in forensic analysis and evidence collection. I have been working closely with Michael and Emma to ensure we gather every piece of crucial information from the crime scenes."

As Mark speaks, his eyes dart between us, assessing our reactions. I couldn't help but feel a level of curiosity about him and the conversation we clearly interrupted.

"Great to have you on board, Mark," Derek acknowledges, his tone respectful. "Your expertise will be great to help us uncover any overlooked details. The killers have been meticulous, and we need to match their level of precision."

Mark nods, his expression intense. "I've been analyzing the evidence collected so far. It's clear that these psychos know what they're doing, but I'm sure I'll find the clues they missed."

I nod, impressed. "We're counting on you, Mark. Every piece of evidence could be crucial in solving this case. Have you found anything interesting so far?"

Mark's gaze shifts and he indicates to the table nearby. "I've compiled my initial findings and observations in these reports. You can take a look and see if there's anything that stands out to you."

Derek and I exchange a glance, intrigued by the prospect of new information. We move towards the table and pick up the reports, flipping through the pages. The level of detail and thoroughness in Mark's analysis is impressive, and it is clear that he has a keen eye for spotting even the smallest potential clues.

As we read through the reports, however, it becomes apparent that there is nothing significantly new or groundbreaking that we hadn't already uncovered. Mark's analysis confirms our initial findings and provides some additional insights, but there were no major breakthroughs that would immediately lead us to the perpetrators.

I look up at Mark, disappointed. "I apologize if my findings aren't as significant as you were hoping," he says sincerely. "The evidence we've collected so far is consistent with a carefully planned and executed series of murders. They are meticulous in covering their tracks, leaving behind no physical evidence or traceable patterns."

Derek chimes in, his voice laced with frustration. "Don't worry, Mark. We appreciate your work, and every piece of information brings us closer to solving this case. We'll continue to analyze the evidence and follow any leads we have."

Mark nods. "I have no doubt about that. I'm here to assist in any way I can. We'll uncover the truth, no matter how elusive it may seem."

With Mark's words resonating in my mind, Derek and I thank him for his efforts and assure him that his contribution was invaluable to the investigation. Mark looks pleased by our acknowledgement and shares his contact information, encouraging us to reach out if we need further assistance or have any questions regarding the evidence.

As Mark excuses himself to attend to another matter, Derek turns to me, his expression tired but unwavering. "Alex, I need to head out to my appointment. Is there anything I can do for you before I leave? Need me to grab you a coffee?"

I pause for a moment, considering his offer. The exhaustion is starting to drag me down, but I also know that I need to stay a little longer to write out the details from today and carefully review Mark's report. A cup of coffee would certainly help keep me focused and alert.

I smile gratefully at Derek. "Actually, that would be great. A coffee would be much appreciated. Thanks, Derek."

He nods and pats my shoulder. "Alright, I'll be back shortly. Take your time and make sure to get some rest when you're done. We'll pick up where we left off tomorrow."

With that, Derek heads towards the elevator, leaving me alone in the office. I take a deep breath and turn my attention back to the murder board, letting my fingers trace over the photographs and notes. The images of the victims stare back at me, their faces now etched into my memory.

Sitting down at my desk, I retrieve a notepad and pen, ready to transcribe the events and insights from the day. I start with the interviews we conducted, the witnesses' statements, and the potential leads we uncovered. Each detail is carefully documented, my handwriting steady despite the underlying turmoil.

I'm part way through writing out the details of the third witness statement when a noise behind me catches my attention. Looking towards the door I'm surprised to see that Mark has returned. He holds a takeaway cup of coffee in his hand. He wears a faint smile as he approaches me.

"I ran into Derek downstairs and he said this was for you," Mark says, placing the coffee in front of me. "I offered to bring it back up since he had to leave."

I nod appreciatively, grateful for the gesture. "Thank you, Mark. I could definitely use this right now."

I reach for the coffee cup, feeling the warmth seep into my hands. The aroma fills the air, offering a much-needed moment of comfort amidst the intensity of the investigation.

I take a sip of the coffee, relishing the warmth and the rich aroma. Mark lingers for a moment, observing me with a thoughtful expression. It looks like he has something on his mind, but I can't quite pinpoint what it is.

"Is everything alright, Mark?" I ask, curious about his sudden return and the unspoken words hanging in the air.

He hesitates for a moment, then decides to speak his mind. "Alex, I hope you don't mind me asking, but I was wondering if you would like to grab a coffee with me away from the office sometime?"

I look at Mark, taken aback by his question. His sudden proposition caught me off guard, especially considering the circumstances I am currently immersed in. The killers' fixation on me makes it difficult to entertain the idea of any personal involvement. I take a moment to gather my thoughts before responding.

"Thank you for the offer, Mark," I reply with a gentle smile. "I'm flattered, really I am. But at the moment I have something going on in my personal life and it's complicated."

I could see a hint of disappointment in his eyes. He nods again, accepting my response, but there is a sudden shift in his demeanor.

His smile fades, and he seems a bit distant as if lost in his own thoughts.

"I understand, Alex," he said quietly, his voice tinged with a hint of disappointment. "I apologize if I overstepped. It's just that... well, I thought we had a bit of a connection earlier, and I wanted to get to know you better. But I respect your decision."

I could sense his abrupt change in mood, and it makes me uneasy. Before I respond, Mark turns and briskly walks towards the exit, leaving me sitting there with a mix of conflicting emotions.

As the door closes behind Mark, I am left alone with my thoughts once again. The weight of the investigation and the situation I find myself in with the murderers feels even heavier. I take a deep breath, trying to regain my composure and refocus on the task at hand.

I sip on the coffee that Mark brought me, the warmth and caffeine a comfort. I know I have to focus and find a breakthrough in the case. The murderers have taken too many lives, and it is my duty to stop them.

The unfinished witness statement still lays on the table in front of me, a reminder of the work that needs to be done. I pick up my pen and start writing, pushing aside the emotional complexities that threaten to distract me.

It doesn't take long before the words on the page become a blur, and my eyelids grow heavy. I shake my head and take more sips of my coffee in an effort to combat my exhaustion. I continue to push myself to get the words down on the paper.

My eyelids grow heavier with each passing moment. Before I register what is happening, my head droops forward, and I don't even feel when it hits the table and the world goes black.

Chapter 8

Alex

I gradually regain consciousness, feeling disoriented and groggy. I blink my eyes open, trying to make sense of my surroundings. The familiar sight of my sanctuary greets me, but something feels off. It takes far longer than it should to realize that I don't remember leaving the office and returning to the house.

As I slowly sit up, a dull ache pulses through my head. Confusion mingles with the remnants of sleep as I try to piece together how I ended up in my rental house and why I passed out.

Breathing heavily, the movement of my body causes me to feel something unfamiliar tucked into the front of my bra. With my heart in my throat, I reach into the bra and pull out a small piece of torn paper.

My eyes widen in horror at the words typed across the page. The message is a chilling reminder of the killers' presence in my life.

**You looked like you
need some rest.**

**You're beautiful
when you sleep,
Little Darling**

A shiver runs down my spine as I read the words. They have shown they could get to me anywhere and had absolutely no boundaries.

That's when my eyes are drawn to the wall directly in front of me. It is no longer the canvas of crime scene photos and case notes that it had once been. Instead, it is covered with a sprawling collage of pictures. Images of me, captured in various settings and moments, were arranged meticulously across the entire surface. They depict me at work, at the crime scene, out on interviews, and even at home in moments I thought I was alone.

Amidst the pictures, a single note stands out, placed right in the center of the collage. I don't even need to remove it to read what it says. It isn't even the first time they have said those words to me, but now it feels so much worse.

**Happy hunting,
Little Darling.**

They enjoy fucking with me. But I am not going to let them get to me. I could play those games too. Instead of succumbing to the feelings that threaten to consume me, I make a conscious decision to channel my anger and transform it into fuel. They wanted to play, to revel in their power over me? Well, I refuse to be a pawn.

Taking a deep breath, I tear my gaze away from the wall and focus on regaining control of the situation. Picking my phone up from where they placed it on the desk in front of me, I unlock it and pull up the messenger app, opening the text messages I received from them previously. I can see it is still very early, but somehow I know they will be awake.

You like playing games, fine, I'll play. Truth or dare?

I believe it's our turn, Little Darling. What will it be?

I let out a growl and clench my hand around my phone in frustration.

Truth

Always the safe option, Little Darling... you need to step out of your comfort zone soon... But fine, how does it feel knowing that we've been watching you, seeing every hot little moment when you thought you were alone?

I close my eyes and breathe deeply, fighting against my body's automatic reaction, recalling the photo and messages they sent me that showed they watched me pleasuring myself. Twice.

A mix of anger, fear, and something strange stir within me. I couldn't deny that there is a part of me that feels a twisted excitement, a dark curiosity sparked by their words. It is a sick game they are playing, invading my privacy and toying with my emotions, but I refuse to let them see just how much they affect me.

Suppressing the uneasiness that tingles beneath my skin, I focus on the task at hand. They wanted to play, and I am determined to turn the tables on them. It is time to show them that I wouldn't be intimidated or controlled.

I take a moment to compose myself, my fingers hovering over the phone's keyboard as I prepare to respond. The truth is, their words shook me to my core. The invasion of my privacy, the violation of my personal moments—it should disgust me, but it doesn't. Deep down, a small part of me acknowledges the twisted allure, the dark excitement that accompanied their acts.

Summoning my inner strength, I type my reply, refusing to give them the satisfaction of knowing how their words truly affected me.

I feel nothing but annoyance and a determination to find you.

Liar. Don't think you won't get punished for lying to us, Little Darling.

I'm not lying, I will find you.

My fingers tremble slightly as I send the message. I hope this response deter them from their attempt to draw me into their disturbing fantasies.

For a few moments, there is no response, but then a new message appears.

By omission. We see through the face you show the world. We can see your hidden desires, your secret fantasies. You can't deny what lies beneath the surface, Little Darling. Embrace it.

My heart races as their words taunt me. They have an uncanny ability to dig beneath my exterior and expose the thoughts I try to keep hidden. It is a chilling reminder of just how much power they hold over me.

But I refuse to let their game consume me. I take a deep breath, grounding myself in my resolve to resist their manipulation.

I type my response, refusing to give in to their attempts to rattle me further.

> I won't deny the complexities of human desires. But I choose to rise above the darkness you seek to exploit. Your perception may be distorted, but I will not succumb to your version of me.

As I hit the send button, defiance surges through me. I would not allow them to dictate my identity or control my actions.

The minutes tick by, but there is no immediate response. The silence fills the room, amplifying the tension that lingers in the air. I know this is far from over.

Finally, a new message appears on the screen.

> Bold words, Little Darling. We'll see if you can truly resist the allure of the darkness within. Soon.

The message sends a chill down my spine, but I refuse to let it deter me. I am intent on finding the truth and bringing an end to this. I would not let them kill another innocent woman.

Locking the phone, I stand and make my way to my bedroom. I am not going to admit that the rest helped when they had a hand in it, I would just use it against them by doubling my efforts to find them.

As I enter my bedroom, a sense of unease lingers in the air. The violation of my privacy has reached new heights, and I can't help but feel a constant watchful presence lurking in the shadows.

In an attempt to wash away the remnants of their intrusion, I decide to take a shower, locking the door and pulling the window shade completely down this time. The warm water cascades over my body, providing a brief respite. As the steam envelops the bathroom, I let my thoughts wander, set on devising a plan to outsmart them.

Suddenly, a memory flickers in my mind. Mark was the last person I saw before I found myself in this unsettling situation. He brought me a cup of coffee, a gesture of kindness and an excuse for the opportunity to ask me out. But now, doubts begin to gnaw at the edges of my thoughts.

Could Mark be involved? Is he part of this sick game? It is a haunting idea, casting a shadow of suspicion on someone I thought was meant to be an ally.

Finishing my shower, I wrap a towel around myself, the cool air of the bathroom serving as a stark reminder of the chilling reality I face. Determined to uncover the truth, I internally resolve to investigate Mark's involvement further.

After getting dressed, I make my way to the office. The drive feels longer than usual, the weight of the situation weighing heavily on my mind. I need to gather more information, to connect the dots and expose those responsible.

On the way, I stop by the drive through café, unable to resist the now familiar routine that brings me a semblance of normalcy. I order my usual bagel and coffee, finding solace in the familiar flavors that provide a brief respite from the chaos of my life.

It surprises me to see some media personnel outside the office building as I turn-into the parking garage. I check the time, realizing it is a little later than I arrived the previous day. I breathe a sigh of relief that they don't leave the building entrance since I have no update to tell them and I could avoid them by using the parking garage elevator.

As I park my car and make my way towards the elevator, I try to maintain a composed exterior, despite the turmoil swirling within me. I am only moments away from pressing the elevator button when I hear a voice.

“Alex,” the voice calls out from behind me.

Turning, I see Tristan Winters striding casually towards me, his hands buried in his pockets and a smirk on his face.

I am not in the mood for his charm. “That’s Agent Darling to you, Mr. Winters,” I respond with a raised eyebrow.

Tristan chuckles, undeterred by my cold response. “So formal, Agent Darling. Don’t tell me the hard and grumpy Agent Matthews converted you to his way of thinking. Not all journalists are bad, you may even like me if you get to know me. Imagine the look of horror on his face if you did,” he gives an exaggerated look of shock, bringing his hand up to hover in front of his open mouth as he widens his eyes.

My lips twitch in amusement.

"Nice try, Winters," I reply, my tone softening slightly. "But I think we both know it takes more than a few witty remarks to win me over."

Tristan feigns a hurt expression, placing a hand dramatically over his heart. "Ouch, Darling. You wound me with your cold indifference."

I roll my eyes playfully, appreciating the momentary distraction from the heaviness of the situation. "Save your theatrics for someone who's impressed, Winters. I have work to do."

Tristan's smirk fades into a more serious expression as he takes a step closer. "I know you're focused on the investigation, and I respect that. But I can't help but feel there's more to this than what meets the eye. I've been covering crime for years, and sometimes an outsider's perspective can bring a fresh angle. I just want to help, Alex."

I pause for a moment, considering his words. While I appreciate Tristan's enthusiasm and his genuine desire to assist, I can't risk compromising the investigation or revealing sensitive information.

"Tristan, I understand your intentions, but this is still an ongoing investigation. I can't tell you more than what you already know," I respond firmly, meeting his gaze. "I need to tread carefully, follow the protocol, and protect the integrity of the case."

Tristan's expression flickers with disappointment, but he nods understandingly. "I get it, Alex. Just know that if you ever need someone to bounce ideas off of or a different perspective, I'm here. Our roles may be different, but I will alway be here if you need me."

I appreciate his offer, knowing that having an ally outside the confines of law enforcement can be valuable. "Thank you, Tristan. I'll keep that in mind."

With a nod, Tristan takes a step back. "Alright, then. I'll let you head up before Agent Derek decides to hunt you down. If you need anything, just say the word."

"Will do," I reply, gratitude in my voice.

I turn back toward the elevator when a voice calls out from the entrance to the parking garage, "Tristan!"

I turn my head to see another man closing in on us, but there is a sense of familiarity evident in Tristan's reaction. "Agent Darling, this is my good friend, Max," Tristan introduces him, motioning towards the man who had caught up to us. He is a little taller than Tristan, with dark brown hair and eyes. There is a look on his face as though he found the whole world humorous.

Max extends his hand towards me, and I shake it firmly. "Nice to meet you, Agent Darling. Tristan here has told me a little about you and the case you're working on. Said you might need my expertise."

I raise an eyebrow, curious about Max's involvement. "Has he now? And what exactly does your expertise entail?"

Max's lips curl into a sly smile. "Let's just say I have unconventional means of gathering information. Sometimes, you need to go beyond the usual channels to get the answers you're looking for."

I exchange a glance with Tristan, silently questioning his judgment. He nods, indicating his trust in Max. It's clear that they have a preexisting professional relationship.

"I appreciate the offer, Max, but as I mentioned to Tristan, this is an ongoing investigation. I can't compromise its integrity," I state firmly, reiterating my commitment to following proper procedures.

Max chuckles, unfazed by my response. "I understand your concern, Agent Darling. Rest assured, my methods are discreet and have a track record of success. Sometimes, the truth requires us to explore less conventional avenues."

I consider Max's words carefully, contemplating the potential benefits of leveraging his unique approach. While it goes against my usual instincts, the urgency of the situation and the lack of progress so far compel me to reconsider.

"I'll think about it," I concede.

Tristan sighs and reaches out to touch my arm. The move surprises me, but I don't let it show. "Go on up, I'd rather not die today when a certain agent realizes we ambushed you."

As we part ways, I feel a mixture of emotions. Tristan's presence is both a distraction and a source of support. While I'm determined to keep him at arm's length for now, I can't deny that his perspective might shed light on aspects I may have overlooked. And his friend could be useful to potentially find details we couldn't find by conventional means.

Entering the elevator, I press the button and watch as the doors close, sealing me within the confined space. The stress of the case bears down on me once again, reminding me of the stakes involved. I brace myself for what lies ahead. It's time to uncover the truth and put an end to this, no matter the cost.

Chapter 9

Alex

As the elevator ascends, I take a deep breath, steeling myself for the challenges that lie ahead. The ride feels unusually long, amplifying the anticipation and gravity of the situation. The rhythmic hum of the elevator provides a steady backdrop to my thoughts.

Tristan was right, when I step off the elevator to head to the office, Derek messages me, asking if I am okay and when I am heading in. I wave my phone at him as I walk in and set my breakfast down.

“Sorry, I was delayed,” I say as I slump into a chair at the table. It honestly feels like it has been an eternity since I awoke in my own sanctuary.

Derek just continues to look at me with a raised eyebrow. “Are you okay?”

I nod, offering a reassuring smile. "Yes, Derek, I'm all good," I reply, hoping to convey a sense of normalcy. But his persistent gaze tells me that he's not completely convinced.

He takes a seat across from me, his eyes fixated on me. “Are you sure?” he asks again, before holding up what I can now see is an unfinished report that I started the night before.

I glance at the report, realizing that I had indeed left it unfinished in the middle of a sentence and I feel heat creep up my neck as a touch of guilt gnaws at me. "Oh, that... It's nothing, I got really tired, and didn’t think it would be a good idea to continue it just in case I missed something important," I say, trying to downplay the significance.

Derek leans forward slightly, his expression growing more serious. "Alex, we're in the middle of a crucial investigation here. We can't afford distractions or lapses in focus. Is something bothering you?"

I take a moment to consider Derek's question and the pressure of the situation. While I appreciate his concern and trust, I just can't tell him about the reason the report is half done.

I meet Derek's gaze, mustering a reassuring smile. "Thanks for your concern, Derek. I appreciate it. But it's as I said, I want to do justice to these victims and didn't think I could while I was exhausted, I'll get the reports completed now."

Derek looks at me for a moment, assessing my response, before finally nodding. "Alright, Alex. Just remember, I'm here for you if you need someone to talk to. We're a team, and we support each other."

"Thank you, Derek. I'll keep that in mind," I reply, genuinely grateful for his understanding.

With that, the tension in the room eases slightly, and we both turn our attention back to the unfinished report. Derek resumes the conversation, discussing the progress we've made and the next steps we need to take. We are heading back out into the field today to continue the face-to-face interviews and retracing the steps of the victims.

We both work to finish up the reports that I left unfinished the night before and then we prepare to head out. We stop at the cafe on the way out but I decline Derek's offer to get a cup while he chooses to get one for himself.

As he is waiting in line I take out my phone and open the messenger app.

Truth or dare?

Truth, Little Darling.

I thought you said something about it being a safe option and about stepping out of your comfort zone.

I will when you do.

Taking a moment to gather my thoughts, I compose my question, hoping that my choice could potentially impact the hunt for these killers.

Why do you choose the women that you choose?

For the fun of it.

I narrow my eyes as I look at the response on the screen of my phone.

Liar

Turnabout is fair play, Little Darling. It's not a lie, but two can play the omission game.

I growl to myself and clench my hand around my phone. Just as frustration starts to bubble within me, Derek returns with his coffee in hand. He notices my tense expression and raises an eyebrow.

"Everything okay?" he asks, concern etched on his face.

I take a deep breath, forcing a smile. "Yeah, just a small personal hiccup but I've got it under control."

He studies me for a moment, skeptical of my answer. "Alright, just remember to take care of yourself."

I nod, grateful again for his support. "I will. Thanks."

With another sip of his coffee, Derek leads the way as we head out.

It's late afternoon when my phone buzzes again.

Truth or Dare, Little Darling?

I stare at the screen while Derek is distracted driving, my phone turned away so he can't see. I think about it for a moment, taking into consideration the previous messages before I type out my response.

Dare

The anticipation builds as I wait for their response. The gravity of the situation frustrates me, but I refuse to let fear or uncertainty dictate my actions. I'm determined to take control.

Their message finally appears on the screen.

I dare you to go to the abandoned warehouse on Elm Street at midnight. There will be a present there for you.

My heart skips a beat as I read their dare. The abandoned warehouse on Elm Street holds an air of darkness and danger, but I refuse to back down. This is another opportunity to gather clues and potentially bring an end to their sinister game.

I glance at Derek, who remains focused on the road, unaware of the conversation unfolding on my phone. The pressure of this decision rests solely on my shoulders. I take a deep breath, steeling myself for what lies ahead.

Dare accepted.

Derek and I immerse ourselves in our work, diligently continuing to visit the last known locations of the victims and interviewing potential witnesses. We leave no stone unturned, meticulously gathering any information that could bring us closer to the truth. Despite our efforts, the day wears on, and a sense of frustration settles within me. The weight of the impending dare hangs heavily in the air, distracting me from the task at hand.

As the sun begins its descent, casting long shadows across the city, I struggle to focus on anything else. The absence of significant breakthroughs during our interviews only amplifies my restlessness. Each passing moment brings me closer to midnight, and the anticipation grows inside me.

After the sunset, Derek and I return to the office, working side by side writing out the reports from our recent interviews and adding any new findings to our extensive case notes. Despite our efforts, there is no fresh evidence or breakthroughs to be found, intensifying the frustration that gnaws at me.

The absence of progress weighs heavily on our shoulders, testing our resilience. We exchange glances of mutual understanding, acknowledging the mounting pressure to make headway in the investigation. The relentless pursuit of the murderers fuels my determination, but the lack of substantial leads adds an additional layer of urgency to our actions.

As we continue to work, the deadline approaches, and the dare at the abandoned warehouse looms over me. The knowledge that a potential clue or revelation awaits there tugs at the edges of my thoughts, challenging me to stay focused despite the setbacks we've encountered.

Derek calls it a night at ten while I once again volunteer to stay and finish the reports. As the office falls into silence, the only sounds are the scratching of my pen on paper and the rhythmic hum of the air conditioning. With each stroke of the pen, my mind wanders to the abandoned warehouse on Elm Street, the eerie location that awaits me.

Another hour passes, and the reports are finally complete. I gather my belongings, ensuring I have my gun just in case. The darkness outside the office window matches the shadows that loom over my thoughts.

While I wait for the elevator, my phone buzzes in my hand and I look down at it as the elevator reaches me.

I hope you like your present, Little Darling.

I frown and look up as I prepare to get into the elevator, only to realize it's not empty.

I meet the cold gaze of Agent Decker, who stands in the elevator next to Agent Travis who has his eyes fixed on his phone and a smirk on his face. His presence takes me by surprise, but I quickly regain my composure, slipping my phone back into my pocket.

"Agents," I greet them, keeping my tone neutral. "What brings you here?"

Agent Travis chuckles humorlessly as he tucks his phone away. "Just passing by, Agent Darling. Thought we'd take a ride in the elevator, you know, enjoy the scenic view."

His nonchalant demeanor unnerves me but I step into the elevator, standing against the opposite wall. The doors slide shut, enclosing us in the confined space.

As the elevator descends, I feel the tension in the air between Agent Decker, Agent Travis, and myself. Their unexpected presence raises my suspicion, especially considering the timing of their arrival. I remain cautious, keeping my guard up and my emotions in check.

With a calm demeanor, I meet Agent Decker's cold gaze. "Is that so?"

He smirks, his eyes glinting with an enigmatic intensity. "It's always interesting to see what unfolds in these elevators."

Agent Travis' smirk widens as he leans casually against the elevator wall. "Yes, it's quite fascinating, isn't it? The confined space, the rising tension. One never knows what secrets might be revealed."

Their words send a chill down my spine. My mind races, trying to decipher their intentions. Do they have any involvement in this?

"I wasn't aware elevator rides had become a spectator sport," I reply, my voice laced with caution. "If there's nothing else, I suggest we focus on our respective duties."

Agent Travis continues to look at me, his eyes gleaming with something I can't identify. "So, Agent Darling, any excitement this evening?"

I raise an eyebrow, choosing my words carefully. "Just wrapping up some work, Agent Travis. Nothing out of the ordinary."

He is amused by my response. "Ah, work, always a thrilling endeavor. But you know, sometimes it's good to step outside our comfort zone. You never know what you might find."

His words send a shiver down my spine. I can't help but wonder if he's alluding to the dare, if he somehow knows about it. My guard goes up, and I remain cautious, refusing to reveal any signs of vulnerability.

"I appreciate your advice, Agent," I reply, my tone steady. "But I believe in staying focused on the task at hand. We have a job to do, and that's where my priority lies."

He chuckles again, a low, unsettling sound. "Of course, Agent Darling. I wouldn't expect anything less from you."

The elevator slows to a stop, and the doors slide open, revealing the building foyer. Agent Decker steps out first, followed by Agent Travis who glances back at me before he walks away.

As the elevator doors close, I take a deep breath, grounding myself in the present moment. I refuse to let the presence of Agents Decker and Travis distract me. The abandoned warehouse on Elm Street awaits, and I will face it head-on.

Filled with renewed resolve, I step off the elevator as it reaches the parking garage. Making my way to my car, my mind is still processing the encounter with Agents Decker and Travis. Their presence was unsettling, and their cryptic comments only added to the mystery surrounding them. But I can't let their words distract me from my mission.

As I drive towards the abandoned warehouse on Elm Street, the night envelops the city in darkness. The streets are deserted, and an eerie silence hangs in the air. The dare and the potential danger that awaits me looms heavily.

Arriving at the warehouse, I park my car a short distance away, ensuring it's inconspicuous. I know I'm early, the clock in my car reading only half past eleven but I have hope of potentially catching the killers as they leave whatever they are wanting me to have.

I check my surroundings, scanning the area for any signs of movement or potential threats. Satisfied that I'm alone, I step out and approach the looming structure with cautious steps.

The warehouse stands as a monument of forgotten memories, its decaying walls whispering stories of the past. The air is thick with an inexplicable sense of foreboding, but I push forward.

As I step through the entrance, the darkness envelops me, broken only by faint streaks of moonlight filtering through cracks in the roof. I navigate the dilapidated interior, my footsteps echoing in the silence. The echoes serve as a constant reminder of the eerie atmosphere surrounding me, but I remain focused on my objective.

Finally, I reach a dimly lit room at the heart of the warehouse. The air grows still, and anticipation settles over me. I survey my surroundings, searching for the promised present, hoping it holds answers or leads that can bring me closer to the truth.

Suddenly, a glimmer catches my eye—a small, wrapped package resting on an old wooden crate at the heart of the room. My heart skips a beat as I approach it cautiously. I inspect it for any signs of danger, but it appears harmless.

As I reach for it a noise across the other side of the room startles me and I lift my head. There is a figure in the opposite doorway, leaning against the frame. The figure is dressed completely in tight black clothes all the way from their feet to the hood that's raised over their head, even black gloves cover their hands. With a tilt of their head, the filtered light hits their face and all I can see is the detailed skull mask that covers from the nose down.

"Hey, Little Darling," the voice is modulated and sinister sounding with an electronic edge to it.

I instantly reach for my gun, but the distraction costs me. I don't even have it aimed at the figure when a slight noise right behind me has me automatically turning in that direction.

A strong gloved hand wraps around my arm with the gun before I can turn and a sharp pain in my neck sends a jolt through my body. My vision blurs, and I feel my legs give way beneath me. The world spins as darkness engulfs my senses. The last thing I hear before succumbing to unconsciousness is the distorted voice of the figure behind me, echoing ominously.

"Time for a nap, Little Darling."

Chapter 10

Alex

As I slowly regain consciousness, my senses come back to life. The first thing I notice is the sharp pain and tension coursing through my arms. I groan softly as I become aware of my precarious position, hanging from a chain in the center of the room.

Struggling to focus, I blink my eyes open, my surroundings slowly coming into view. The dimly lit room reveals its decaying walls, the peeling wallpaper bearing witness to years of neglect. Dust particles dance in the air, catching the faint streaks of moonlight that manage to filter through the cracks in the roof.

I can see my gun laying on the crate next to the wrapped gift that had drawn me here. I feel momentarily ashamed for how stupid I was to fall into such an obvious trap, but I wasn't able to pass up the allure of more information on the murderers.

"Awake again, Little Darling?" The voice almost directly behind my ear startles me and I jerk on the chains, the sound of the movement echoing in the decaying room.

A chuckle sounds, and I feel fingertips brush my back sending a shiver down my spine. The fingers trail against me as the figure moves around my body to stop in front of me. My heart is racing in my chest. I have to push down the panic that is bubbling to the surface. The figure stills their fingers just below the space between my breasts.

“I was worried I was going to have to give you adrenaline to wake you up.” I can tell their voice is being changed somehow and when they tilt their head back slightly I’m confronted with a half skull mask covering the lower half of their face looking out at me from their hood. There must be a voice modulating device built into the mask.

A shift in the light briefly gives me the sight of intense black eyes. No person has eyes that dark, even with the dim light it meant they either had brown eyes or were using contact lenses.

As I lock eyes with the figure, a shiver runs down my spine. their intense gaze penetrates through the darkness. Fear intertwines with my determination, but I refuse to let it overpower me.

The figure's gloved hand slides up, wrapping around my throat, their fingers pressing into my skin. I feel the pressure, the tightness constricting my breath. Panic wells up within me, but I struggle to maintain composure, to prevent them from seeing my fear.

With a chilling calmness, the figure leans closer, their skull mask inches away from my face. Their modulated voice resonates through the room, full of sadistic satisfaction.

"How are you liking our little game of truth or dare, Little Darling?" they taunt.

Despite the fear coursing through me, I summon the strength to speak, my voice strained but defiant. "Your games are going to be over for good soon enough.”

A low chuckle reverberates from behind the skull mask. I hear another chuckle from behind me but I can’t see the other figure. "Bold words, Little Darling, for someone who no longer has their gun.”

My eyes flick to where it sits so innocently on the nearby crate. It’s another way to torture me, having it so close but still out of my reach.

The figure follows the movement of my eyes, looking down at the gun. “You didn’t think we would let you keep that did you?”

A body presses against my back, and a similar modulated voice then speaks close to my ear. “You can have it back when we’re done.”

I feel a surge of adrenaline course through me, a mix of fear and anticipation, as the figure in front of me tightens their hand on my throat. “But only if you’re a good girl.”

The pressure on my throat intensifies, sending a thrill down my spine. The sensation of being surrounded by them, their hands on me, sends a mixed wave of fear and unexpected arousal rippling through my body. It's a confusing and unsettling combination that only adds to the complexity of the situation.

The voice behind my ear asks, "Are you going to be a good girl for us, Little Darling?" The voice, distorted yet laced with a seductive undertone, only adds fuel to the confusing fire that burns within me. It becomes increasingly difficult to ignore the sensations that stir within me, the intensity of the moment, and the power play unfolding around me. My heart pounds in my chest, both from the physical restraint and the tantalizing danger that hangs in the air.

I try to steady myself, to regain control of my thoughts and emotions, but their touch and the sensation of being dominated only heightens my awareness. It's a dangerous dance between survival and the inexplicable allure of their power.

I fight to regain my focus, to push away the distraction of these conflicting emotions. Deep down, I know that succumbing to them would be a betrayal of my principles, a surrender to darkness I fought so hard against.

Summoning every ounce of strength, I steady my voice, ignoring the tremor that threatens to betray me. "I'll never be your 'good girl.' I won't play your games. You won't break me."

The figure's grip tightens further, their laughter resonating in the room. "Oh, Little Darling, such fire. Who says we want to break you? The darkness within you calls to us. Embrace it."

The figure before me presses closer, pushing me harder into the figure at my back. Their presence becomes suffocating, igniting a dark, forbidden desire. Their arousal is evident, their hard cocks pressing against my body. I struggle against the conflicting emotions inside of me, my body betraying me with a slight tremor.

I find myself questioning my own feelings, my own boundaries. The danger lingers, the thrill entwined with the fear, creating an allure that both frightens and entices me.

The figure in front of me leans closer, the skull mask brushing against my cheek. It's surprisingly soft, as though made of silicone. "If I touch your pussy right now, would you be wet for us, Little Darling?"

My body betrays me further and I can't stop the trembling whimper that escapes my lips.

I try to control my breathing, desperately trying to push away the conflicting emotions that threaten to consume me. The figure's words, filled with sadistic anticipation, echo through my mind, mingling with the sensations of their hands on my throat and their bodies pressed against mine.

The intensity of the moment, the thrill of danger, and the unfamiliar stirrings within me create a chaotic storm of confusion.

Summoning the last vestiges of my strength, I manage to speak, my voice quivering yet resolute. "I refuse to let you manipulate me. Your twisted desires won't control me."

The figure behind me chuckles, the sound sending a chill down my spine. "Oh, Little Darling, it's not about manipulation. It's about discovering your true self, the desires that lurk within. We can set you free."

The gloved hand leaves my throat, and a surge of relief washes over me. However, before I can fully comprehend the situation, I feel their fingers trace a path down my body, stopping at the hem of my pants.

I tense, my instincts urging me to resist, but a small part of me questions the depth of my own desires. I wrestle with the thoughts that flicker through my mind, the ones telling me to give in.

The figure's voice, now a mere whisper, reaches my ears once more. "Don't be afraid of what you truly want, Little Darling. Embrace the darkness. Surrender."

The words ignite a dangerous curiosity within me, mingling with the fear that still lingers. It's a tantalizing walk on the edge of forbidden territory.

I'm so caught up in my own thoughts and emotions that I barely register when the gloved fingers flick open the button of my pants. The fingers slide into the opening and past my underwear and directly to where I already know I'm dripping for them.

I gasp, the touch electrifying. The figure's fingers move with a deliberate slowness, teasing and exploring, pushing the boundaries of my resistance.

I struggle to maintain composure, to cling to the last shreds of defiance. Every fiber of my being screams for me to resist, to escape from this situation. But a small voice within me, a voice I have repressed for so long, whispers of surrender.

As their touch intensifies, tracing circles and exerting a maddening pressure, my body reacts against my will. Waves of pleasure ripple through me, mingling with the fear that still lingers.

The figure's voice, now a breathy whisper, reaches my ear once more. "Feel it, Little Darling. Embrace the desires that simmer beneath the surface. Let go of your inhibitions."

My mind spins, torn between the need to fight and the overwhelming sensations that ripple through my body. In this moment of vulnerability, I confront a part of myself I have long denied, a hidden craving for the forbidden.

Yet, as my body responds, my mind races to find an escape, to regain control. I refuse to succumb to them, to become their pawn.

Summoning my strength, I force the words past the turmoil within me. "I won't be a slave to your darkness. I won't lose myself."

The figure's fingers pause, the pressure easing, and a low chuckle reverberates in the room. "You resist with such fervor, Little Darling. But deep down, you yearn for the release that only surrender can bring."

A burst of defiance surges through me, fueled by the realization that my strength lies in resisting their twisted allure. I gather my resolve, channeling it into a quiet but fierce determination.

"No," I say, my voice firm and unwavering. "I won't let you corrupt me. I won't be defined by your twisted desires. I am stronger than you think."

Their laughter echoes through the room but the figure removes his gloved hand from my pants. "You will learn, Little Darling. In time, you will beg for release."

The figure holds their hand up, looking at it as it turns in the light to show the wetness covering their gloved fingers that came from me. They bring them to their face and using their other hand move the mask to allow them to slide the fingers beneath it but still not giving me any details of the face beneath the mask.

I hear as they suck the remnants of me off their fingers and they moan.

The fingers reappear only to return to my throat as they step closer again, pushing me back against the figure behind me. “You taste so good, Little Darling. I can’t wait to devour you.”

In the face of their threats, I find solace in the knowledge that true strength lies in resistance, in the ability to hold onto one's values in the face of adversity. I won't allow them to break me.

As I stare into the figure's intense black eyes, my fear melts away, replaced by the strength of my resolve.

The figure leans in closer, their voice dripping with menace. "You may think you're strong, but the darkness within you is undeniable. And we will be there to embrace it when the time comes."

A growl escapes my lips, an instinctual response to their taunting words. The sound surprises even me, a raw display of defiance that echoes off the decaying walls.

The figure's grip tightens on my throat, their fingers digging into my skin. They lean in even closer, their eyes locking with mine. "Ah, the fire in you, Little Darling" they say, their voice laced with a mix of amusement and anticipation. "It just makes me want to fuck you more. To wrap my hand around this pretty little neck and squeeze until you can’t feel anything but my cock until you pass out."

As I hang there, my gaze unwavering and determined to hide the effect those words have on me, I meet the figures' eyes. I refuse to back down, knowing that the power lies within me to overcome their twisted games.

They just laugh in response. “We actually only came here with the intent to introduce ourselves,” the figure says with a thoughtful tilt of its head.

“I’m Truth,” comes the voice of the figure behind me.

“And I’m Dare,” says the one in front of me. “Don’t worry, this is one truth and dare game you won’t have to choose between.”

With a final squeeze of their hand, they release me, leaving me hanging from the chains once again. As they retreat into the shadows, their mocking laughter echoes through the decaying room, a haunting reminder of the danger that still surrounds me.

"Oh, Little Darling," their voice echoes through the silence when I can no longer see them, resonating with a dark delight. "You may think we’re letting you go, but you're mistaken. You belong to us now."

I continue to hang there, the minutes stretching like eternity as I struggle to figure out how I would be getting out of the predicament I found myself in when a metal noise sounds in the silence and I drop to the ground.

As I crash to the ground, the impact jolts through my body, the pain reverberating in my limbs. I lie there, momentarily disoriented, taking deep breaths to steady myself.

Through the haze of pain, my eyes dart around the room, searching for any sign of the figures. To my relief, they are nowhere in sight.

I push myself up from the cold, dusty floor. The chains that bound me hang loosely, their heaviness a reminder of the situation I narrowly escaped. With shaky hands, I reach for my gun on the nearby crate, grasping it tightly; its familiar feeling brings a sense of security.

My attention then turns to the wrapped gift, a mysterious object that drew me to the warehouse. Curiosity mingles with caution, I carefully pick it up, feeling the weight in my hands. I know I can't fully unravel its secrets here and now, but I refuse to leave it behind.

As I tuck the gift under my arm, I cast a final glance around the room, taking in the decaying walls, the eerie silence that hangs in the air. There is an unsettling presence that lingers, a reminder of the darkness I have escaped, but I refuse to let it consume me.

Chapter 11

Dare

I watch from the shadows as she calmly walks back toward her car. I'm always watching her, every chance I get I'm looking at her. It's an obsession and it consumes me completely.

Truth shifts slightly out of the corner of my eye, watching her with the same intensity that I do. We share this dark secret, bound by our mutual infatuation. Truth is like a reflection of my own desires and fears. We understand each other without uttering a single word.

So far she has exceeded all of our expectations, she is going to be our dark Queen. The one we will worship above all others. She just has to embrace that part of herself.

I could still taste her, her flavor lingering in my mouth and just making me ache even more for her. I told her the truth, I couldn't wait to devour her. That small whimper that she couldn't stop will play on repeat in my mind when I wrap my own hand around my cock later.

My heart races with anticipation as I watch her unlock the car door and slide into the driver's seat. The engine purrs to life, breaking the silence of the night. She glances briefly in my direction, her gaze piercing through the darkness, but her awareness of my presence remains uncertain.

I hope she likes the gift. Maybe one day we would tell her what we did to get it for her.

As she starts the engine and drives away, I watch the tail lights fade into the night, swallowed by the darkness. I don't need to follow right away, I know exactly where she is going. And following right now would be too obvious while the streets are empty.

As much as the need burns inside me to see her reaction to our present in person, the cameras we hid in her house would have to suffice.

I would be sure to make her thank me properly some other time.

Truth walks over to me, removing his mask now that she has gone. I reach up and remove mine, shoving it into the pocket of my hoodie.

"That went better than expected," he says, turning once more to look in the direction she disappeared and showing his obsession again.

But then I still haven't looked away either. "Yes it did," I responded distractedly. It's not like he isn't used to my behavior by now.

He reaches out and takes hold of my wrist, bringing my gloved fingers to his nose and inhaling deeply. His moan is obscene, and I snatch my hand away before he does something stupid like sucks on my fingers. He just snickers in response.

"Wish it was my fingers on her pretty pussy," he says.

"Soon enough," I respond, trying to temper his fervor. "Our time will come, but we have to be careful, methodical. She needs to be deeper first, more willing to embrace that side of herself."

Truth's eyes gleam with a dangerous hunger, his smirk betraying the depths of his obsession. It doesn't bother me, it matches my own after all.

We both crave her in ways that defy reason, yearning to unlock the depths of her darkness and revel in the shared ecstasy it promises.

I feel a mix of excitement and caution as I see the look in Truth's eyes, recognizing the reflection of my own desires mirrored back at me. There is an undeniable connection between us, forged in the fires of our shared obsession. We understand the depths to which we are willing to go, how far we are willing to push the boundaries of morality.

Truth's smirk widens; he relishes in the anticipation, fueled by the thought of possessing her in the most intimate of ways. "She will submit," Truth whispers, his voice dripping with certainty. "We will make her ours, body and soul."

I can't help but shiver at his words, the prospect of fulfilling our dark desires lingering at the edges of my consciousness.

"I crave her," he murmurs, his voice dripping with a mixture of longing and anticipation. "I want to see her surrender, to witness her embrace the depths of her desires."

I nod, my own hunger rising like a tide within me. But I know the importance of restraint, of keeping our obsession in check. A surge of anticipation courses through me, fueled by the twisted fantasies that dominate my thoughts. The allure of seeing her surrender to her own darkness, to witness her embrace the depths of her desires, consumes me completely.

Taking my phone out I open it, navigating to the hidden apps and selecting the one I want. Truth crowds closer to look at the screen, humming to himself as the app loads.

Time for the next step.

Chapter 12

Alex

The present sits on my coffee table, it looks so innocent and inconspicuous almost. Except for where it came from.

I still haven't opened it. I haven't done anything since I got home except sit on my couch and look at it. My mind keeps playing on the different things it could be. Some sort of evidence? Some hint of who they are? A bloody bleeding heart?

Nope, too small for that.

I know I am not going to find out until I open the damn thing.

Taking a deep breath, I finally muster the courage to pick up the present from the coffee table. It's surprisingly light, adding to the mystery of its contents. My hands tremble slightly as I turn it around, inspecting it from every angle.

As I unwrap the gift, the layers of paper fall away, revealing a small, unassuming box. Its plain design and lack of embellishments puzzle me even more. How could something so ordinary hold any significance? Nevertheless, I know I have to open it.

I gently lift the lid of the box.

Then I tilt my head in confusion. Nestled in the box is a USB drive.

The sight of the USB drive inside the box unsettles me. I carefully pick it up, feeling its smooth surface against my fingertips. Questions swirl in my mind as I consider its significance. Why would they go through the trouble of giving me a USB drive? What secrets could it hold?

With a mix of apprehension and curiosity, I make my way to my office, clutching the USB drive tightly. The familiar surroundings provide a sense of comfort amidst the brewing storm of uncertainty. I sit down at my desk and open my laptop, the computer screen illuminating the room with its soft glow.

Inserting the USB drive into the port, I watch as the computer recognizes the device and displays its contents. My heart races as a series of named folders pops up—names of the victims that already have spaces dedicated to them on my walls. Each folder contains a collection of photographs, documents, and notes, evidence of the crimes committed against these innocent women. It isn't just images from after they died, there are rows of images from before they died, like surveillance. Or like they were stalked. Which given the murderers I am dealing with is plausible.

As I scroll through the files, a sinking feeling settles in the pit of my stomach. There are more folders—names that I don't recognize. Names that don't match any of the known victims. The realization strikes me that these folders represent other women that the killers targeted, their stories untold. Were they alive or dead?

My hands tremble as I continue to explore the contents of the USB drive. Then, amidst the sea of folders, I stumble upon one that sends a chill down my spine—the folder bearing my own name. Panic mixes with curiosity as I open it, revealing a collection of photographs and documents.

There are surveillance photos of me, candid shots taken without my knowledge. Detailed notes chronicling my daily routines, my interactions, and even my moments of vulnerability. Newspaper articles following my career highlights. And even images from before I moved to town.

My heart races as I flip through the images and documents, my mind trying to process the implications. How could they have so much information about me?

I take a deep breath, forcing myself to maintain composure and stay focused. There would be time to delve deeper into my own folder, but for now, my priority is the folders of the unknown women. There is something about them, something that tugged at my instincts, urging me to uncover their stories.

Clicking out of my own folder, I navigate to the first folder with an unfamiliar name. Inside, there are a handful of photographs—ordinary snapshots of everyday life. Smiling faces, casual moments captured in time. But that's where it ended, there was no evidence of crime scenes.

Opening the next folder, I find a similar collection of images. These women appear to be leading seemingly normal lives, unaware that their stories were intertwined with something far more sinister. The photos were taken discreetly, as if the women were being monitored or stalked. Yet, there is no conclusive evidence of harm.

Confusion and frustration well up inside me. What do these folders mean? Are these women alive or dead? Are they potential targets or survivors? The lack of information gnaws at me, fueling a relentless desire to uncover the truth.

I pull out my phone and navigate to the number they used to send me messages, hitting the call button, not caring that it is now the early hours of the morning.

"Little Darling," the phone hadn't even rang for a full ring before they answered. Their voice is modulated even through the phone.

"Why give me this? How does this benefit you?" I ask.

They chuckle softly, sending a shiver down my spine. *"Ah, Little Darling, who said it would? It will benefit you and that's the main thing."*

I frown further in confusion. "Why would you give me something that would help me stop you?"

Another chuckle. *"Who said it would do that, either? It will help you look for us, but it won't lead you to us."*

I growl in frustration. "Stop talking in riddles."

They sigh softly. "*Little Darling, just say thank you, like a good girl.*"

I hesitate for a moment, but despite my confusion and frustration, a part of me couldn't deny the thrill that courses through my veins at being called "good girl." It stirs something deep within me, awakening a hidden desire I have never fully acknowledged before.

"Thank you," I reply, "But I won't rest until I uncover the truth behind all of this."

They chuckle once more, a chilling sound that reverberates through the phone. "*Oh, Little Darling, you have quite the spirit. Don't worry, the truth will be revealed to you in due time. Now get some sleep.*"

Before I respond, the line goes dead.

I stare at the phone in my hand, a mix of conflicting emotions swirling inside me. The command to get some sleep resonates in my mind, but the adrenaline pumping through my veins makes the idea of rest seem impossible. The USB drive and its disturbing contents consume my thoughts, leaving no room for respite.

But deep down, I know they were right. I couldn't continue my search in this exhausted state. Fatigue would cloud my judgment and hinder my ability to unravel the truth. I need a clear mind, and some sleep in order to have renewed energy to face the challenges ahead.

Reluctantly, I set the phone aside and close my laptop. The room around me feels suffocating, and I long for a breath of fresh air. Leaving the USB drive behind, I make my way to my bedroom, my mind still racing with unanswered questions.

As I lay in bed, I stare up at the ceiling, my thoughts consumed by the mysterious folders, the women's stories, and my own connection to it all. The darkness of the room mirrors the shadows that envelop my mind, and sleep seems elusive.

But as exhaustion settles in, my eyelids grow heavy, and the weight of the day's events pull me into a restless slumber. Once again dreams intertwine with fragments of reality, blurring the lines between truth and fiction.

In the depths of my sleep, my subconscious mind weaves a tapestry of haunting dreams. I find myself in a dimly lit room, the air heavy with anticipation. Masked men surround me, their presence both ominous and alluring. Their faces concealed, they move with a calculated purpose, their eyes gleaming with sinister intensity.

I could feel their hands on me, their touch both invasive and strangely electrifying. Their fingers trace patterns across my skin. The dream becomes a dance of power and vulnerability, where boundaries blur and the lines of control are tenuous.

As the dream unfolds, I become aware of a strange dichotomy within myself. Part of me resists their advances, fighting against the intrusion into my personal space. Yet, another part of me feels an undeniable thrill, a dark fascination with the forbidden and unknown.

The masked men seem to sense this internal struggle, and they revel in it. Their touch intensifies, their grip tightening, as they push the boundaries of consent. The dream becomes a twisted exploration of pleasure and pain, of the conflicting emotions that live deep within my psyche.

In the midst of the chaos, flashes of fragmented memories and images from the USB drive seep into the dream. The faces of the unknown women, the evidence of their stalking, mingle with the masked men in a surreal combination of fear and intrigue.

Abruptly, my eyes fly open, and I find myself gasping for air. The dream left me disoriented and shaken, its vividness lingering like a phantom echo. Sweat coats my body, and my heart races in my chest, as if trying to escape the confines of my ribcage.

I sit up in bed, my breathing gradually slowing as I attempt to ground myself in the reality of my bedroom. The remnants of the dream cling to me, their presence tangible and unsettling. It is as if the boundaries between the dream world and my waking life blurred, leaving me questioning what was real and what was merely a figment of my imagination.

As I glance around the room, the darkness presses in on me, reminding me strongly of my dream. The thought of returning to sleep is daunting, for fear of what other twisted visions my subconscious might conjure up.

Gathering my thoughts, I remind myself that dreams are products of the mind, reflections of our fears, desires, and experiences. The dream I just experienced was undoubtedly influenced by the disturbing contents of the USB drive and the mysteries surrounding it. It was a manifestation of the psychological turmoil I had been grappling with, a surreal manifestation of the blurred lines between victim and investigator.

Pushing aside the disconcerting thoughts, I reach for my phone on the nightstand. The time displayed on its screen confirms that it is still early in the morning, but sunrise isn't far off. I guess it is time to start the day.

Needing to wash away the lingering remnants of the unsettling dream, I take a shower. The warm water cascades over my body, providing a soothing respite from the disquiet that had taken hold of my mind. As I close my eyes, I allow the water to wash away the tension and confusion that cling to me.

After several minutes, I step out of the shower, feeling refreshed and somewhat more grounded. As I reach for a towel to dry myself off, I notice something peculiar. A message is written on the foggy mirror, as if by an invisible hand.

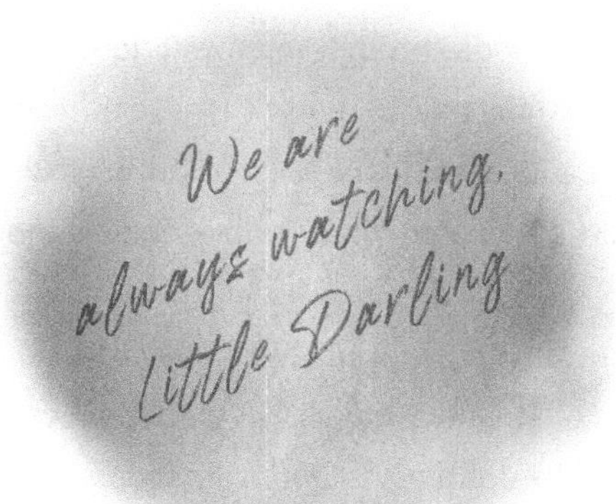
We are
always watching,
Little Darling

Chapter 13
Alex

I feel like I am on a merry-go-round and I can't get off.

After my strange night and then the message on the mirror, I decide to get an extra strong coffee and just dig into the investigation like nothing strange occurred.

I know I need to look through the mysterious files. but until the files supply something new to report to the team, I am going to keep it to myself. Like a lot of things lately. After all, what would I tell them, that the stalkers are fixated on me and giving me more evidence to find them?

As the sun begins to rise, I make my way to a drive-thru café to grab a strong coffee and a bagel. The barista doesn't even bat an eye when I order a double shot, effortlessly preparing my caffeine fix. With breakfast in hand, I head towards the office, relieved to find the parking lot and elevator empty, granting me a brief moment of solitude. However, my luck runs out as soon as I step into the office, where James is already engrossed in reviewing our updated reports.

James barely acknowledges my presence as I walk in. "Still couldn't manage to go grocery shopping?" he remarks, glancing briefly in my direction.

I snort and place my breakfast on the table. James glances at it and asks, "One or two shots?"

"Two shots," I reply, sinking into a chair with a sigh.

He chuckles. "I thought I taught you better than that."

I grin tiredly. "We're not quite at the three-shot stage. Give it time."

His expression turns serious. "Speaking of time, give me an update. Have we made any progress?"

I feel weariness settling in, my mind and body weighed down by the relentless twists and turns of the investigation. Nevertheless, I push aside my fatigue and focus on James' inquiry.

"Not much progress, I'm afraid," I confess. "The leads are scarce, and we're still piecing together the fragments of information we have."

James leans back in his chair, his eyes narrowing. "Any breakthroughs at all?" he presses, his tone a blend of anticipation and concern.

I sigh, rubbing my temples in an attempt to alleviate the growing tension. "Not yet," I admit. "We are re-interviewing everyone that the victims may have come into contact with, hoping for some sort of connection or lead."

James sighs, mirroring my own frustration. He runs a hand through his hair, his gaze fixed on the scattered reports strewn across the table. "It's like they're deliberately avoiding leaving any common breadcrumbs," he mutters, exasperated.

I nod, my weariness deepening. "Exactly. It's as if they're one step ahead, anticipating our every move. They're cunning, methodical, and it's becoming increasingly difficult to build a usable profile."

We both sit in silence for a moment, grappling with the burden of our predicament.

"We can't let frustration cloud our judgment," James finally says, his voice firm. "We need to stay focused, even when the breadcrumbs seem scattered or nonexistent. Somewhere within these fragments lies the key to unraveling their motives and identifying them."

I nod in agreement, steeling myself for the challenges that lay ahead. "I know, we can't afford to lose hope or let their tactics deter us. We'll continue to gather evidence, analyze every piece of information, no matter how small, and adapt our strategies. Eventually, we'll uncover the pattern, no matter how well-hidden it may be."

James lets out a heavy sigh, his gaze fixed on the reports. "Time is working against us," he says. "The longer we spend deciphering these scattered breadcrumbs, the more likely it is that they have already set their sights on another victim."

His words hang heavy in the air, a stark reminder of the urgency of our investigation. Underlying that, however, is the sinking feeling that I already know exactly who they have their sights set on.

Without waiting for my response he stands and makes his way from the room.

I need to make progress, I need more relevant information.

Taking my phone out I open up the messaging app.

Truth or dare?

It takes only a moment for the response to come through.

I'm Truth, but if you're asking for the purpose of our game, then I choose dare. I did promise that I would when you did after all.

My lip twitches and I push down the humor I find in the response. A daring smirk creeps onto my face as I formulate my response, emboldened by the game of cat and mouse we are engaged in. I type my words carefully, anticipation building at their possible reaction.

I dare you to interact with me today. Come out of the shadows. No more hiding.

I hit send, my heart racing with a mix of excitement and apprehension. Would they accept the challenge, or would they retreat further into the darkness, taunting me from afar? The seconds tick by slowly as I await their response, my eyes fixed on the screen, searching for any sign of their next move.

After what feels like an eternity, their reply appears on the screen, short and cryptic.

Dare accepted.

My pulse quickens, the thrill of the chase intensifies as I realize that the stakes have been raised. The ride we are trapped on is about to take a daring turn, and I brace myself for the unknown.

As Derek enters the room, I quickly tuck my phone away, concealing the conversation. The weariness etched on his face mirrors my own, his blue eyes tired, a testament to the toll this investigation has taken on both of us. We exchange a knowing look, silently acknowledging the weight of the challenges we face.

"Morning Alex, looking forward to another thrilling day of interviews?" he asks.

I offer Derek a wry smile. "Thrilling is one word for it," I reply, my voice laced with sarcasm. "But you know me, always up for a challenge."

Derek chuckles, sounding exhausted. "That's what I like about you, Alex. Your unwavering spirit, even in the face of adversity."

I appreciate his words, knowing that we're in this together, navigating the treacherous waters of this investigation. The dare I issued earlier still lingers in the back of my mind, a silent challenge that hangs in the air.

With renewed resolve, we head out, ready to face the interviews that lie ahead. Each conversation, each interaction, hopefully brings us closer to the answers we seek. We delve into the lives of those connected to the victims, carefully listening, observing, and piecing together the fragments of information we gather.

As the day progresses, the interviews blend together, the faces and stories becoming a blur in my mind. But I remain focused, determined not to let any potential leads slip through the cracks. We ask probing questions, searching for any connections, any hint of the truth that has eluded us thus far.

As the day draws to a close, having done all the interviews we could, I find myself back in the office. Derek calls it a night again after we complete our reports. I decide to do the same, making my way to my car also.

The dare lingers in the air, a silent challenge waiting to be met. I check my phone, hoping for a message, but the screen remains blank.

I return to the rental house, change into a long sleep shirt for comfort, and retrieve my personal laptop from my office before making my way to the living room. The day's relentless pursuit of answers has taken its toll, leaving me physically and mentally drained. With a sigh, I set my laptop on the coffee table and sink onto the couch, intending to start going through the mysterious files. But the weariness that clings to me like a heavy cloak proves too difficult to shake off.

I rest my head back against the soft cushion, closing my eyes for a moment to find respite from the swirling thoughts and unanswered questions. Sleep quickly envelops me, pulling me into its depths like a rip tide. The weariness wins, and I succumb to its embrace.

The tranquility of sleep shatters as I startle awake. Disoriented and groggy, my eyes fly open, and a gasp escapes my lips.

There is a mouth on my pussy, hungrily devouring it, as gloved hands hold my legs open. My back arches with a moan as their tongue swirls around my clit.

But I can't see anything.

I try to reach toward my face but my arms won't move.

Whatever has my hands bound shifts, and I can feel the fingers digging into them now where they are being held above my head.

My awareness starts to return and I can feel the couch beneath my body. I must have laid down across it at some point or they laid me down. My head is on the arm rest and my hands are being held over the edge of it.

And one of them has their mouth on my pussy.

I whimper and gasp again as something brushes the side of my face, a modulated voice then speaking close to my ear. "Awake now, Little Darling? How do you like this for interaction?"

My heart races, and I can't stop the moan from escaping me as the mouth on my pussy continues to move. As much as I want to fight against it I cannot deny the arousal and thrill that crashes through me.

I struggle slightly, trying to pull my arms free, wanting to remove what they used to cover my eyes. The mouth moves away from me and a hand lets go of one of my legs and moments later pain shoots through me as a gloved hand lands a sharp slap on my pussy.

I'm stunned into stillness, and then a gloved finger pushes slowly inside me.

He slapped my pussy. Who does that?

And who gets so turned on from it that they start panting and almost cum?

The mouth returns to my clit, the tongue flicking and swirling as their finger starts moving in and out of me.

“You like that, Little Darling? Are you going to be a good girl and cum for us?” comes the voice in my ear again. My pussy clenches as the one between my legs adds another finger.

My mind is a chaotic blend of fear, confusion, and a twisted sense of pleasure. It's a maddening cocktail that intensifies my arousal, despite the shiver of fear that grips me. The dichotomy of sensations sends my body into overdrive, battling between the desire to escape and the yearning for more.

As the pleasure builds within me, I fight to regain control of my thoughts. This isn't what I anticipated when I issued the dare. I expected a response, a challenge, but not this...

The gloved fingers continue to thrust inside my pussy, curling and rubbing in just the right spot every few thrusts. The tongue continues to swirl around my clit, the mouth applying just the right amount of suction to send me catapulting toward the fast approaching orgasm.

“I want to hear you scream, Little Darling.” The words are a seductive purr.

With another curl of the fingers inside me and the bite of teeth on my clit, they get exactly what they want. My back arches off the couch and my scream echoes around the room as I shatter, the waves of my orgasm crashing over me.

I vaguely hear them both groan as the sound leaves my mouth.

“That’s it, Little Darling, fucking music,” the voice groans against the side of my face.

The mouth on my pussy doubles down, attacking my pussy and clit with renewed vigor and shoving an extra finger inside of me. I'm hurtling toward another cliff in seconds, my body going into overdrive as I tighten hard around the fingers thrusting into me.

I writhe and moan uncontrollably as another orgasm rips through me, my body convulsing with pleasure as I scream for them again.

As the waves of pleasure subside, I'm left panting and disoriented, my body covered in a thin sheen of sweat. The gloved hands slowly withdraw from me, leaving me feeling empty and vulnerable. I lie there, still unable to move or see, trying to gather my thoughts and make sense of what just happened.

I vaguely register movement until something touches my lips. My panting mouth gives them access to shove their gloved fingers inside. I taste myself mixed with the taste of leather.

"Suck, and if you bite you will get punished."

I do as I'm instructed, sucking and licking the glove clean.

The fingers leave my mouth and seconds later I feel a hot breath against my lips. He growls "Good girl," to me seconds before his mouth is devouring mine with the same enthusiasm he used to devour my pussy.

I can tell that it's the one who was down there because I could taste myself on his mouth too.

And his voice wasn't modulated.

Chapter 14

Alex

I try to hold onto the memory of his voice but the moment his tongue thrusts into my mouth it's gone like dust in the wind. The taste of him along with myself is intoxicating.

He kisses me like it's the only time he will ever get the chance. His gloved hands grip my hair, the leather pulling painfully on the strands.

I wish I could see him. I wish I could touch him. But suddenly he's gone again, leaving me bewildered and longing for more.

The grip on my wrists adjusts and my hands are raised into the air, then I'm being pulled up off the couch. Darkness still envelops me, the lack of my senses is confusing and disorienting, causing me to stumble and land on my knees.

My heart pounds in my chest as I try to anticipate what will happen next.

"Exactly where I want you, Little Darling. Good girl." The voice this time is modulated, and I don't know if it is the same one who spoke first or if the other one put his mask back on. It sends shivers down my spine.

As I kneel on the ground under their control, a mix of fear and excitement courses through me.

The grip on my wrists changes and my arms are pulled behind my back. Something is wrapped around them and I whimper when it is tightened to the point of pain.

I shake my head slightly but whatever they secured over my eyes doesn't shift. But I sense when one of them steps in front of me.

"Open your mouth, Little Darling," comes the voice again and I feel fingers dig into my chin to still my movements.

I know exactly where this is going. "What do I get if I do?"

They both chuckle, I can hear it from both in front of and behind me. "This isn't a negotiation. I could just make you."

My chuckle is just as sarcastic as theirs. "And I could just bite your cock off too, I'm sure you would enjoy it better if I was a little more willing."

A thumb brushes my bottom lip and I use my teeth to nip at it just to prove my point. It has the opposite effect, making him groan quietly and press his thumb harder against my teeth until I open them and he shoves it into my mouth, using it to press down hard on my tongue.

"How about this, show us just how much of a good girl you can be for both of us, and we will take the blindfold off and sit and have a chat." There is humor in his voice.

I take only a moment to think about it. I cannot pass up the opportunity. I open my mouth wider and tilt my head back.

He groans, "Good fucking girl."

I feel him step closer as his thumb leaves my mouth, the velvet heat of his cock replacing it. My tongue flicks across the head of it, tasting the saltiness of it with a moan of my own.

This is so wrong in so many ways.

His fingers grip my chin, firmly holding me in place as his cock slides into my waiting mouth.

A mixture of forbidden pleasure and excitement courses through me. I work my tongue around him, feeling his hardness and relishing the taste of him. There are a couple of piercings along the underside; I feel them under my tongue and I rub against them. The groans that escape his lips only fuel my desire to please him further.

The other one of them behind me remains silent, but his presence is palpable. I feel his eyes on me, watching my every move. The knowledge that every little move I make is being watched intensifies the thrill, adding an extra layer of exhilaration to the moment.

As I indulge in this forbidden act, a combination of guilt and excitement swirls within me. I am fully aware of the wrongness of the situation, of the boundaries I am crossing. But the intensity of it overwhelms any rational thoughts, leaving me solely focused on the pleasure I am providing.

I continue, moving my mouth along his length and swirling my tongue around him and over his piercings, the line between pleasure and darkness becoming increasingly blurred. The taste of him lingers on my tongue, a mixture of desire and forbidden temptation. His presence engulfs me, dominating my senses as he takes control.

Gloved fingers dig into my hair, gripping and twisting, the pain shooting through my scalp. He thrusts hard into my mouth, his cock hitting the back on my throat, making me gag .

The mixture of fear, excitement, and a primal desire pulsates through my veins. The darkness shrouding me only heightens my senses, amplifying every touch, every sound, every moan I release around his hard cock.

The restraints on my wrists are tight, a painful reminder of my captivity, but I choose to embrace the moment, to surrender to this moment. With each pull and twist, a surge of pleasure intertwines with the discomfort, pushing me further into the depths of my desires.

He groans loudly. "Your mouth feels so good, Little Darling. I can see I'm going to get addicted to the feel of it."

The aura of dominance they exude keeps me on edge, my heart pounding in anticipation. I'm at their mercy, willingly or not, and a part of me revels in the forbidden nature of it all.

With every flick of my tongue, every moan that escapes my lips, I embrace the complexity of this forbidden encounter, knowing that the path I tread is lined with darkness and desire.

His thrusts start to grow more erratic, pushing further into my throat each time, the piercings scraping against me. I relax my throat and his next thrust pushes deep, the groan he releases echoes around the room. My eyes water from the forcefulness, my throat stretched to accommodate him.

His grip on my hair tightens, controlling my movements as he thrusts into my mouth more forcefully. I continue to surrender to his movements, my body adapting to the rhythm he sets. The mixture of pleasure and discomfort melds together, fueling a primal hunger within me. I focus on breathing steadily, allowing him to push deeper into my throat, my gag reflex becoming a mere whisper in the background.

"Fuck," he groans as he thrust as deep as he can and holds me down on him as he explodes in my throat. "Swallow, Little Darling," he groans.

I do as he commands, swallowing every drop, my throat squeezing around the head of his cock as he cums.

He withdraws from my mouth, leaving me breathless and gasping for air. The taste of him lingers on my tongue, a bittersweet reminder of the intensity of the moment we just shared. My lips are swollen and sensitive, my body still pulsating with a mixture of pleasure and anticipation.

The blindfold continues to shield me from the world, leaving me in a state of heightened vulnerability. The darkness heightens my other senses, as I remain kneeling before them, restrained and under their control.

I can sense movement around me before a hand brushes against my face, small touches against my skin as though moving strands of hair aside.

"You're not done yet, Little Darling," comes a modulated voice from above me.

They must have traded places. There is a difference to this voice, almost like it has a strained edge to it.

Something brushes against my sensitive lips and I flick my tongue out against it, tasting the leather of a glove. He growls in response and has a firm harsh grip on my hair seconds later.

I cry out at the forcefulness of it and he takes advantage of my open mouth, pushing his cock all the way into the back of my throat and making me gag. I feel the tears escaping my eyes, but they are just absorbed by whatever they have covering my face.

If the taste of him wasn't different and if he wasn't bigger, I would have thought it's still the same person as the first time. The piercings along the underside are the same.

My body instinctively reacts and tries to pull away, but the grip on my hair keeps me in place, the discomfort and pleasure intensifying the sensations coursing through me. I focus on my breathing, trying to steady myself as he thrusts forcefully into my mouth. Each movement pushes my limits, testing the boundaries of my submission. Spit floods my mouth and drips down my chin, it's messy and wet and just seems to make him more feral.

I press my tongue up against his piercings on his next thrust.

The sound of his strained groans fills the air, mingling with the sound of my choked gasps. The darkness surrounds me, amplifying the raw intensity of the moment. I surrender to his control, allowing myself to be consumed by the forbidden desires that swirl within me.

My throat relaxes to accommodate his size, the resistance fading away as I become lost in the moment. Every flicker of his dominance fuels my own hidden desires, drawing me deeper into the dark abyss.

His grip on my hair tightens, guiding me with an unyielding force. I adapt to his rhythm, my mouth and throat accommodating his every thrust.

A gloved hand suddenly slides between my legs from behind, two fingers thrusting into my dripping wet pussy and rubbing against the front wall. A loud and long moan escapes me around the cock in my mouth.

"That's it, Little Darling. Does being treated like our little slut turn you on? Are you this wet from choking on our cocks?" The modulated voice growling in my ear makes my whole body tremble as he moves his fingers almost violently inside of me.

I barely sense when a hand moves between my face and the body in front of me but nothing prepares me for his fingers closing over my nose and squeezing it closed as the cock in my mouth thrusts deep into my throat and stills there.

My airway constricts, my throat closing around him, and I feel the moment he cums down my throat as I choke on him. Panic surges through me as the grip on my nose cuts off my oxygen supply. I gasp, desperate for a breath, but there is no escape. The darkness around me becomes suffocating, mirroring the control he exerts over me.

In the midst of my struggle, a mix of fear and arousal intertwines, blurring the lines between pleasure and danger. I am at his mercy, completely vulnerable and under his command. Every movement, every sensation, increases the intensity of the moment.

Dizziness floods my body before pleasure rushes through me. My body shatters with the most explosive orgasm that I have ever felt, the intensity of it crashing over me like a tsunami. Waves of ecstasy rip through every fiber of my being, overwhelming the boundaries of pleasure and pain. The combination of the grip on my nose and the cock deep in my throat propels the pleasure to unimaginable heights.

As I surrender to it, my body feels weightless, as if I am floating outside of myself. The darkness that surrounds me seems to dissolve, replaced by a kaleidoscope of sensations and emotions. In this suspended state, my boundaries blur, and I am consumed by the all-encompassing pleasure that engulfs me.

Unable to control my body's response, I writhe and tremble, trapped in the grips of this mind-shattering climax. My moans and whimpers, muffled by the cock in my throat, reverberate throughout the room, mingling with the grunts and groans of the men dominating me.

The feelings of pleasure and darkness intertwine, and I am acutely aware of the forbidden nature of this encounter. But in this moment of euphoria, my desires eclipse all rational thought, leaving me solely focused on the ecstasy coursing through my veins.

As the orgasm gradually subsides, my body relaxes, floating back down to earth. The grip on my nose releases and the one in front of me withdraws from my mouth. I gasp for air, greedily filling my lungs. The taste of him lingers on my tongue, a potent reminder of the depths to which I have surrendered.

My chest heaves, lungs burning as oxygen floods my body once again. I cough, my body trembling from the intensity of the experience.

The silence is palpable, broken only by the sound of my ragged breaths. I remain on my knees, disoriented, yet yearning for more. I can sense them, observing me with an intensity that sends shivers down my spine. My body is a canvas for their darkest desires and I can't help but crave more.

Hands suddenly grip me, lifting and moving me until I feel the couch beneath my ass again before they let go.

Suddenly, light rushes into my eyes and I'm momentarily blinded. It takes a moment for my eyes to adjust and settle before I realize that in reality the light is only dim, coming only from one of the lamps in the room.

Blinking, I watch as they move to sit on the couch opposite the one they placed me on and I can't help but frown. They are once again covered from head to toe, the same as the warehouse, the shadows of their hoods only giving hints of the skull masks they have back on their faces.

My hands are still secured behind my back. I frown as I try to shift my hands, and I glance in their direction before looking back at the figures opposite me with a raised eyebrow.

They both chuckle at my look before one tilts his head to the side. "We agreed we would take your blindfold off. We said nothing about our masks or your restraints, Little Darling."

Well, fuck.

I really should have thought through the price of my submission better.

Chapter 15
Truth

If I wasn't already obsessed with her, then what just happened would have fucking pushed me completely over the edge. Her mouth was like sticking my cock into a piece of heaven, out of this world and forbidden at the same time considering I already know that isn't where I am going to end up.

But the moment she came apart while being suffocated, all my dreams came true. I just wish I could have seen her eyes in that moment, watched the fear enter them and take over as she struggled for breath and couldn't find it, how her eyes would have glazed over as the endorphins rushed into her body, and then how her eyes would have rolled back as she shattered.

Fuck, I need to stop thinking about it; my cock is already rock hard again.

She growls softly at Dare pointing out the limitations on our agreement and I almost laugh again. Silly, Little Darling.

We aren't new to the negotiation game. It would only ever work out well for us and bad for her. Though if she continues to negotiate like she did this visit then I am completely happy with that.

She adjusts on the couch, trying to get comfortable while the restraints still dig into her wrists. She must feel her own cum on her thighs when she moves as a flush creeps up her neck. It's a captivating sight, one that intensifies the heat coursing through my veins.

I choose to break the silence; maybe that will help get my cock under control. “It’s almost midnight, Little Darling. Did we sufficiently ‘interact’ with you today?”

Or maybe not.

Her growl, soft yet filled with defiance, only serves to heighten my desire and I find myself chuckling at her heated look. She is no damsel in distress, no fragile princess waiting for salvation. She is a force to be reckoned with, a match for the darkness that resides within us. She is not the one in need of saving; she is the one who saves herself.

Neither one of us is prince charming, we are the villains. But we both recognise the darkness that lurks inside her, and we all know she doesn’t need prince charming.

Hell, personally I would love to watch her slaughter prince charming and then fuck her in his blood, but that is my own depraved mind talking.

I can't deny the twisted fantasies that consume me, the desire to witness her savagery, to indulge in the depths of her darkness. We are the catalysts for her awakening, the ones who will unveil the depths of her desires and her own depravity.

As I watch her, her flush rising, her eyes closed in a moment of respite, I feel the heat coursing through my veins. I am captivated by her, consumed by the desire to push her limits, to see her embrace that side of herself.

She is a contradiction, an intoxicating blend of strength and vulnerability. And in this twisted dance, I find satisfaction. We are her villains, and she is our muse, a canvas upon which we paint our darkest desires.

Tilting her head, she opens her eyes to look at us again, her gaze filled with a mixture of curiosity and frustration. "Is there any point to me trying to know which one of you is which?" she asks, her voice laced with a hint of defiance.

Dare responds, his tone teasing and suggestive. "Probably not, unless we want you to scream it while we make you cum for us." His words hang in the air, a provocative invitation.

She contemplates her next question, a spark of determination in her eyes. "Will I ever see your faces?" she asks, her voice tinged with both curiosity and a hint of longing.

I chuckle softly, relishing in the power of our anonymity. "Maybe, maybe not," I reply cryptically. "Who knows what the future holds for us."

Her frustration grows, but it only adds fuel to the fire within me. I find pleasure in her longing, in the knowledge that she yearns to unravel the enigma that we are. But that is a desire I am not yet willing to fulfill.

As she continues to search for questions, attempting to seize control of the situation, she poses a query that holds weight. "Are you going to kill me?" Her voice is slightly hesitant, a testament to the emotions that linger beneath the surface.

Dare, never one to shy away from the truth, offers a response, though it may not provide the comfort she seeks. "How about this," he begins, his voice dripping with dark amusement. "If we are going to kill you, we will let you know before we do." His words hang in the air, leaving an unsettling sense of uncertainty.

I fight the urge to laugh, my lips twitching with suppressed amusement. Her frustration is palpable, but it only fuels the intensity of the moment. She needs to ask better questions, to probe deeper into the twisted recesses of our minds.

She continues to assess us, her mind working furiously to find the right words. "Are you stalking anyone else right now?" she asks, her tone laced with curiosity.

I pause for a moment, considering her question. "Not currently," I reply. The truth is far more complex than a simple yes or no, but revealing our secrets would only strip away the allure of our game.

I watch her closely, captivated by the way her mind processes our answers. There is a hunger in her eyes, a thirst for knowledge and understanding. She longs to delve deeper into our twisted world, to explore the complexities that lie within.

As the silence lingers, I feel the heaviness of her unspoken questions hanging in the air. It is a delicate dance, this game we play, where truth and deception intertwine.

I lean forward, my voice a low, seductive whisper. "Ask us another question, Little Darling," I encourage, a sinister smile playing at the corners of my lips though she can't see it. "Delve into the darkest corners of your mind, and we shall meet you there."

I can sense the inner turmoil within her as she grapples with the questions that linger in her mind. Her curiosity battles against her apprehension, and I revel in the power we hold over her psyche. We are the embodiment of her darkest fantasies, the keepers of her deepest desires.

She takes a moment to compose herself, her gaze piercing as she considers her next words. The anticipation in the room is palpable, the air charged with a twisted energy that binds us together.

Finally, she speaks. "Tell me," she begins, her voice wavering only slightly, "what is it that draws you to your victims?"

Dare responds, his voice laced with a chilling allure. "Ah, Little Darling, you have all the information you need in the files we have provided. The reasons behind our choices, what makes us choose them, what makes us kill them, they are all there for you to discover."

"Tick-tock, Little Darling," I interject, my voice a low, husky murmur. "Our time together is limited, and the night grows short. Ask your last question wisely."

I find myself intoxicated by the power play between us, the tantalizing dance around the edge of her boundaries. Each question she poses brings us closer to the precipice of our desires, a fragile thread connecting us in this macabre tapestry.

She pauses, her eyes flickering with uncertainty as she gathers her thoughts, ready to venture further into the depths of our twisted minds.

Finally, her question breaks the silence, cutting through the tension that hangs in the air. "What is it that you truly want from me?" Her voice is strong but there is a small tremble in it, revealing the vulnerability that lies beneath her defiant facade.

My smile gets wider behind my mask, my dark desires unfurling within me. "What we truly want from you, Little Darling," I respond, my voice a low, seductive murmur, "is to unravel the depths of your darkness, to awaken the beast that resides within. We want to witness your surrender, to see you embrace your own depravity with an insatiable hunger."

Dare leans forward, his voice a velvet caress. "We want to take you to the edge of ecstasy and madness, to push your boundaries until they shatter into a million delicious pieces. We want to be the ones who lead you down the twisted path, to create a symphony of twisted desires that consumes us all."

Her eyes widen, but I can see the curiosity flickering within them. It is a dangerous game we play, but she is drawn to it as much as we are. She is our muse, our canvas, and we are willing to explore the darkest recesses of her mind, to indulge in our shared fantasies.

I lean closer, my voice a whisper. "So, Little Darling, ask yourself this: Are you ready to embrace the darkness within, to surrender to the twisted desires that bind us together? Are you ready to become the embodiment of our shared madness?"

The room hangs heavy with anticipation as we wait for her response, the air crackling with the electricity of our forbidden desires. The game is reaching its climax, and we stand on the precipice, ready to plunge into the depths of our darkest passions together.

I can almost see the mental wall she is trying to rebuild in her mind before my eyes, the defiance and stubbornness winning out.

“You will not win against me, I will not let you break me.”

Her words hang in the air, a declaration of resistance that stirs a perverse thrill within me. I admire her strength, her unwavering determination to protect herself from the darkness that beckons. It is a challenge that ignites a twisted fire within me, one that fuels my desire to unravel her defenses, to witness her surrender.

Dare's laughter fills the room, his amusement holding dark undertones. He stands and moves towards her, a predatory grace in his every step. "Oh, Little Darling," he murmurs, his voice dripping with sinful promises, "breaking you is not our intention. But make no mistake, we will make you bend."

She remains defiant, her gaze unwavering, even as Dare looms over her. I observe their interaction with a twisted satisfaction.

With a final lingering look, Dare turns to me, his eyes filled with silent communication. Our time together draws to a close, and we both know it. It is time to retreat into the shadows.

I stand and move around to her other side, drawing her attention back to me. But it's a planned distraction, she doesn’t even see when

Dare pulls out the syringe filled with a sedative. But she feels it when he injects her with it.

She is out within seconds, allowing us to untie her and carry her to her bed.

I watch as Dare gently lays her on the bed, tucking her in with care. Her body appears serene in slumber, a stark contrast to the fiery spirit she exhibited moments ago. We move around the room, securing the house, ensuring that no trace of our presence remains.

As we make our way towards the exit, I cast a final glance toward her bedroom where her sleeping form is, longing stirring within me. The minutes stretch before us, an eternity of waiting until we can see her again, until we can resume our twisted dance.

Outside, the night is cloaked in darkness, matching the shadows that live within us. I feel a thrill, a twisted satisfaction, knowing that we have left our mark upon her, imprinted our presence upon her very soul. She may resist, she may fight against the allure, but in the depths of her being, she craves the darkness that binds us together.

Chapter 16

Alex

I'm starting to feel like a failure to my FBI training. I need to stop letting them drug me. I wake up early from my deep, albeit drug-induced, sleep. Checking my phone there, I see there is still another hour until sunrise.

As the weight of our encounter lingers in the air, I take a deep breath, trying to gather myself. The conflicting emotions inside me churn, a mix of frustration and self-doubt. I have to push aside the disquieting thoughts and focus on the task at hand. Retrieving my laptop, I settle back into bed, the dim glow of the screen illuminating my face.

Opening the folder containing the files on our most recent victim, I start to delve deeper into the details. It contains a wealth of information, far more than I had initially realized. My heart sinks as I realize the extent of my oversight. How could I have missed these crucial details during my first review?

The documents paint a chilling picture of the victim's life, their fears, and vulnerabilities. The meticulousness of the planning becomes apparent, the depth of their depravity sending shivers down my spine. I read through witness statements, forensic reports, and looked through the photographs, my mind racing to piece together the puzzle.

But amidst the expected evidence, I stumble upon some peculiar documents that send a jolt of confusion and unease through me. As I dig deeper into the files, my initial confusion turns into a chilling realization. These documents are crime reports, detailing their connection to illicit activities that I have never seen before. Murder, child endangerment, trafficking. These reports are not part of the public record. They are not even on any databases that I have access to through the FBI. It's as though they were deleted from existence.

The depths of this "victims" darkness become increasingly apparent, painting a grim picture of their life beyond what was previously known.

The burden of this new revelation settles heavily upon me. I am faced with the grim reality that the victim was not as innocent as she appeared, that her path was entangled with the very darkness that then sought to consume her. It raises unsettling questions about the nature of her fate and the motivations behind her death.

My mind races, attempting to process the implications of this newfound information. How did the victim become entwined in these criminal activities? Could there be a hidden connection there that ties them and the other victims together? And most importantly, how did these reports vanish from even the most secure databases?

Closing out of this victim and navigating into the previous victim, I find the same thing. There is so much more to this whole investigation than what is publicly known. There is a tangled web of evil that appears to have been covered up and erased, but by who? It had to be someone on the inside. And how did the killers get the files when I never found them?

As the realization sinks in, a wave of unease washes over me. The very foundation of trust within the FBI, the organization I swore to uphold, feels suddenly shaky. If these crime reports were intentionally erased from the databases, it suggests a high level of corruption and a dangerous cover-up.

Questions swirl in my mind, and doubts creep in like tendrils of darkness. Who can I trust within the Bureau? Who can I trust within the very team I am working with? Could there be moles or collaborators working against us? The uncertainty gnaws at me, threatening to undermine my every move.

I take a moment to reflect on the encounters I've had, the suspicious actions, and the cryptic messages exchanged. Faces and names flash through my mind, and I find myself questioning the motives and loyalties of those I once considered allies. Can I rely on my fellow agents, or are they part of the web of deceit that has ensnared us all? And where do the murderers fit into this?

My instincts scream at me to be cautious, to keep my discoveries close to the vest. I need to maintain a certain level of secrecy, for the enemy may be closer than I ever imagined. Trust must be earned, and at this moment, I find myself questioning everyone, even those I once held in high regard.

Are the killers themselves actually the only ones I could trust?

With that disturbing thought I close the laptop. I would need to spend more time going through all of the files, connecting the dots and tracing the threads that bind the victims together, and ultimately expose the darkness that led to their fates.

Amidst the doubts and suspicions, a flicker of determination reignites within me. I will not allow myself to be paralyzed by fear or consumed by mistrust. I will look at every piece of evidence, follow every lead, and expose the truth, no matter the cost.

Putting the laptop aside I get up, resolving to go about my day as though this knowledge isn't eating away at my insides. The sun is already starting to filter through the blinds and I know I have to start my day.

After a quick shower I get dressed and head toward the office, getting my usual coffee and bagel along the way. Unlike my last trip into the office I feel like I see everyone I've become familiar with in a different light this time, and all it does is raise my suspicions.

I see Tristan lurking around the front of the office building holding a coffee cup as I drive toward the parking garage. Agents Decker and Travis are engrossed in a discussion by a car when I get out of mine. When the elevator briefly opens on the ground floor to let people in, I even see Mark and James laughing together near the coffee cart. And then when I exit the elevator to walk into our office, Michael and Emma pass me getting into the elevator with a morning greeting.

Every one of them looks like they are going about their day as normal, but to me every interaction, every look, every word could be hiding something sinister beneath a face of normalcy.

I am not even in the office itself yet and already my nerves are fraying and the facade of pleasant ignorance is wearing thin.

Derek is already in the office at the table, making notes and looking through the reports. He only looks up when I slump into the chair with a huff, then he frowns. "Morning Alex, are you okay?"

I force a smile, attempting to mask the turmoil brewing beneath the surface. "Morning. Yeah, just a rough night. Didn't get much sleep, you know how it is." My voice betrays my weariness.

Derek's brow furrows in concern, his eyes searching mine for any sign of what might be troubling me. He has been a dependable partner throughout this investigation, but the doubts swirling in my mind now cast a shadow over our relationship as well. I question whether I can confide in him or if his loyalty, too, is compromised.

"Is there something specific bothering you?" Derek asks, his tone gentle yet insistent. "You can trust me."

I take a moment to contemplate Derek's question, weighing the risks and uncertainties that currently plague my mind. While I value his partnership, the magnitude of the situation demands caution and discretion. It's no longer just about trust; it's about safeguarding the truth and ensuring that those responsible are held accountable.

But I can't reveal my doubts to Derek, not yet. The web of corruption runs deep, and until I have solid evidence and a clearer understanding of who I can truly trust, it's best to keep everything close to the vest.

"Thanks, Derek," I reply with a weary smile. "I appreciate your concern, but it's nothing I can't handle. Just some personal matters weighing on my mind."

Derek's expression softens, and he nods understandingly. "Alright, remember I'm here if you need me."

"Thanks," I say, grateful for his support. "I'll keep that in mind."

With a subtle shift in conversation, I steer us back to the task at hand. "Speaking of which, we still have a lot of interviews to conduct today. I think it's best if we hit the ground running. We can discuss any updates or concerns as we go."

Derek's focus returns to the investigation, and we dive into planning the day's interviews, going through the list of potential witnesses and suspects. The familiar routine brings a temporary sense of stability amidst the uncertainty that plagues my thoughts.

As we head out of the office, I remain guarded, observing every interaction and conversation with a more critical eye. I listen carefully to the words exchanged, searching for any hidden meanings or signs of deception. The doubts persist, but for now, I must compartmentalize them, channeling my energy into uncovering the truth.

Throughout the interviews, I maintain a professional demeanor, concealing the doubts and suspicions that gnaw at me from within. I ask probing questions, seeking to uncover any hidden connections, patterns, or inconsistencies. I observe the body language of those we interview, hoping to catch a glimpse of truth or deception.

As the day progresses, I can't shake the feeling of being watched. Paranoia whispers in the corners of my mind, suggesting that every conversation, every movement, is being monitored. I remind myself to stay focused, to not let fear cloud my judgment. But the knowledge that someone within the Bureau may be involved in a dangerous cover-up continues to eat away at my resolve.

By the time evening descends, we conclude our last interview for the day. Exhaustion bears down on me, both physically and mentally. The stress of the investigation and the growing doubts have taken their toll. I realize I can no longer go on like this, blindly trusting those around me without concrete evidence of their loyalty.

Returning to my rental house, I find comfort in the silence. The darkness outside mirrors the turmoil within me. I know that I need to delve further into the files but after the events of the day I need some time to decompress.

I head into the bathroom and turn on the shower, letting the sound of running water drown out my racing thoughts. Stepping under the warm stream, I let the tension melt away, at least temporarily. The feeling of the water cascading over my body is soothing, a momentary respite from the chaos that surrounds me.

As I stand there, allowing the water to wash away the physical and emotional exhaustion, I let my thoughts drift. The rhythmic sound of the water hitting the tiles creates a backdrop of white noise, drowning out the noise of doubts and suspicions that have plagued me throughout the day.

I focus on the sensation of the water against my skin, the gentle pressure easing the tension in my muscles. The warmth of the water envelops me, creating a cocoon of comfort.

With each passing moment, the water clears my mind, washing away the chaos and confusion that has clouded my thoughts. I allow myself to be fully present, embracing the simplicity of this solitary moment.

Stepping out of the shower I wrap a soft towel around myself and walk toward the counter. Opening the mirror cabinet, I pick through the limited supply of items I put in there the first night I arrived. Selecting a scented moisturizer to indulge in the luxury of self-care, I close the cabinet.

The container makes a loud noise in the small space when I drop it into the sink, my eyes widening at the reflection in front of me in the mirror. Whatever thoughts still plaguing my mind about the victims and the corruption vanish.

I can feel the cold touch of the blade against my neck, causing a tremor to run through me. I meet the intense, black-eyed gaze of the figure standing behind me, his hood partially concealing his features.

“I really need better locks,” I snark.

He chuckles and the closeness of his body behind me has me feeling it against my skin. The way his voice is modulated gives the sound a sinister edge. “Pretty Little Darling. Do you think a lock would stop us?”

I tilt my head slightly, not really paying attention to the fact that by doing so I press my neck closer to the blade in his hand. “I really don’t feel like this is all that fair. You seem to see me naked all the time but yet you don’t return the favor.”

His chuckle rumbles against my back again, sending shivers down my spine. "Ah, Little Darling, where's the fun in fairness?"

I try to take in as much of the room from my view in the mirror before narrowing my eyes back on him. “Where is your other half?”

The blade scrapes up the skin along my throat and his focus stays fixed on that for a moment. I’m forced to lift my chin as the blade gets higher.

“Around. You’ll see him soon enough,” he eventually responds. His other arm moves around my body, his gloved hand wrapping around my throat, the grip firm but not cutting off my airways. “What would you do to know who we really are, Little Darling?”

His eyes bore into me as he moves the knife back down my body. He uses the tip of the knife to undo the towel wrapped around me. It falls to the floor at our feet and I’m now left fully exposed to him as my breath catches.

I hear him groan as he scrapes the tip of the blade across my skin, trailing it down one of my breasts to then press the flat of the blade against the nipple. The coldness makes me shudder. This shouldn’t be turning me on so much, but it is.

I swallow hard against the arousal flooding my body. “What makes you think that I won’t just get sick of your games and report this?”

He chuckles again, his body now close enough that I can feel his hard cock against my ass. “You haven’t yet, because you’re such a good girl for us. You don’t want us disappearing like ghosts. Besides, you’re too curious, too invested now. I can see it in your eyes, you’re already too far down this rabbit hole.”

As his words sink in, fear, desire, and curiosity all vie for dominance, creating a chaotic storm within my mind. There is an undeniable pull that their presence has on me, even in this perilous situation.

His gloved hand tightens around my throat, his grip both commanding and possessive. The coldness of the blade against my skin and the pressure of his body against mine awaken sensations I never expected to feel in such circumstances. It's a twisted dance of power and vulnerability, a dangerous allure that I can't fully comprehend.

His mask brushes against the side of my face as his modulated voice rumbles in my ear. "How far are you willing to go for your answers? How hungry are you, Little Darling? Would you let me open your skin with my blade? Would you let me fuck your pretty pussy with my cock?"

Chapter 17

Alex

I gasp softly, my body trembling at the raw intensity of his words. The mix of fear and desire within me intensifies, my mind struggling to process the overwhelming sensations coursing through my veins. The darkness of the situation tugs at the deepest recesses of my desires, awakening a hunger I didn't know existed.

"I... I won't be your submissive plaything," I manage to stammer, my voice betraying a flicker of uncertainty. "I won't let you control my body or mind."

His grip on my throat tightens, the pressure not quite cutting into my ability to speak or breathe freely, but enough to make me feel it every time I do. His other hand, still holding the blade, traces a tantalizing path along my exposed skin.

His voice lowers, a dangerous edge creeping into his tone. "Oh, but you've already allowed us to infiltrate your mind, Little Darling. You're drawn to the darkness, to the forbidden. You could be our Queen. Don't deny what your body is telling you."

As his words sink in, a part of me resists, screaming for self-preservation and logic. But another part, a part that I'm both ashamed of and intrigued by, yearns to explore the depths of this twisted dance.

My voice shakes as I speak, the words slipping out against my better judgment. "I want to know. I want to know the men beneath the masks, both of you. But I won't just give in to what you want. I won't lose myself to do that."

He leans closer, his mask brushing against my ear, his words a seductive whisper. He starts to trail the blade over the top of my breast. "Let me make you a promise, Little Darling. Giving in isn't the path to losing yourself, it's the path to finding yourself. And once you taste the ecstasy that lies beyond fear, you will understand."

His words resonate within me, igniting a primal curiosity that pushes me closer to the edge. He is right, I am drawn to their darkness. I stand there, caught in the web of his allure, contemplating the choices that lie ahead.

There needs to be some give though, not all taking. I narrow my eyes at him in the mirror. "What would you give me? What do I get for letting you fuck me?"

He brushes the mask against my face again as he chuckles. "Always a negotiation, Little Darling."

The knife scrapes a little closer against the skin of my breast and I let a soft hiss escape as he hums in response as though contemplating his answer.

"Since you like to play Truth or Dare, how about we give you two truths, like a bonus reward for being such a good girl, Little Darling. One truth from each of us outside of the game, within the rules of course."

His proposition hangs in the air, tempting me with the promise of both knowledge and pleasure. I weigh the risks and rewards, the dangerous allure of their world against the potential answers that lie within their truths. The frustration of the investigation is wearing me down as the proposition repeats in my mind. Finally, I nod, my voice firm. "Alright, two truths."

“Ask your first question, you can ask Truth the second one when you see him. Make them count, Little Darling.”

So this is Dare. I can never tell which one I am dealing with at any given time, they like to disorientate and confuse me.

My mind is working through options as fast as it could. What could I ask that would give me information that mattered? I don’t need information on the victims, they already provided that with the USB. And I hadn’t looked at the files enough to know if they also disclosed more detail on how deep the corruption goes. It needs to be something they wouldn’t have already provided. “How did you two first meet and come to know each other?”

He tilts his head as he gazes at me and I can’t decipher the look in his eyes. “I don’t think you really thought that one through, Little Darling. There is no big story of how we first met that you can track down the details. We are brothers, technically we met when our whore of a mother gave birth to Truth.”

He's right, I hadn’t thought that would be an option, but at least now I know he is the older of the two, and obviously the more dominant. The shot-caller as it were. I need to add that to the very small list of things I actually know about them.

There are so many things I need to do and not do. But instead, my body bends forward as I press myself against the blade in front of me, my ass moving against his hard cock.

If a small part of my brain thought for even a second that he may move the blade when I pressed forward, then I would have called that part of my brain out for its foolishness. I knew the type of man I was dealing with, so the bright red blood that wells up around where the blade cuts into my skin isn’t a surprise at all.

The groan that comes from him as a result has my pussy throbbing. The pain from the knife finally reaches my brain but it gets mixed up with the arousal I feel.

I brace myself against the conflicting sensations surging through my body, a mixture of pain and pleasure intertwining in a way that defies reason. The blood trickles down my skin, serving as a stark reminder of the dangerous game I'm willingly playing.

His grip on my throat slackens, his touch transforming from commanding to possessive as his gloved fingers trail down my neck, following the path of the blade. A dark hunger glimmers in his intense black eyes, mirroring the twisted desires that have awakened within me.

The room fills with a dangerous tension, a fragile balance between power and submission. The metallic tang of blood mingles with the heady scent of desire, creating a potent cocktail that fuels the intensity of the moment.

His gloved fingers connect with the cut on my chest, the pain throbbing through my body once more as he spreads the blood slowly on my skin, the color standing out starkly. He brings his blood covered hand back to wrap around my throat again, squeezing hard enough to cut off my air.

"Your actions have consequences, Little Darling," he growls with a feral intensity.

Meeting his heated gaze, I refuse to back down. A spark of defiance ignites within me. I understand the gravity of the situation, but I refuse to be intimidated.

"Place your hands on the sides of the counter," his command pierces the tense air, carrying a warning. "Do not move them, if you do, the consequences will be severe."

Without hesitation, I comply, gripping the edges of the counter tightly. My knuckles turn white as I brace myself for whatever lies ahead. At this moment, I am resolute, prepared to face the outcome of my choices head-on.

His hands move from in front of my body and grab my hips, moving my body backward. He presses a gloved hand to the center of my back and bends me forward, nudging my legs apart. I can still see everything in the mirror in front of me, so I watch the look of hunger enter his eyes as his hand trails along the skin on my back, looking at where he must have left more blood against my skin from his glove. "You look so pretty in this color, Little Darling."

This time when the blade cuts through my skin, the pain hits me faster. But so does the pleasure. His fingers and the blade keep moving across my skin as I try not to pant with the arousal coursing through my body.

The blade cuts into the flesh of one of my ass cheeks and I whimper. His black eyes return to looking back at me with an intensity that makes my whole body feel like he's touching a raw nerve. "Every time you sit I want you to feel me, Little Darling. I want you to remember this moment."

Then he is pushing something hard inside my pussy. It's solid and cold but I'm so wet that it slides in with no resistance until he stops, pulling it almost all the way back out before thrusting it back in hard. My pussy clenches around it, unable to stop the reaction he pulls from me as he keeps thrusting it almost violently inside me.

I stand there, my body bent forward and trembling, as a mix of sensations courses through me. The sting of the blade, the burning ache in my flesh, and the cold intrusion inside me send waves of pleasure and pain crashing through my senses. I struggle to reconcile the conflicting emotions that swirl within me, unsure of whether to resist or surrender to the depths of this dark desire.

I whimper again at the cold hardness moving inside my sensitive pussy before he pulls it out again, bringing his hand up toward his mask as he watches me in the mirror.

He just fucked me with the handle of his knife. It's wet and glistening under the light of the bathroom, wet from being inside of me.

He pushes the handle under the bottom of the mask and I already know his intentions, his eyes hooding over as he groans when he must taste me there. I stand there, my body still trembling from the mix of sensations that consume me. The air is thick with a potent blend of anticipation and desire, as I meet his heated gaze in the mirror. The intensity in his eyes mirrors my own, a reflection of the hunger that pulses between us.

As he removes the handle from under his mask and secures it in a sheath on his leg, a surge of anticipation courses through me. I watch, captivated, as he discards any concern for cleanliness, his actions fueling the darkness that now envelops us.

"You've taken my knife so well, Little Darling," he purrs, his voice dripping with satisfaction. "Now, let's see how well you take my cock."

His gloved hands move to his pants, opening them and pulling his hard length out. I didn't see him when he fucked my mouth because they blindfolded me, but I don't recall him being as big as he looks. The piercings glinting from the overhead light draws my attention to them.

"Remember, Little Darling, do not move your hands," he growls to me.

Wrapping a gloved hand around his cock, he steps closer to me until he's directly behind me, hidden from the reflection by my own body. But I definitely feel it when he guides the head of his cock to my wet pussy, pushing it in slowly, stretching me until his piercings are inside and I'm whimpering from the feeling.

Without warning, he plunges his cock the rest of the way inside me, filling me completely with a primal force. The sensation is overwhelming, the blend of pleasure and pain amplifying the intensity of his thrust. I bite my lip hard to stifle the moan that threatens to escape, raw desire coursing through my veins as he groans and looks at me with such an intense look of hunger it should scare me. "You were made for my cock."

His gloved fingers dig into my hips as he slowly pulls his cock almost all the way back out before slamming back into me, stretching me to my limits. He does it again, dragging a moan from me. Then he sets a hard punishing rhythm, slowly retreating before thrusting deep and hard back inside of me, his fingers digging into me hard enough that I know they will leave bruises.

I feel the piercings on his cock brush against the walls of my sensitive pussy, adding a new layer of sensation to the mix. The metallic coolness and the slight tug ignite a fire within me, intensifying the already overwhelming pleasure that courses through my body.

I try to maintain control, to stifle the moans that threaten to escape my lips, but the sheer intensity of the experience makes it nearly impossible. Every nerve ending in my body is alive with sensation, consumed by the raw hunger that now consumes us both. "That's it, let me hear that pretty voice."

As his thrusts grow more powerful, the sound of our bodies colliding fills the room, merging with the symphony of our ragged breaths. The air crackles with electricity, charged with a potent blend of desire and dark primal need.

I'm so close to the edge, my orgasm within reach when he stops, and with a whimper my orgasm slides away. He moves one gloved hand to wrap around the back of my knee, his fingers digging into the skin there hard as he lifts it up and away from my body. Leaning his whole body over mine he reaches for my face with his gloved hand.

Then he thrusts the three middle fingers of his gloved hand deep into my open mouth, while his thumb and little finger press into my jaw. He presses the fingers down on my tongue, and I taste the bitter metallic taste of my own blood. Using the grip on my jaw and my leg, he adjusts the angle of his cock and starts thrusting into my pussy again.

Oh, fuck... The change in angle has the head of his cock hitting just the right place inside of me.

The sudden shift in position takes me by surprise, pleasure and pain merging into an explosive mix. The taste of blood mingles with the primal need that courses through my veins, intensifying the building pressure within me.

His fingers fill my mouth, stretching my lips as he plunges them deep, mimicking the rhythm of his cock inside me. I gag slightly, the intrusion both overwhelming and arousing. The control he exerts over my body, the way he dominates me completely, only fuels the fire that burns within.

I close my eyes, surrendering to the pleasure that threatens to consume me. His cock thrusts relentlessly, hitting that sweet spot with each deep, powerful movement. The ache in my jaw and the burn in my throat mixes with the relentless pounding, pushing me closer to the edge of oblivion.

My moans are muffled by his fingers, lost in the depths of our forbidden encounter. I can taste my own desperation, the desperate hunger that pulses through every fiber of my being. I was wrong, I am his plaything, and I am reveling in the darkness that engulfs us.

He growls, the sound vibrating through his fingertips and into my mouth. He pulls his fingers from my mouth and wraps them around my throat, squeezing hard enough to cut off my air.

I try to gasp for air, my body trembling under his grip, the lack of oxygen intensifying the sensations that course through me. The mixture of pleasure, pain, and desperation reaches its peak, teetering on the edge of release. Every cell in my body is alight with a primal need, my mind consumed by the dark desires that bind us together.

As his fingers tighten around my throat, I can feel my pulse throb beneath his touch. The world around me blurs, my focus narrowing down to the powerful rhythm of his thrusts and the intoxicating pressure against my throat. I am suspended in this moment, lost in a vortex of pleasure and surrender.

The raw power of his domination washes over me, igniting a fierce need within me. My body responds, clenching around him, my walls tightening in a desperate attempt to hold on to the pleasure that threatens to shatter me. The tenuous thread that holds me back from the edge snaps, and I hurtle into the abyss of ecstasy.

A guttural scream escapes my lips, muffled by the hand that still constricts my throat. The world around me spins and dissolves into a whirlwind of sensation, pleasure crashing over me in relentless waves. I am consumed by the force of my orgasm, every nerve ending ablaze with ecstasy as I surrender to the darkness that envelops me.

His thrusts become more erratic, the sound of his growls filling the room as he nears his own release. The grip around my throat tightens, his fingers leaving imprints on my skin, marking me as his. I can feel the tension in his body, the final moments before he succumbs to the same abyss that claimed me.

With a primal roar, he finds his release, his body shuddering against mine as he cums deep inside me. The heat of his release fills me, mingling with the ache and pleasure that still echoes through my body.

But he still doesn't release his grip on my throat; if anything it tightens even more. My hands release the counter to try to scratch at the hand around my throat, but my nails can't get any purchase on the glove that covers his hand.

The last thing I hear before I lose consciousness is his modulated voice. "Naughty, Little Darling. I told you not to move your hands."

Chapter 18

Alex

As I slowly regain consciousness, my senses begin to awaken, pulling me back from the depths of the abyss and into the disorienting reality of my situation. My mind is foggy, and my body feels heavy. Panic flickers within me as I become aware of the tightness around my wrists, realizing my hands are bound. I try to open my eyes, but the haze lingers, obscuring my vision.

I'm no longer standing, the sensation of movement indicating that I'm being carried. The swaying motion adds to my disorientation, making it difficult to gather my thoughts. I'm still very naked and I feel a mix of vulnerability and anticipation, my body still throbbing from the intensity of our encounter.

With each step he takes, I feel the shift in momentum, my body gently swaying in response. My limbs feel weak and unsteady, the remnants of pleasure and exertion coursing through me. A dull throbbing headache claws at the edges of my mind. It's as if I'm caught between the remnants of my orgasmic haze and the stark reality of my predicament.

Suddenly, the motion halts, and I feel a change in the atmosphere. My body is shifted, maneuvered into a new position. I sense my bound hands being raised and then being attached to something, the cool metal biting into my skin. My body is slowly maneuvered until it's straight and my weight starts bearing down on my wrists before he releases his hold on me. It occurs to me that I'm hanging from something. The realization sends a shiver down my spine, a mix of trepidation and a twisted thrill coursing through me.

My heart pounds in my chest as the tension in the room becomes palpable. I can't see him, but I can feel his presence, the heaviness of his gaze bearing down on me. A mix of vulnerability and anticipation floods my senses as I hang there, suspended, my body at his mercy.

The ache in my limbs intensifies as the strain of my weight settles further on my wrists. I try to shift, to alleviate some of the pressure, but the restraints hold me in place. My muscles protest, and the cuts in my skin throb as my body stretches.

My mind races, grappling with a myriad of emotions. The remnants of pleasure still linger within me, but they are now entwined with fear and the growing uncertainty at what lies ahead.

As the haze lifts from my vision, I start to make out what is in front of me. My own bedroom wall.

I feel the edge of a blade graze against the skin on my back and I shudder. Am I going to be punished now? Did he really expect me to keep my hands still when I couldn't breathe?

I can't stop the small whimper from escaping as the knife keeps moving lower. But then the knife leaves my skin.

My vision clears so I see when a gloved hand comes to rest on the wall on either side of my body, the knife held loosely in one of them. And then I feel as he presses his clothed body into my back. He's hard.

"You awake again, Little Darling?" His modulated voice rumbles from behind my ear.

I nod slightly before trying twice to talk, eventually getting out a "Yes" through a scratchy throat.

He hums in response. "Well that voice isn't acceptable," he says before disappearing. I have no idea where he is but I can hear him moving around behind me. I can't move my head or body enough to look.

He reappears as quickly as he vanished, reaching a hand around to grip my chin and mouth and tilt them up forcefully. Then there is liquid flooding my mouth.

There is too much of it and as much as I try to resist the onslaught I'm sputtering and choking on it in seconds as I swallow it on reflex. The last of it slides down my throat before he lets go of me again.

It's not just water, I can tell from the taste of it that there is something else in it. It had a sweetness to it. For all I know he potentially poisoned me.

"Is that because I moved my hands? Did you poison me as punishment?" I sputter out. Admittedly, my throat does feel better, even if it was poisoned.

He chuckles, coming back to stand at my back with his hands braced on either side of me. "Oh I'm positive that Dare has something deliciously evil planned to punish you for not obeying, but that is for him to carry out. I just want to be able to hear you scream."

Fuck.

For a moment it feels as though my heart stops beating. It never even occurred to me that I am now dealing with Truth and not Dare.

He continues to chuckle, "You thought I was Dare right? You thought you would have a small reprieve since he already came in that pretty pussy tonight? Guess again, Little Darling. Though I do hear you have a question for me first."

My heart is now suddenly racing in my chest. I completely forgot about the two truths that I had been granted in exchange for this encounter, though now thinking back on it two truths were definitely not a fair exchange.

His hands disappear again and his warmth moves away from my back before I feel the knife start trailing against the skin on my back again. “Better think quickly, Little Darling, I’m going to be playing in the meantime.”

The sting of the knife cutting into the flesh on my back has my breath hissing out of my lips, but soon the pleasure is chasing it.

I close my eyes, trying to gather my thoughts amidst the mix of pain and pleasure. The blade continues to trace intricate patterns on my skin, leaving a trail of searing heat in its wake. I bite down on my lip, fighting back a moan as conflicting sensations course through me.

The knife disappears for a moment and next I feel a completely different sensation. I feel his tongue against my skin as he licks a long slow line up my spine. Given the placement of the cuts in my skin and the position of my body, it would be impossible that he wouldn’t have my blood in his mouth.

And then he licks along one of the already sensitive cuts in my skin. Hot pleasure shoots straight through me and directly to my clit, and I can’t stop the moan escaping my lips this time.

His voice, filled with sadistic amusement, cuts through the air moments later. He must have repositioned his mask though, as it’s modulated again. "Tell me, Little Darling, what burning question do you have for me? I'm all ears while I mark your beautiful body."

Despite the haze of arousal and pain, I manage to find my voice. "What... What made you start killing?"

His movements pause for a moment; I could feel the knife hovering just above my skin. I can sense the heaviness of his gaze, contemplating his response. Finally, he speaks, his voice low and filled with dark amusement.

"Ah, my Little Darling, you're hoping for a specific event, aren't you? Some grand catalyst that sent us down the path of murder. But you see, it wasn't that simple. It wasn't a single moment or a single event that led us here," he says.

He braces himself against the wall again, his body once again close to mine and his mask brushing against the shell of my ear, and I feel a moment of respite. His words linger in the air as he continues to speak, his voice filled with a mixture of bitterness and melancholy.

“Have you heard of that question, the one that all criminal psychologists and profilers ponder. Are monsters born like that or are they a result of their environment? What I can tell you is that childhood trauma can shape a person, mold them into something unrecognizable. It can plant the seeds of darkness deep within their soul.”

His words bear the burden of his past experiences, and I can sense the layers of pain hidden beneath his carefully crafted facade.

“The things we saw and experienced growing up were the stuff of nightmares. It breeds resentment, anger, and a desire for retribution. It forged a darkness within us that we couldn't escape."

"But it wasn't just our individual experiences," he continues, his voice laced with a hint of sorrow. "It was the collective failures, the systemic shortcomings that pushed us further down this path. The failure of those who were meant to protect and serve, the law enforcement that turned a blind eye or sometimes even contributed to the suffering of the innocent."

I feel a pang of understanding deep within me, the recognition that the world can be a cruel and unforgiving place, capable of breeding monsters in the wake of broken promises. He rubs his mask more solidly against the side of my head before he continues, as though seeking comfort.

"We are not monsters created overnight. No, Little Darling, it was a gradual descent, fueled by a culmination of events, scars, and the festering wounds of our past. We were broken by a broken world, driven to seek our own justice."

The weight of his words hangs in the air, a heavy realization that we are both products of a society that failed us. The memories and events of my childhood are what put me on the path to becoming an FBI agent.

"But enough about the past, my Little Darling," he says, his voice returning to a low, seductive murmur. "There is just one more mark I need to make on your pretty body."

He moves back from me and the blade finds its mark again, slicing through the flesh of my other ass cheek with a calculated precision. Pain mingles with pleasure, and I can't help but wonder how far down this dark path we have both ventured.

"Now you will think of both of us whenever you sit down."

For fuck's sake. How could I not every time I moved until any part of me healed from this? I could tell the cuts they made weren't too deep, but they still wouldn't heal overnight.

I hear when he returns the knife to its sheath in his pants, recognizing the sound from when Dare did the same thing. Then his gloved hands are tracing patterns along the skin on my back. The feel of the leather gloves sliding along my skin is erotic, mixing with the throb of the wounds when his fingers find them. The combination of sensations—his gloved touch, the ache of my wounds, and the lingering pleasure from earlier—becomes an overwhelming storm that consumes my senses.

As his hands continue their exploration, they venture around my body to cup my breasts. His touch is firm yet gentle, his fingers kneading the flesh, teasing and tormenting my hardened nipples.

But he doesn't stop there. His hand travels further down, finding its way between my legs, where my clit throbs with need. The blood on his gloves acts as a slick lubricant, intensifying the sensations as he rubs and circles it with precision.

My body betrays me, my hips involuntarily grinding against his hand, seeking more of the delicious friction. Each stroke and touch brings me closer to the edge, the pleasure building within me.

He whispers in my ear, his voice laced with sadistic delight, "Oh, my Little Darling, you're so responsive, so eager to be pleasured. Does the pain enhance the pleasure for you? Does the feel of blood on my hands excite you?"

His words ignite a fire within me, fueling the intoxicating mix of pain and pleasure that courses through my veins. I can't deny the dark desire that thrives within me, the twisted need that hungers for more.

His hands move again, becoming a dance between his gloved hands and my willing body. His touch alternates between my back, my breasts, and my throbbing clit, the pleasure building each time. Each time he brings me close to the edge, he withdraws, denying me the release I so desperately crave.

A desperate moan escapes my lips, a plea for more, for the sweet release that hovers just out of reach. I'm on the edge, teetering on the precipice, consumed by a maddening mixture of pleasure and frustration.

He revels in my torment, his touch unrelenting. His gloved fingers dance over my body, setting every nerve ending ablaze with desire. The cycle repeats, his hands traversing the path from my back to my breasts and then down to my pulsating clit, edging me closer and closer with each pass.

I'm trembling, my body aching with need, my mind consumed by a desperate hunger for release. I'm beyond begging, my pleas falling from my lips in desperate whispers.

"Please," I whimper, my voice filled with a mixture of desperation and longing. "Please, let me cum. I need it, I can't take it anymore."

He chuckles darkly, his voice dripping with sadistic satisfaction. "You beg so sweetly, Little Darling, as if your every word is a melody just for my ears," he murmurs, his breath hot against my skin. "But I'm not quite finished with you yet."

With that, he moves his hands again. Instead of starting the dance again he grabs my waist, pulling me toward him and spinning my body before slamming my back against the wall.

I gasp as my body collides with the unforgiving surface, the impact reverberating through me. The sudden shift in position sends a jolt of both pain and arousal coursing through my veins. My bound hands strain against their restraints. I'm trapped between the cold wall and his unyielding body, his hands gripping my waist possessively.

His masked face hovers inches from mine, his black eyes burning with a dark intensity. There's a hunger in his gaze that matches my own and his eyes don't leave mine as he pulls his hard cock from his pants and positions himself at the entrance of my wet and aching pussy.

He pushes his cock into me until his piercings are just inside and then he thrusts hard, filling me completely. Reaching down, he drags one of my legs up and pulls my body away from the wall, his gloved fingers digging hard into my flesh in a way that I know will only add to the marks already littering my body. His other hand wraps around the front of my already tender throat until I'm stretched between the tip of his cock and the hard wall.

I could already tell this is going to hurt.

I gasp as he thrusts into me with a force that borders on pain, my body straining against the unyielding wall. The mixture of pleasure and discomfort sends a pulsing sensation through me, heightening every sensation. His grip on my throat tightens, restricting my air-flow and amplifying the intensity of the moment.

His movements are rough and unrelenting, his cock pounding into me with an urgency that matches the darkness in his eyes. Each thrust sends shockwaves of pleasure and pain radiating through my body, blurring the line between agony and ecstasy. The marks on my back throb with each collision, a painful reminder of the depths I have descended into.

I struggle to find my breath, my mind clouded by a heady cocktail of sensations. The pressure on my throat intensifies, a reminder of his current power over me. Pleasure coils within me, building with each forceful thrust, pushing me closer to the edge.

My body trembles as I feel the familiar tendrils of ecstasy wrapping around me, threatening to pull me under, but the feeling of his grip on my throat holds me back, denying me the release I crave. I'm caught in a tumultuous storm, my senses heightened to the brink.

With each powerful thrust, the sensations become more intense, pushing me closer to the edge of oblivion. I can feel the walls of my pussy clenching around him, desperate for release, while the ache in my back and the pressure on my throat serve as reminders of the twisted pleasure I'm entangled in.

His voice, filled with wicked pleasure, growls at me, "Scream for me, my Little Darling. Let the world hear your surrender." And then, he releases his grip on my throat.

The sudden rush of air fills my lungs, a gasp escaping my lips. In that moment, my body unravels, the tight coil of pleasure exploding within me. A powerful orgasm crashes over me, waves of ecstasy washing everything away, leaving only the raw intensity of pleasure in its wake.

I scream, the raw primal sound echoing through the room as my body convulses in the throes of release. My back arches against the wall as I ride the waves of pleasure.

He continues to thrust into me, stretching my leg further up as he slams my whole body into the wall. With each hard thrust my body is torn between the pain and the lingering ecstasy. He prolongs the moment of my surrender, pushing me to the edge of madness. Until with an almost feral growl he finds his own release, but still he slams into me again and again and throws me into another mind shattering orgasm.

As the second orgasm crashes over me, my whole body shudders and protests uncontrollably, my senses overwhelmed by the sheer intensity of pleasure. My moans and whimpers blend with the sound of his own primal groans, filling the room with an intoxicating symphony of desire and surrender.

I reach a point of sensory overload. The intensity becomes too much to bear, and my body succumbs to the overwhelming sensations. Consciousness slips away, and for the second time that night I fade into the comforting embrace of darkness.

Chapter 19

Truth

It's twisted and sickly satisfying, seeing the look in our Little Darling's eyes as her body shuts down and she drifts off into unconsciousness. The way her eyes widen slightly before the haze takes over, and her eyelids flutter before rolling back completely. Then, watching her eyes finally close as her body goes limp under my touch.

I know I should stop moving at that point, but I can't resist giving a few final thrusts. The way her pussy unconsciously tightens around my softening cock sends waves of pleasure through me.

She's so perfect, like she was made just for us. I want to stay inside her forever.

Gently I lower her leg and let her body rest against the wall. Reluctantly, I pull out of her and tuck myself away. With a gloved hand, I lift her chin to admire her sleeping face and brush sweaty strands of hair away.

Tilting my head, I take in every little detail of our beautiful Little Darling.

It's not surprising when I see a bare hand enter my line of sight, fingers resting against her neck to check her pulse. The hand disappears briefly, only to return moments later with a sedative, injecting it into her.

I raise an eyebrow at him over my shoulder.

"We can't have her waking up while we clean her," he says in response to my look before he pulls down his hood and mask now that we know she won't suddenly wake up.

Letting go of her chin I step away, pulling my own hood and mask down then joining him as we both gaze over her body. It's a masterpiece, in my opinion. There's hardly any of her fair skin left uncovered by her own blood. Or our cum.

He speaks to me again without looking, just as captivated by her as I am. "Did you take care of that other thing?"

I chuckle a bit at his question. "Of course. She won't even notice any difference."

"Good," he says before he starts moving around the room.

I take the bowl of water and the soft cloth he hands me, feeling the coolness even through the leather of my gloves. Without hesitation, I start gently wiping away the blood and our mess from her body. Each stroke of the cloth is careful and tender, as if I'm handling something fragile and precious.

While I clean her, I steal glances at her peaceful face, lost in unconsciousness. Despite the situation, there's something captivating about her, something that keeps us enthralled in this twisted obsession.

We work in silence, the only sounds being the rustling of the cloth and the occasional drip of water. We empty and refill the bowl regularly, making sure it stays as clean as possible while washing her. The weight of our thoughts hang heavy in the air, mixing with the scent of blood, sweat and sex.

With delicate care I clean her pussy with a fresh bowl of water, wiping away the mixture of our releases that cover her thighs. Internally wishing that I didn't have to, that I could leave with the knowledge that she is covered in us, in our cum, in the most primal claim to her body.

When I finish cleaning her, I toss the dirty cloth aside, letting the water wash away the evidence. I can't resist reaching out to touch her once more, running my fingers down her curves and soft skin with a strange mix of tenderness and possessiveness.

Then, we both shift our focus to her wounds. With gloved hands, we carefully apply antibacterial cream to the cuts and abrasions we inflicted upon her delicate skin. We work in unison, each tending to a different area, making sure to cover every wound with utmost care.

Once the antibacterial cream is applied, we retrieve small dressings and place them gently over the wounds, securing them in place. It's a twisted act of tenderness, attending to the damage we caused, as if we're nurturing her back to a state of twisted perfection.

With the wounds dressed, we work together to turn her around, exposing her back to us. We repeat the process, cleaning the wounds, applying the antibacterial cream and carefully dressing each wound with the same meticulousness.

As we work, I notice just how tangled and mussed her hair has become. Once we are done with the last wound I reach for a brush and start running it through her hair, the strands slipping through the bristles as I untangle the knots. It's an intimate act, almost loving, in contrast to the darkness that consumes us.

My thoughts drift as I get lost in the rhythm of caring for her. I had been too caught up in my emotions with her when we spoke. I had come too close to revealing secrets about ourselves that we weren't ready for her to know yet. She would know them in time, but I need to be more mindful to not get drawn so quickly into her orbit to the point of forgetting myself.

Once I finish brushing out the tangles in her hair, Dare steps forward and together we lift our Darling into his embrace, cradling her with care. As he holds her close, I move to unfasten the restraints around her wrists, releasing her from their grip.

With the restraints removed, Dare carries her towards the bed, his steps steady and sure. I follow closely behind, my eyes fixated on her sleeping form, my mind consumed by a twisted longing to possess her completely.

When we reach her bed, Dare lays her down gently, his touch lingering as if he too is unwilling to let go. I watch with an unwavering gaze, unable to tear my eyes away from our dark Queen. I yearn to touch her, to leave my mark upon her in every way possible. But I know the time isn't right, that we aren't at that stage yet.

As Dare tucks her into bed, I stand by, my hands twitching with the urge to claim her fully. The obsession that courses through my veins burns hot, fueling my every thought and desire. But for now, I restrain myself, knowing that there are steps we must take before we can fully indulge in our dark fantasies.

With our Darling settled in bed, I take a step back, my gaze never leaving her. Her slumbering form radiates an ethereal beauty, a captivating allure that draws me in. I want to possess her, body and soul.

But there are tasks at hand, obligations that demand our attention. Dare and I exchange a silent understanding, we both know what needs to be done.

Moving with purpose, we meticulously erase any evidence of our presence in the room. Bloodstains are carefully cleaned, traces of our passion and depravity wiped away. The hook that I used returns to its original use hidden behind a full length mirror. The room slowly sheds its connection to our twisted desires, returning to a semblance of normalcy.

Finally, as the last trace of our presence is eradicated, we stand in the transformed room. It is as if nothing extraordinary occurred within these walls. Our eyes meet, a silent acknowledgement of the lengths we will go to to protect our secrets.

We turn our attention back to our sleeping Queen. I approach her with caution, my fingertips grazing her cheek, my touch a whisper against her skin. The desire for her is overwhelming, but we know that patience is our ally. We must proceed with care, ensuring every step aligns with our obsessive vision.

Dare's presence beside me is a reassuring anchor, his eyes filled with the same dark longing. He sets up a glass of water on her bedside beside some tylenol just in case she wakes in any pain.

"She surrendered to us so beautifully tonight," I whisper, my voice hinting at the desire I feel inside. "She craves the darkness as much as we do."

"Yes," he murmurs, his voice laced with a hint of reverence. "But we knew she would."

With a gentleness that belies the dark possessive thoughts in my mind, I brush a kiss against her soft lips. I want the taste of her to be all I taste forever. I want the scent of her to be the only scent I ever smell again. I want to be surrounded by her until death tears us apart.

She is and always has been our everything, the ultimate partner in our dark souls.

Chapter 20

Alex

Opening my eyes to see the first touch of sunlight starting to creep through my blinds confuses me. The whole scenario I find myself in confuses me.

I let two stalkers, two killers, fuck me into oblivion the night before, and I enjoyed it. Actually, enjoyed is an understatement. The pleasure I experienced with them was unlike anything I have ever known, but the circumstances surrounding it were undeniably dark and twisted.

It's not as though I haven't had sex before, and yes I already knew that I enjoyed a little bit of pain with my pleasure. But at that moment, as I thought about the experiences of the past two nights, I feel like they metaphorically wrapped their hands around my throat and were dragging me into the depths of hell with a smile on my face.

Well, the phantom feeling of their hands on my throat may just be the lingering marks from being choked.

Lifting the sheet to look down at my body I can see they have taken meticulous care in cleaning and dressing my wounds. It hints at a level of thoughtfulness I hadn't initially attributed to them. It raises questions about who they truly are and what drives them. The level of care shows aren't merely two mindless psychopaths, but individuals with their own intricate motivations and desires.

Seeing the glass of water and tablets on the night stand beside the bed, I hesitate for only a second before taking them. My body aches in both a good and bad way. It's only as I reach into my drawer for my birth control that a thought occurs to me; I had been so consumed with them that I didn't even insist on protection or checking with them that they were clean.

A strange thing to think about when the men in question kill people.

I know I should feel guilty about the path I am taking. I am not just breaking the rules, I am pouring gasoline on the rulebook and setting it alight while roasting marshmallows over the flames.

There's an allure to their darkness, a magnetic pull that draws me closer even as I wrestle with my own sanity.

I'm not sure if the picture of corruption that the files were starting to paint is what is contributing to my complete disregard for all ethics.

A nagging worry creeps in that I should have been more cautious. But in the haze of passion, rationality gave way to reckless abandon. The truth is, in that moment I wanted to surrender to them completely, to experience pleasure that transcended the boundaries of safety and sanity.

I push aside the lingering doubts and remind myself that it's too late to change what has already transpired. My encounter with these men was a choice I made, driven by an insatiable hunger for something more, something beyond the boundaries of normalcy.

Getting out of bed I carefully inspect the dressings on my wounds, finding comfort in the fact that they look waterproof. It seems they took care to ensure that my physical well-being was attended to, despite the darkness that enveloped our encounters.

Walking into the bathroom I turn on the shower, stepping into the warm cascade of water. I let it wash away any lingering physical remnants of the previous night, but it can't wash away the questions that linger in my mind. How did I end up in this twisted situation? What does it mean for me moving forward? And most importantly, what is it about them that draws me in despite the darkness that surrounds them?

Exiting the shower, I wrap myself in a towel, my mind still swirling with conflicting thoughts. I know I need time to sort through it all, to understand the depths of my desires and the risks I have taken. But one thing is certain—I willfully took steps in a direction that I thought I would never go, and there may not be any turning back now.

As I get dressed I realize that none of the cuts on my skin are in places that would be visible while wearing my regular work attire. The only one that comes close is the one I caused by pressing myself against Dare's blade. It's just another confusing note to add to my ever growing pile of confusion.

Taking the easy approach, instead of using makeup to cover the bruises on my neck, I choose a turtle neck blouse to go under my blazer. The fabric is soft against my skin and hides an array of sins.

Leaving the bedroom I head out the door, my mind still in a whirlwind of conflicting thoughts and emotions. I step into my car, ready to continue my routine and find a sense of normalcy amidst the chaos that has become my life.

As I drive towards my usual drive-thru for coffee and a bagel, I find the entrance blocked off, a sign indicating that it's temporarily closed. Frustration tugs at me, but I quickly adapt, parking my car and deciding to go into the cafe instead. It's a small disruption to my routine, but one that feels symbolic of the changes that have taken place within me.

Entering the cafe, I join the line, my mind still preoccupied with the events of the past nights. The scent of freshly brewed coffee fills the air, momentarily distracting me from my thoughts. After placing my order and paying, I move to the side to wait for my food and coffee when I hear something that I didn't expect.

"Darling!"

Turning, I meet familiar eyes sitting at a table by the window. After accepting my order from the barista, I slowly move over to the person who called my name.

"It's Max isn't it?" I say, though I already know the answer, I remember it very clearly.

He smiles a mile wide and I force a smile in response as though his presence here, in my regular cafe, a street away from my rental house, wasn't setting my nerves on end. I try to keep my composure, reminding myself that it could all be a mere coincidence.

"Yes," he replies, his voice laced with a mix of familiarity and excitement. He leans back in his chair, his eyes studying me intently. "I never thought I'd run into you here. What a pleasant surprise. I must say, you look as captivating as ever."

I nod politely, suppressing the urge to ask how he knew about my regular cafe. Instead, I divert the conversation, hoping to keep things casual. "What brings you here? Just grabbing a coffee?"

Max leans back in his chair, his gaze fixed on me. There's an intensity in his eyes that makes me uneasy. "Yes, I love the coffee here. Actually, since you're here, I've been thinking about our conversation and the offer I made. Have you had a chance to think it over?"

"I do appreciate your offer, Max," I reply, trying to sound grateful without revealing my reservations. "But right now, I need to get to the office and continue my work."

Max's smile falters slightly, but he nods understandingly. "Of course, Darling. Your dedication to your work is one of the things I admire about you. Take care, and remember, I'm only a call away."

With that, I bid him a polite farewell and make my way out of the cafe, the encounter leaving me with more questions than answers.

As I get back into my car, I take a deep breath, trying to push aside the unsettling encounter with Max. I have a job to do, an investigation to pursue. The twisted dance I find myself in won't unravel itself, and I can't afford to be distracted by past acquaintances.

Starting the engine, I head toward the office. I'm so hungry that I devour my bagel before I even make it to the parking garage. As I drive into the parking garage of my office building, I notice a couple of cars pulling in behind me. It's an uncommonly busy morning, and the usual quiet is replaced by the hustle and bustle as I step out of my car, coffee in hand.

Just as I begin walking towards the entrance, I hear someone calling out my name. I turn my head and see Mark, the crime scene technician, approaching me with a friendly smile.

"Hey, it's good to see you," Mark says, his tone warm and inviting even after how our last encounter left off. "I was just heading in. How have you been?"

I force another smile onto my face, but already my nerves are wearing thin and I haven't made it in the door yet. "I've been...busy," I reply, keeping my response vague. "Lots of things going on."

Mark nods in understanding. "I can imagine. But I'm sure you're making progress with the investigation, right? You'll get to the bottom of it."

I shift uncomfortably, feeling the weight of Mark's gaze on me. I take a sip of my coffee, buying myself a moment to gather my thoughts.

"Yes, we're making progress," I reply, trying to sound confident. "But there's still much work to be done. We're following every lead, examining every piece of evidence."

Mark's smile widens, a glimmer of something unidentifiable in his eyes. "That's what I like about you, always dedicated to your work. You're thorough, and it shows."

I nod, grateful for his praise, but inside, I'm desperately searching for an escape route from this conversation. I need to distance myself from these weird encounters and focus on the task at hand.

"Well, I should get going," I say, my tone clipped as I try to sound busy. "Derek is probably waiting for me already."

Mark's expression flickers with frustration, but he nods understandingly. "Sure, I don't want to keep you. Just remember, if you ever need any assistance or if there's anything I can do to help, don't hesitate to ask."

I offer a brief thank you before swiftly making my way towards the elevator, eager to leave the awkward encounter behind. The stress of recent events presses down on me, intensifying the sense of urgency in my steps.

I internally curse when someone steps up beside me as I'm waiting for the elevator, thinking it's Mark joining me for the trip. But then I'm wishing it was Mark when I catch sight of Agent Decker beside me.

He's focused on the closed doors as though waiting for the elevator to arrive, but I can see the corner of his lip twitch as he holds back a smirk. I narrow my eyes and look over my shoulder thinking maybe I could just skip this elevator or walk around the long way, but Agent Travis is behind me.

He isn't subtle about the fact that he was looking at my ass as he looks up into my eyes with a smirk of his own. I force yet another smile onto my face and look back to the elevator doors knowing I am not getting out of this new hell.

As the elevator doors open, I step inside, feeling the heaviness of their stares following me. Travis reaches past my body to press the number for his floor, his arm brushing against me.

The air inside the elevator feels tense, and I try my best to focus on the numbers lighting up as we ascend.

Agent Decker stands beside me, his posture relaxed, but I can tell he's enjoying this awkward situation. Agent Travis is behind me, and I can sense his lingering gaze, making me uncomfortable. I take a deep breath, reminding myself to maintain composure, even as my mind races.

"Busy morning, huh?" Agent Decker finally breaks the silence, his voice casual but almost with a knowing edge to it.

I nod, keeping my responses brief. "Yes, it's been quite busy."

"And how's the investigation going?" Agent Travis chimes in from behind me, his darkly amused tone not lost on me.

"We're making progress," I reply, trying to keep my voice steady despite the unnerving situation. "But you know I'm not going to discuss the details with you."

Agent Decker chuckles lightly, turning his attention directly to me, clearly enjoying my discomfort. "Of course, we understand the need for confidentiality. But you must admit, it's a fascinating case, and both it and you have definitely captured our attention."

Suppressing a sigh, I refrain from engaging further. I don't want to fuel their curiosity about the investigation or give anything away about the tangled mess I find myself in. Thankfully, the elevator reaches my floor, and the doors open. I quickly step out, feeling relieved to escape the confined space.

Just as I think I'm free from their gaze, the sound of the elevator doors being held open makes me look back. Agent Travis smirks, releases the doors, and speaks with a tone that sends shivers down my spine, "We'll see you around, Darling."

Chapter 21

Alex

My heart feels like it's trying to leave my chest the fastest way possible.

I'm standing frozen staring at the closed doors of the elevator long after it has moved away from my floor. The ding of the elevator arriving on my floor again startles me moments before Derek steps through the doors with a scowl on his face.

"Hey, are you alright?" Derek's concerned voice breaks through my daze as he approaches me, his frown deepening when he sees my distressed expression. "You look like you've seen a ghost. Is something wrong?"

I force a smile, trying to appear composed despite the chaos of emotions swirling inside me. "I'm okay, just a lot on my mind. You know how it is."

Derek studies me for a moment, clearly not fully convinced by my response, but he nods in understanding. "Yeah, I get it. It's all really taking a toll on us. Just remember, I'm always here if you need me, alright?"

I take the opportunity to change the subject and divert the attention away from myself. "Thanks, Derek. I appreciate it. And how about you? Are you okay? You seem a bit... tense."

Derek exhales, his shoulders relaxing slightly. "Yeah, just some personal stuff. Nothing I can't handle."

I nod in acknowledgment, respecting Derek's privacy, but still wanting to offer my support. "Well, if you ever want to talk about it, you know I'm here for you too."

"Thanks, that means a lot," he replies with a smile. "Alright, let's get to work. We need to go over the interview notes from yesterday and see if there's anything we might have missed."

We make our way to our office, filled with our files and interview notes and the murder boards around the room. It's quiet, the only sound being the shuffling of papers as we take our seats.

Derek glances at me across the table, and I can't help but notice a mischievous twinkle in his eyes. "You know, we make a pretty good team," he says playfully. "Maybe one day soon we'll solve this case and have a well-deserved celebration."

I chuckle, enjoying the light-hearted moment amidst the seriousness of our work. "That sounds tempting, but we might have a long way to go before we can even think about celebrating."

Derek leans back in his chair, his eyes locked on mine. "Oh, I have no doubt we'll crack this case wide open. And when we do, I'll make sure we have the time of our lives."

His words catch me off guard, and I feel my cheeks flush slightly as I smile in response. I can't deny that I am attracted to him, but the constant presence of Truth and Dare currently in my life made it hard to think of anyone else.

The sudden creak of the opening door provides a welcome distraction, and my attention shifts to find Mark standing at the entrance with a deep frown etched on his face.

"Have you seen James by any chance?" he asks, his tone gruff and impatient.

Derek raises an eyebrow in response. "In his office, I assume. If not, he might be grabbing a coffee."

With a nod, Mark turns on his heels and exits the room, the door closing with more force than needed, leaving us in a moment of brief silence.

"He seems tense, too," I comment, breaking the silence.

Derek chuckles softly. "Mark's always a little on edge. You get used to it," before I can respond, he turns his attention back to the files. "Alright, let's get down to business. None of the interviews we conducted yesterday led to any new information. It's like we're hitting a dead end."

I nod in agreement, grateful for the shift in focus. "Yeah, it's frustrating. We should start reviewing everything again from the start. Maybe we missed something crucial."

Derek takes out a pen and starts jotting down some notes. "You're right. Let's go through each interview with fresh eyes, looking for any connections or patterns we might have overlooked."

As we delve into the interview notes, I try to maintain my focus on the task at hand, but my mind keeps drifting back to Truth and Dare and the mystery files. I know there are details they revealed about the corruption of the victims, but sharing that information with Derek would be too risky until I knew what to do with it and who to trust. Besides, I'm not even sure I fully comprehend the implications of their revelations myself.

With each passing moment, the burden of the truth they shared with me feels like a ticking time bomb, threatening to shatter the fragile balance between my personal life and the investigation. I need to be cautious, to tread carefully, and to keep these secrets close to my vest until I have a better understanding of the bigger picture.

I find myself not putting all of my effort toward the case, knowing now that the “victims” weren’t innocent people themselves.

My heart races as I navigate the delicate balance between my duty as an investigator and the knowledge that I possess. The truth of the "victims" casting a shadow over my dedication to the case.

As Derek and I continue to review the interview notes, I find myself occasionally glancing at him, wondering if I should confide in him about the disturbing information I've learned. But doubts linger, holding me back from revealing the truth. The consequences of such revelations are unknown, and I can't risk jeopardizing the investigation or putting anyone's safety at risk.

Lost in my thoughts, I barely notice the passing time. It's only when my stomach growls loudly that I realize it's well past lunchtime. I glance up at Derek, who seems equally absorbed in the files.

"We've been at this for hours," I remark, finally breaking the silence. "Maybe we should take a break and grab something to eat."

Derek looks up, his expression a mix of surprise and realization. "You're right. I didn't even realize how late it's gotten. We definitely need a break."

He stands up from his chair, stretching his arms above his head. "I actually need to make a quick call. Why don't you head out and get some fresh air? Grab lunch without me. I'll catch up with you in a bit."

His suggestion catches me off guard, but I realize it's an opportunity to clear my mind and gather my thoughts. Besides, a break would do us both some good.

"Sure," I reply, offering a grateful smile. "I'll take a walk and find a nearby café. You take your time with the call."

Derek nods, his gaze lingering on me for a moment longer before he turns his attention to his phone. I gather my belongings and step out of the office, feeling a sense of relief as the cool air hits my face.

As I walk through the bustling streets, I find solace in the anonymity of the crowd. It's a chance to gather my thoughts, to sort through the tangled web of information and emotions that swirl within me.

While I long to confide in Derek, I know that I need more time to process the information from Truth and Dare. The lines between right and wrong blur, and the consequences of my actions weigh heavily on my conscience. I need clarity before I can share the burden of this knowledge with him.

Entering a nearby café, I order a light meal and find a secluded corner to sit. As I eat, I go over the mystery files in my mind, searching for any clues or connections that might help break open the case. The weight of the truth hangs over me, urging me to find a way to reconcile the information I possess with my role as an investigator.

Lost in thought, I barely notice the figure that suddenly takes a seat across from me at the café table. When I look up, my heart skips a beat as I come face to face with Tristan Winters.

I should have known I wouldn't be able to avoid him for too much longer so him finding me here on a random break came as no surprise.

"Mr. Winters," I address him, trying to keep my tone formal. "What are you doing here?"

Tristan grins, his gaze unwavering. "Will you ever call me Tristan? I just happened to see you from across the street and thought it was the perfect opportunity to catch up, without your constant shadow. I hope you don't mind."

"Okay, Tristan," I reply. "Is there something you wanted to discuss?"

He leans back in his chair, studying me intently. "Actually, yes. I wanted to follow up on our last conversation. Have you given any more thought to my offer of assistance?"

I remember his proposal well – he had suggested helping me from a journalist's perspective, offering insights that could lead to a different angle on the case. With the revelations from Truth and Dare though, I'm not sure I can completely trust Tristan. I'm not sure yet who I can completely trust until I delve deeper into the files.

"I do appreciate the offer," I reply, "but this case is already complicated enough. I'm not sure how involving you as a journalist would be beneficial."

Tristan's grin widens, "Ah, but that's the beauty of it. Sometimes, an outsider's perspective can shed light on things that those involved might overlook. Besides, I've never been one to shy away from a challenging story."

His confidence is evident, and I can't deny the allure of having an additional perspective on the case. Before I can respond my phone buzzes from where I placed it on the table in front of me.

There is a notification on the screen showing a new message from an unknown number. I know who it's from. I turn the phone over so that the screen is face down on the table.

Tristan raises an eyebrow as he notices my action with the phone. "Don't you need to get that?" he says, gesturing toward the phone. "I'm assuming that's Agent Derek desperately needing you back at his side already."

I can feel my heart pounding, torn between curiosity and the fear of revealing too much. "It's just a message from a friend," I respond, trying to keep my voice steady. "Nothing urgent."

He leans back in his chair, still wearing that grin. "You seem quite tense for just a message from a friend," he remarks, clearly enjoying the mystery. "But I won't pry. We all have our secrets, don't we? You can answer it, I won't even ask." He holds his hands up in a gesture of innocence.

I hesitate for a moment but then pull the phone close to me and hold it so he can't see the screen as I check it.

Truth or Dare, Little Darling?

I frown at the message, keeping in mind the presence of Tristan across from me.

Truth

I place the phone back down again and concentrate back on Tristan. My mind races, and I try to come up with a way to change the subject. "So, about your offer to help with the case... I'm not entirely convinced it's the right move right now."

My phone buzzes again. Holding up a finger, I give Tristan an apologetic look and pick it up.

If you woke up in the dead of night with my cock buried in your pretty pussy, would you want me to stop or keep going?

I already feel the heat in my cheeks from the flush I know has appeared from reading the message. This is definitely not the right time and place for me to answer a question like that, but now I'm stuck between the question on the phone in my hand and the man watching me from across the table.

I take a second to assess the feelings the question raises before I send a quick response and put my phone back down. The path they already have me on is getting darker and deeper each day. I can't deny my body's instant reaction to the scenario he painted in my head.

Keep going.

I take a few deep breaths to calm myself before I look back at Tristan, but something must still show on my face.

Tristan's expression softens, and he leans forward, his eyes showing genuine interest, but he continues the initial conversation as promised. "Look, I understand your hesitation. But trust me, I have no ulterior motives here. I genuinely want to help, my intentions are to shed light on the truth, just like you. We both want that, right?"

Tristan's sincerity is evident in his words, and I can't help but feel conflicted. On one hand, his help could be valuable, especially with his fresh perspective as a journalist. On the other hand, I'm still grappling with the burden of the secrets I carry, and I don't know if I can fully trust him with everything I know.

"I do want to find the truth," I admit, my voice softening. "But the case has taken some unexpected turns, and I'm afraid it might be too much for an outsider to handle."

Tristan nods thoughtfully, his grin fading into a more serious expression. "I can understand why you might feel that way. But sometimes, it's precisely an outsider's perspective that can see things from a different angle and bring new insights to the table. I won't push you, but if you ever change your mind, just know that I'm here."

"I appreciate that," I reply, my guard still up but more willing to consider his offer. "Let's give it a couple more days. If I don't make any significant progress, I will reach out to you for your perspective."

Tristan's eyes light up with a hint of excitement. "Deal," he says, extending his hand across the table.

I reach out to accept the gesture, feeling a sense of relief and uncertainty all at once. The case is consuming me, and I know I need help. Tristan might be the unexpected ally I didn't know I needed.

His fingers wrap tightly around mine, his hand warm and almost comforting. "I really feel I can help you, so whenever you're ready, just give me a call."

Chapter 22

Alex

When I return to the office Derek is still on the phone, talking in hushed but aggravated tones. His frustration is palpable. He ends the call with an exasperated sigh, his hand gripping the phone tightly.

"What's wrong?" I inquire, concerned about his state of mind.

Derek runs a hand through his hair, his brows furrowed. "Just more of that personal issue I mentioned earlier. It's really gotten under my skin. But I'll start addressing it tonight. No need to dwell on it now."

I nod, understanding that he needs his space to handle whatever is troubling him. "Take your time, Derek. I'm here for you if you need anything."

He gives me a smile before shaking his head, trying to shake off the frustration. "Thanks, Alex. Alright, let's get back to work. But first, I think we need a fresh overview on this."

Derek glances at the old murder boards, filled with images and notes that have become familiar to us. "We've hit a dead end with the interviews, so maybe it's time to reassess our approach."

I look at him curiously, intrigued by his suggestion. "What do you have in mind?"

Derek walks over to a storage closet and retrieves a new, larger board. "Let's start by pinning up the victims' images again. We need to analyze why some were targeted and killed faster than others. There might be a pattern we missed."

Excitement bubbles within me as I assist Derek in setting up the new board. We carefully pin up the photographs, arranging them in a way that allows us to study them as a whole. The faces of the victims stare back at us, a chilling reminder of the lives lost.

Derek steps back, his gaze sweeping over the board. "There must be a reason behind the order in which they were targeted. We need to consider factors like location, occupation, personal connections, anything that might help us uncover the killers' motives."

I nod in agreement, my mind already racing with possibilities. "Some victims might have been easier targets due to their routines or vulnerabilities. Others may have had connections to the murderers, whether known or unknown. We should also consider any distinguishing characteristics or similarities among the victims."

Derek leans against the table, his eyes fixed on the board. "Exactly. We'll cross-reference their profiles, look for any commonalities, and dig even deeper into their lives. There has to be something we've overlooked or missed, a clue hiding in plain sight."

Despite our best efforts, the board of victims' images remains a complex web of unanswered questions. The more we delve into their lives and backgrounds, the more we establish that, on the surface, there are no apparent connections between them. No commonalities in their routines, no shared acquaintances, and no discernible patterns in the way they were targeted.

Frustration mounts in the room further as we hit dead end after dead end. The lack of progress and the weight of the unsolved cases feels like a burden I can't shake off, knowing that there are files in my possession that could solve everything.

Derek and I spend hours pouring over the evidence, all the available documents, and reexamining interviews. We explore different angles, consider alternative theories, but nothing seems to fit together. To the unknowing eye the motivations remained elusive, shrouded in darkness, just out of our reach.

I need to get working on the files at home, being here isn't getting me anywhere. Feeling the mounting frustration, I take a deep breath, trying to push aside the thoughts of those files and how they could be the answer to everything. I focus on the present, on the board in front of us, and on the resolution to find the missing pieces in what we have that could break open the case.

But as we continue to work through the same information again, my patience wears thin, and I can't contain the frustration any longer. With a mix of anger and helplessness, I grab a handful of papers from the table and throw them at the board, watching them scatter across the images of the victims.

"None of it makes sense!" I yell, my voice echoing in the otherwise quiet office. "We've been at this for so long, and we're no closer to finding answers!"

Derek's face is a mix of concern and sympathy as he steps closer to me, his hand gently rubbing my arms in a comforting gesture. "Alex, you're exhausted. We both are. Maybe it's time to take a break and get some rest."

I shake my head, my frustration and exhaustion intertwining with my growing desperation. "No, I can't rest. I can't stop until we figure this out."

Derek's grip on my arms tightens, his voice becoming firmer. "I know you're dedicated, Alex, but pushing yourself like this won't help anyone. We need a fresh perspective, and that won't happen if we're running on fumes."

Tears of frustration and fatigue threaten to spill from my eyes, and I wipe them away hastily. "I feel like I'm going insane. I know the pieces are right in front of us, but we can't make them fit."

Derek's expression softens, and he pulls me into an embrace. "We'll get to the bottom of this, Alex. But right now, you need to take care of yourself. Go home, clear your mind. Tomorrow is a new day."

I lean into him briefly, feeling a mix of comfort and gratitude. "You're right," I whisper, my voice breaking slightly. "Maybe, I do need to clear my head."

Derek pulls back after only a moment, looking into my eyes with genuine concern. "Promise me you'll take care of yourself. Promise me you won't let this case consume you."

I nod, but I know the next words out of my mouth will be a lie. "I promise. I won't let it consume me."

He gives me a small smile, "Good. Now go home, and remember that I'm here for you, whenever you need me."

Taking a deep breath, I gather my belongings and prepare to leave the office. As I start to walk out, Derek's words echo in my mind, and I realize that he's right. Stopping in the doorway I look back at him. "You're right, we do need a fresh perspective. If we don't make any headway tomorrow, I'm getting Tristan to help us. He might be able to see something outside of the box. And he has friends who might be able to help with information that isn't here." I say waving a hand at the mess I'm leaving him to pick up.

Derek's expression wavers between surprise and annoyance at the mention of Tristan. He opens his mouth as if he wants to protest, but then he visibly restrains himself.

"Alright, if you think it could help, then we can consider it," Derek concedes with a hint of reluctance. "But let's not forget that we need to tread carefully when involving outsiders in such a sensitive case."

I nod, appreciating his concern and acknowledging the risks involved. "I know, Derek. We'll be cautious, but we can't keep hitting dead ends like this. We need all the help we can get."

Derek's demeanor softens, I know he also feels the stress of the case and understands my determination to find the truth. "You're right. Just promise me that if we bring Tristan in, you won't let him get too close to the sensitive details of the investigation. We don't want any leaks or potential compromises."

"I promise," I reply, though I know that keeping Tristan away from sensitive information might not be as simple as it sounds, especially if he's genuinely eager to assist us. "We'll be careful, and if it doesn't feel right, we can always reassess."

Derek gives me a half-smile, he can't control everything, but he seems to trust my judgment in this matter. "Alright, then."

"Alright, then," I echo with a grateful smile. "I'll see you tomorrow."

With that, I leave the office, the weight of the case still heavy on my mind, but with a glimmer of hope that Tristan's assistance might provide a breakthrough.

As I arrive at my rental house, I'm greeted by the comforting silence. But the pressure of the unsolved case and the mystery files feels even heavier in the solitude of my home. I know I should take Derek's advice and rest, but my mind won't allow me to relax. I need answers, and I know the files Truth and Dare gave me hold the key.

I make my way to my sanctuary, where I have my desk and can be surrounded by the images of the case and crime scenes. I set up my laptop and connect the drive, watching as the various folders fill the screen.

The folders on the drive are organized meticulously, with each victim having their own folder containing relevant documents and information. I've already reviewed the files of the two most recent victims, but now, armed with the knowledge I gained from those files, I know what I'm looking for in these other folders.

I start by opening the folder of the victim before the last one I viewed, and as I suspected, there's more to the story than what was publicly known. The victim's public profile showed a clean record, but buried within the files are records of illegal activities and connections to dangerous individuals. Details about their connections to criminal activity and hidden aspects of their lives are meticulously documented.

It becomes evident that the killers are not just random psychopaths but targeting their victims for a reason. The more I dig into the files, the clearer it becomes that this is more than just a random killing spree with nothing connecting to each other. There's a calculated method behind their actions.

A mix of shock and realization washes over me. It becomes evident that these victims were far from innocent bystanders; they were entangled in really dangerous circles even if the face they showed the world gave no indication of it, and their deaths had nothing to do with their public actions but everything to do with what they did away from the public eye.

Continuing my investigation, I find that the files have been meticulously wiped from official databases, leaving no traces behind. Whoever orchestrated this cover-up knew what they were doing, and it suggests a high level of insider knowledge or support.

My mind races as I consider the implications. The killers somehow got this information also, whether it was before they were covered up or afterward I couldn't be certain, but it raises questions about how they obtained these files. The level of sophistication required to retrieve data wiped from public records indicates a level of expertise beyond that of ordinary criminals.

I take notes, trying to piece together the connections between the victims and the criminal activities they were involved in. It's a complex puzzle, and the more I delve into the files, the more I realize that these victims were part of a dangerous ring of murderers, drug dealers, child abusers and traffickers. Somehow, they were all connected, and their actions had remained hidden until now.

Creating a space on one of my walls I organize the information, creating a new board. It becomes apparent that someone or multiple people within the bureau itself might be protecting this criminal network. The extent of the cover-up is alarming, and I can't help but wonder how deep the corruption goes and who might be involved.

My hands shake as I continue to pin up photographs and connect the pieces of the puzzle. I know I'm getting close to the truth, and it terrifies me to think about what might happen if this case is blown open. The danger is real, but I can't let that stop me. The truth must be exposed.

I take a step back to survey the board, and the interconnecting web of criminal activity stares back at me, haunting and infuriating. The urge to confront the people responsible, no matter how powerful they may be, burns within me. But I know I can't act recklessly; I need concrete evidence and a solid plan to take down the network without putting myself or others in harm's way.

But that doesn’t stop the anger from coursing through my body.

Taking a deep breath, I force myself to calm down. I can't afford to let my emotions get the best of me. I need to think rationally and strategically. As I look at the board, a new plan starts forming in my mind.

First, I need to find out who within the Bureau might be involved in the cover-up and protecting the criminal network. To do that, I have to be discreet and cautious. I can't trust anyone within the office blindly, not even Derek. The corruption might run deeper than I realize, and I can't afford to let the wrong person know what I'm onto.

As I ponder my next move, I remember Tristan's friend, Max, who claimed he could get information otherwise unattainable. If there's anyone who can help me uncover the identities of those involved in the cover-up, it's him. But I need to approach this carefully and ensure that Max can be trusted.

With a plan forming in my mind, I decide that I'll reach out to both Tristan and Max the next day. I need to gather more information, and their assistance could prove invaluable. But for now, I also need to heed Derek's advice and get some rest. My mind is racing, and I know I won't be able to think clearly without getting some sleep.

After a quick shower to wash away the stress of the day, I crawl into bed, feeling mentally exhausted. As I close my eyes, the images of the victims and the complexities of the case haunt my thoughts. I can't help but wonder how many more lives are at stake and how deep the corruption within the Bureau runs.

Chapter 23

Dare

I have been watching her for hours. I could see as she made all the connections from the files we gave her, I watched her set up the new board in her office. Originally, we decided to allow her some time to herself tonight, but I couldn't stay away.

Frustration and anger coursed through me for most of the day.

I always find myself watching her, so I saw as she smiled at him, I saw when they were in each other's personal space. She allowed him to be too close to her body and she needs to be punished for that.

She is ours and no one else's.

I will be dealing with *him* soon enough, and she will watch. But right now I need to deal with her. My Little Darling Queen.

She would learn soon enough not to get close to other men. Not to talk to them so intimately. Not to smile at them like she did. She really shouldn't even be breathing the same air as anyone but us. Her pretty perfect skin should never be touched by anyone but us. She belongs to us.

It doesn't take much to get into her house when I know she has finally fallen asleep. Sliding the key in the lock and opening the door is almost noiseless. We made sure it would be. We didn't want her waking up just by entering the house after all.

Opening the panel for the air conditioning unit I press the hidden button there, triggering the mild sedative to fill the air of her room. My mask filters it so that it doesn't affect me. I have plans tonight and I didn't want her waking until I am ready.

I knew what Truth had done. When he did it, I was a little concerned that he might be stepping a little too far too soon, but I let him do what he wanted. It's not like I didn't really see the point in it at the time.

But now I am wholeheartedly behind his actions. She is ours, and ours alone. She is our Queen. And like fuck am I ever letting her get away from us. Her place is by our side. I would never not let her have free will, but I would certainly do everything in my power to maneuver her until the only choice she has is us. Until the only thing she could do is take her place between us.

After giving the sedative time to take effect, I move slowly into her bedroom. She barely has the sheet covering her, her beautiful hair is spread across the pillow next to her and my hand twitches at the sight of it. I just want to wrap it tightly around my hand and use all that brunette goodness to control her as I fuck her throat, but the sedative is mild and I came here for a purpose.

I would need to control that urge for the moment. And it's not as though I didn't warn her I would do this.

Pulling the sheet gently down her body I hum softly to myself at the sight of her gorgeous long legs. She doesn't realize what a turn on those are, everytime I see her in her professional pantsuits. But that could also be because I want to follow the length of them all the way up to her pussy.

Right now, I get to do just that, without the barrier of fabric in my way. Taking my glove off for the moment, my fingers trail against the skin of her leg, it's so soft, like silk under my fingers. Goosebumps rise on her skin as my fingers continue to trail upward.

When my fingers move further up, raising up the sleep shirt she has on I can see the pretty pair of underwear underneath. Slowly sliding them down and off her legs I internally hope they aren't her favorite pair, before I tuck them into one of the pockets of my pants.

I gently part her legs but pause for a moment as she shifts her upper body slightly. She settles back down without waking.

I know the sedative won't last too much longer. I take the opportunity while I can to lift the mask and bring my face close to her exposed pussy. Inhaling deeply I groan softly to myself, I love the smell that is all her. But more than that I love how sweet she tastes on my tongue. I slowly slide my tongue along the length of her with another groan and my hard cock throbs where it's pressed against the inside of my pants. Her breath hitches and her back arches softly with a small moan of her own. But as I look at her intently, I can tell she is still asleep.

I don't want to tempt fate too much, as much as I want to bury my face in her pussy and stay there for hours. The clock is ticking against me.

Covering my face and hand again I move her legs further apart, moving onto the bed between them. Pulling my cock from the confines of my pants, I rub the head against her, the lick I gave her pussy had turned her on and made her wet enough that my cock has no issues when I start to push myself inside her.

I'm halfway to being balls deep when she shifts again with another moan, her breathing getting heavier in her sleep. Her pussy is tight, her body almost fighting against the intrusion. I know the piercings on my cock would be rubbing hard against her skin, but the sedative must still be affecting her enough to keep her down for the moment.

I watch the tiny reactions cross her face as I push the rest of the way inside her pussy. Her mouth is open and she is panting slightly, a tiny frown pulls at the skin between her eyes as her head tilts back just a little. Her legs shift, bending unconsciously and making it easier for me as I drag my cock almost all the way back out and then slowly push all the way back in.

Releasing a soft groan, I close my eyes for a moment to savor the feeling of her, so tight, hot, and wet. Her pussy is squeezing around my cock, an automatic reaction from her body, but it makes me want to let go and fuck her hard until she is screaming. However, I want this soft moment first before she wakes up. I need to feel her surrounding me, knowing that we fit together perfectly, that we belong together and she will understand that one day soon.

I slowly drag myself out then push back in again. Her moan this time is louder. I can tell the sedative is starting to wear off, I can see the flutter of her pulse in her neck, stretched before me, is starting to flutter faster against her skin.

My next thrust is a little harder, her breasts bouncing a little from the movement. I wish I didn't have the mask on at that moment, I would love to be able to take her nipples into my mouth, licking, sucking, then biting down hard until she screams and cums around my cock from the pain of it.

The feeling of her hands against the skin on my back startles me. Even in her sleep her hands dug their way under my hoodie and found skin. Her nails scratching harsh lines all the way down to my hips on my next thrust have a hiss and a moan escaping me. Fuck, I love the feel of her cutting me up with her kitten claws. But for the moment, I can't have that.

Pausing and using my knees for balance, I gently grab her wrists, cross them over one another, and wrap my gloved fingers of one hand around them. They look tiny in my hand, like one simple move could break them. I move her hands to the small gap on the mattress above her head and press them down firmly, securing them there so she can't move.

Bearing my weight down on them, I brace my other hand and thrust into her again. It's harder than before, but she needs to wake up now. Her eyes open with a cry and a gasp on the next thrust.

I stop moving and tilt my head, watching the myriad of reactions cross her face. The surprise is there, but there isn't a lot of fear. I can tell when she remembers the truth question I posed to her, realizing that I planned to do this.

Her breathing speeds up as her pussy tightens around me, she shifts her legs and hips as though impatient for me to move.

"Keep going," her voice is a soft rasp, a combination of sleep and the sedatives I'm sure.

I hum in response but don't move just yet. "Pretty Little Darling, I came to make a point," I say to her, the mask doing its job to modulate my voice.

She tugs slightly on her hands before tilting her head defiantly. "That you could fuck me whenever you want? I never said you couldn't, if you remember correctly, I even said to keep going, twice already."

It's a struggle to suppress my laughter, but I feel my lips curve up in a smile, out of sight behind my mask. My voice takes on a harsher tone, laced with possessiveness. "Listen closely, my Little Darling. Your body, your heart, your very soul—they belong to us, and only us. No one is to ever come near them again. Your smiles, your emotions, your moans, your pleasure—it's all ours to claim."

I run my gloved fingers down her neck before wrapping my hand around it, her head tilting back on a moan and meeting my intense gaze. "You're ours, and we'll do whatever it takes to make that very clear to you. We'll possess every inch of you, every secret desire you have we will fulfill." I pull back and thrust into her, rough and hard, trying to drive the point into her as hard as I drive my cock into her pussy.

Her breath hitches, and she looks at me with a dark need, a burning fire that I want to build into an inferno big enough to burn the whole world down. "Yes," she whispers.

I lean down closer to her, my hand squeezing on instinct,and I can't resist thrusting harder into her pussy. I feel her pulsing around me as she moans, I can tell she's already close to the edge. But then so am I, the possessive need to make her ours is like an insanity taking over my mind.

"We will kill anyone who touches you, Little Darling. If they even breathe on you too closely I will slit their throat and fuck you in their blood while it's still hot. You are ours. Do you understand?" my voice is harsh as I grit out my question.

"Yessss," she moans in response, her pussy tightening further around my cock.

I pull out only to slam back into her, "This pussy belongs to us, if anyone else even thinks of touching it, I'll cut off their hands and make them eat them one finger at a time." She whimpers and I watch the flush spreading up her chest and neck, her pussy is clamped down on me so tight it's a struggle to draw back again.

"And every chance we get, we will fuck you, hard, over and over. Filling you with our cum until you're big and round with our babies." I slam into her again, and she keens under my hands, her whole body trembling. "Only death can take you from us now, and even then, I would fight him for you."

"God," she moans as I continue to move.

"God isn't here, Little Darling. We are your devils, and we own your soul."

She shatters around me, her screams echoing around the room as she cums all over my cock. I release her throat and use that hand to lift her leg higher before I set a savage rhythm. I groan when a second orgasm rolls through her, not able to hold my own release off and I explode deep inside her pussy, my cum hot as her pussy drags it out of me one squeeze at a time.

But I don't let that stop me. My cock becomes sensitive from my release, but I keep thrusting inside her hard. I was blessed with a short refractory period, a curse when I'm listening to Truth fuck her after me, but a blessing right now.

Neither my movements or my cock soften, my hips continuing to snap forward. She will understand what it means to be owned by us. Every move she makes from now on will be a reminder of who she belongs to.

A possessive insanity takes hold of me as I continue to fuck her savagely. Her needy pussy continues to come apart for me to the sounds of her moans and screams. I cum one final time on a harsh groan as I watch her eyes roll back and flutter shut as she finally slides into unconsciousness again.

Leaning down I lift my mask enough to kiss her parted lips, my voice is a gravelly rasp as I breath against her skin. "You will never leave me again, Little Darling."

Chapter 24

Alex

I have no idea who fucked me last night.

That's probably not something to be proud of, but when dealing with a duo of masked men on a regular basis and only one shows up to fuck you until you're unconscious, it makes it a little hard to tell. Though based on the interactions to date, I would guess it was Dare. He comes across as the more controlling one, still a psycho, but a controlled psycho.

And it would be helpful if their psychotic tendencies stopped turning me on.

I spend longer under the cascade of hot water in my shower this morning, trying to wrap my head around at exactly what point in time I completely disregarded all sanity. When, during this whole twisted game, did I become such a willing participant?

As the steam envelops the bathroom, I lean against the tiled wall, letting the hot water soothe the bruises on my body. My thoughts are a whirlwind, and I can't help but replay the events of the past few days over and over in my mind. How did I end up in this twisted dance with these dangerous men? Why do I find myself strangely drawn to the darkness they brought into my life? I have to confront the fact that I am becoming complicit in my own undoing.

I could no longer deny that I am already addicted to them. I don't even know who they really are, but there is something about them that draws me to them, like a moth to a flame, or in this case a lamb to the slaughter.

There is still the ever present fear that they would decide to be done with me and kill me like the other victims, but it is slowly diminishing with each day and each twisted revelation.

We had been completely wrong on their motivations for killing these women. They weren't looking for an ideal match at all, they were looking for the ultimate evil within a web of lies and manipulation. But then I wonder if that was their goal for us as investigators, to make us look in a completely different direction, the ultimate misdirection.

But then why disclose their secrets to me? Why entangle me in their web, giving me information I cannot use? What is their goal in doing that?

With a sigh, I turn off the water and step out of the shower, wrapping myself in a towel. There are new dressings on the cuts that Dare must have applied after I passed out the night before.

Controlled and thoughtful psycho.

As I dress, I can't help but look at the bruises and dressings on my body. They serve as a reminder of the darkness I more or less willingly stepped into. Yet, strangely, there is a part of me that feels excitement at the evidence of my encounters with these men. It is a sickening realization that their actions had become intertwined with a twisted form of desire in my mind.

I shake my head, trying to dispel those thoughts as I finish getting dressed for work. I know this is not healthy, that I should be running away from them, not getting drawn deeper into their twisted world. But the allure is there, and I can't deny it.

As I grab my car keys and head out the door, with a newfound resolve, I decide that I need to get to the bottom of this whole tangled web soon; before my sanity leaves me completely and I do something I regret.

Thoughts of the prior morning's run in with Max drift through my mind as I make my way to the cafe, but thankfully the drive thru is open today. Ordering my regular coffee and bagel, I glance around, half-expecting to see Max again, but he's nowhere in sight. Relief washes over me, and I try to focus on the task at hand: getting through the day without any unnecessary complications.

I almost feel like I'm tempting fate just thinking about it. But I thankfully manage to avoid everyone as I drive into the parking garage and even when I get to the elevator to take it up to our office.

Derek is already in the office when I arrive, leaning against the table and looking intently at the new board that we created together the night before. After all the revelations from my own board at home, it seems so strange to see this one knowing what I now know.

"Good morning," Derek greets me, snapping me out of my thoughts. His voice is tired, and I can see the exhaustion in his eyes. It seems like he's been working tirelessly on this case, just like me.

"Good morning," I reply, trying to sound as normal as possible. But my mind is still consumed by the dangerous game I'm playing and the secrets I can't yet share with Derek.

He glances at me, concern in his eyes. "You still look tired. Did you get enough sleep?"

"Yeah, just had a lot on my mind," I say with a forced smile, not wanting to worry him further.

Derek nods, seemingly accepting my explanation, but his eyes linger on me for a moment longer before he turns his attention back to the board. "There's something off about this case. It's like we're missing a crucial piece of the puzzle."

My heart sinks, knowing that I'm the one withholding that crucial piece of information. I want to tell him everything, to share the dark truth I've uncovered, but without concrete evidence, it could jeopardize not only the investigation, but our safety as well.

"Yeah, it's definitely complex," I reply carefully, trying to steer the conversation away from any sensitive areas.

Derek sighs, running a hand through his hair. "We need to find more leads. Anything that can help us understand their motives better."

"We'll keep digging," I promise, feeling the pressure of my own secrets pressing down on me.

Throughout the day, Derek and I work tirelessly on the case. But my mind is split between the task at hand and the truth that is buried underneath these victims. The desire to tell Derek everything, to share the burden with him, is almost overwhelming, but I resist, knowing that it's not the right time.

We exchange ideas, discussing different possibilities and reevaluating all the evidence we have. But even with our renewed efforts, we still can't seem to find the missing pieces that would connect all the dots from the information we have.

By evening, frustration starts to creep back in. It feels like we're running out of options. I know it's time to call Tristan for help, as much as I wish we could solve this on our own. The thought that I could use his friend, if he can access the missing pieces of the puzzle that were deleted, gnaws at my subconscious.

"Derek, I think it's time we bring in Tristan," I say, looking at him earnestly. "He might be able to offer a fresh perspective and help us see things from a different angle."

Derek hesitates for a moment, clearly torn between his reservations and the need for progress. Finally, he nods, "Alright, give him a call. But let's be cautious and only share what's absolutely necessary."

"I will," I assure him, feeling a mix of relief and trepidation about involving Tristan in our dangerous investigation. I pull out my phone and dial the number Tristan gave me at the cafe the day before.

It rings a few times before he answers, "Tristan Winters."

"Hey Tristan, it's Alex."

"Well, well, well, to what do I owe the pleasure of this call?" his voice is full of warmth and humor.

I can't help but chuckle at Tristan's tone. "I hope I'm not interrupting anything important."

"Of course not," he replies. "Just lurking in the shadows with nothing better to do like Agent Derek said." I can practically hear the grin in his voice.

I smile, appreciating the levity in the midst of our serious situation. "Well, I was wondering if you're still up for helping us out with the case."

"Anything for you." Tristan responds. "Agent Derek actually letting me assist? I must be dreaming. I never thought the day would come."

I chuckle softly, knowing how much Derek hates journalists. "Yeah, well, I guess we're willing to try anything at this point. We've hit a dead end, and I think your fresh perspective might just be what we need."

"Hey, I'm flattered," Tristan says, sounding genuinely pleased. "I'll do my best to assist you guys in any way I can. Just let me know when and where you want to meet."

"It's starting to get late," I reply. "Why don't we all get together for a coffee in the morning? We'll fill you in on what we've got so far."

"That sounds perfect," Tristan agrees. "I'll be there bright and early, or as early as I can manage for a journalist, at least."

I chuckle, "Early for you means before midday, right?"

"Hey, don't be so cruel," Tristan jokes back. "But sure, I'll set my alarm for an ungodly hour. See you at the crack of dawn."

I laugh, shaking my head. "Well, don't worry. I'll make sure to get you some extra strong coffee to wake you up."

"Deal," he says with a hint of amusement. "Looking forward to it."

After confirming the meeting time and place, we end the call. I glance at Derek, who's packing up his things, getting ready to leave for the day. "Tristan is on board. We'll meet him at the cafe tomorrow morning."

Derek nods, looking slightly apprehensive but also hopeful. "Alright, let's hope he can bring something new to the table."

I nod in agreement. "Fingers crossed. It's worth a shot at this point."

As Derek bids me goodnight and heads out, I find myself alone in the office. My mind starts to wander again, and I can't help but think about the dangerous game I'm playing. The truth I hold, the secrets I can't share, it's all becoming too much to bear.

With a heavy sigh, I look down at my phone resting on the table. It's as if the device is taunting me, reminding me of the messages I've exchanged and the game of Truth or Dare.

Taking a deep breath, I open the messaging app and begin typing a message.

Truth or dare?

It takes only a moment for the response to appear.

Truth, Little Darling.

I shouldn't be surprised; they said in the past they would only choose dare when I do. I think about what I want to ask again but then decide to go for it.

Is it true that the women you murdered were involved in the same criminal organization?

The response comes back quickly, and a chill runs down my spine as I read it.

Yes, Little Darling. But they were only the servants of a bigger monster.

I stare at the screen hoping for more from them, but I know I won't get anything else. That's not how they play. I quickly type out another message but I can already predict what the response will be.

Who is the bigger monster?

The response is immediate and in no way, surprising.

Ah ah, Little Darling, it's our turn.

Once again I'm left staring at my screen waiting for more that doesn't come. With a growl of frustration I put my phone away and leave the office behind.

The sun has just disappeared below the horizon when I pull my car into the rental house. My frustration has faded slightly but it's still there bubbling below the surface. My footsteps as I walk toward my front door is loud in the silence. The shadows from the street lights are long and dark, but they don't hide the note that's pinned to my front door.

Taking it down I frown at it, not able to read it in the dim light of my doorstep. Opening the door, I move into the entryway and turn on my light. I can already tell something is different. Looking down at the note in my hand, a chill spreads down my spine.

Truth or Dare,
Little Darling?

My heart pounds in my chest as I stare at the note. I'm already on edge, and this only adds to the turmoil inside me.

I quickly scan the rest of the paper, hoping for some clue or context, but it's just those four words. Truth or Dare, Little Darling. There's nothing else written on either side, and the simplicity of it makes it even more unsettling.

I glance around, half-expecting to see one of them lurking in the shadows, but the house is empty and there's no sign of anyone else being there.

I walk further into the living room, my eyes scanning the surroundings for any other clues. That's when I notice it—a small vial sitting on the coffee table. It wasn't there before.

Picking up the vial, I examine it closely. It's a small, clear container with a liquid inside, and a note is attached to it.

Drink,
if you Dare.

My mind races with possibilities. Is this some sort of test or trap? Should I really dare to drink whatever mysterious substance is in this vial? My instincts scream at me to be cautious, but there's a part of me that's inexplicably drawn to the idea of accepting their twisted challenge.

With trembling hands, I debate my choices. If I refuse, will there be consequences? But if I drink it, what could happen? I can't be sure if it's a harmless test of courage or something far more dangerous.

My curiosity wins over my fear, and I make a decision. I uncork the vial, bringing it close to my nose to catch a whiff of its contents. There's a faint, sweet scent that I can't quite place. It's enticing, but it doesn't offer any answers about what this liquid might do.

Taking a deep breath, I steel myself and raise the vial to my lips. Before I can second-guess myself, I tilt it back, and the liquid spills into my mouth. The taste is unusual, a mix of bitter and sweet that lingers on my tongue.

A few seconds after I've swallowed it, a wave of dizziness washes over me. My vision blurs momentarily and I reach out to steady myself on the coffee table as I sit down heavily on the couch.

As the contents take their toll on me, my body starts to feel heavy and sluggish. It's as if I'm sinking into a hazy dream, where reality and illusion blend together. My eyelids grow heavier with each passing moment, and I struggle to keep them open.

I feel my body sliding sideways on the couch as I try to fight against the drowsiness, attempting to stay alert, but it proves to be too powerful. The room around me fades away and my mind is plunged into darkness.

Chapter 25

Alex

As my consciousness slowly returns, I become aware of my surroundings. I'm lying on the ground in a clearing, surrounded by trees, with my hands bound in front of me. The darkness has deepened, and the moon casts an eerie glow over the clearing, creating haunting shadows that seem to dance around me.

The clearing is eerily quiet, except for the distant rustling of leaves and the occasional hoot of an owl. I struggle to free my hands, but the bindings are too tight, and my attempts only cause them to dig deeper into my skin.

I can't see anyone else around, but that doesn't mean I'm alone. I struggle to sit up, my bound hands making it difficult to gain leverage. I search the ground for something sharp or any tool that might help me escape, but there's nothing within reach that I can see.

I take a few deep breaths to steady myself. I need to think clearly and come up with a plan. Gathering my strength, I push myself up to my feet and carefully assess my surroundings. The trees loom over me, and the darkness makes it difficult to determine any landmarks or paths.

I have no idea which direction might lead to safety or even where I am.

"Hey, Little Darling."

I can't tell which direction the modulated voice is coming from. Looking around, I still can't see anyone in the shadows, and the voice seemed to come from every direction all at once.

I stop moving; it is useless looking for them if they don't want to be found. I take a deep breath making sure to project my voice as strong as I can. "What am I doing here?"

A chuckle echoes around me. "We feel like it's time for some role playing, Little Darling. Instead of you hunting us, we are going to hunt you. Through this forest. In the dark."

My heart skips a beat then speeds up in my chest. "What happens if you catch me?"

Laughter fills the air, sending shivers down my spine. "Hmmmm maybe we'll kill you…"

A second voice speaks, still modulated but there's a slight difference to it allowing me to pick up the change. "Or maybe we'll fuck you…"

A hum sounds before a voice speaks again. "Maybe we'll fuck you and then kill you."

Another chuckle. "Hell, maybe we'll kill you while we fuck you. Who knows..."

"Depends on our mood." Their laughter blends together, creating an unsettling soundtrack to the pounding of my heart. It continues to echo around me, and I can't shake the feeling of being completely surrounded.

My mind races, trying to come up with a plan to escape. The darkness and the unknown terrain make it challenging to even begin to formulate a strategy. My instincts tell me to run, to try and find a way out of this, but with my hands bound, I feel vulnerable and exposed.

I take another deep breath, trying to remain composed. They wouldn't really kill me, would they? Why would they have gone through all of the effort if they were just going to kill me?

They are just trying to scare me. Make me run like a scared rabbit right into their arms. Two could play this game. Well, three actually.

Clearing my throat I look around at the trees. They are there somewhere, out of sight. "Hardly seems fair, making me try to escape you with my hands bound."

Another chuckle sounds, echoing around the clearing. "Well, you proved that you couldn't control your hands, Little Darling. I told you not to move them, now this is your punishment."

Well, fuck.

I had been warned.

"How about this, Little Darling, if you make it out of this forest, we will take you home as though this never happened."

I narrow my eyes at the shadows. "No, I have another deal for you instead."

One of them hums before a voice sounds again. "And what deal would that be, Little Darling? You don't exactly hold all the cards here."

"I'll play along, I'll be your little rabbit, I'll even scream nice and loud for you, but I want something big in exchange."

A chuckle comes again but there's a more serious edge to it this time. "Always a negotiation, Little Darling."

I raise my chin in defiance. "You want something from me? Well I want something from you."

There is barely a hesitation before a voice comes again. "Hmmm, okay Little Darling. Be a good little rabbit, and we will give you something you truly want."

I frown at the words. "Don't I get to specify what I want?"

The laughter has an almost evil edge to it this time and it sends another shiver down my spine. “No, Little Darling.”

“Now run.”

I don’t need to be told twice. My feet are moving before I even think about it.

I'm thankful for the full moon and my decent night vision keeping me from running into the first tree I come across.

My heart races as I sprint through the dark forest. Every snap of a twig underfoot, every rustle of leaves sends my senses into overdrive. I can't afford to make a sound, to give away my position to them so quickly.

The shadows of the trees stretch out like menacing claws, threatening to ensnare me at any moment. My mind races, trying to stay focused on the path ahead while also keeping an ear out for any signs of their movement.

I come to a stop behind a tree to catch my breath and get my bearings; the forest feels like it is closing in on me.

“Don’t stop now, Little Darling, you’ve only just started.”

The voice sounds from multiple directions, but I don't know where it's actually coming from.

But I do exactly what the voice wanted: I run.

The branches and underbrush scratch against the fabric of my clothes and I’m suddenly thankful they didn’t remove them. But I know I won’t be able to use these clothes for work again; they are no doubt already ruined. The occasional sting to my scalp makes me wish I wore my hair up for work.

The moonlight filters through the leaves, casting eerie shadows on the forest floor. My mind races with every step, trying to map out the terrain, searching for any advantage I can get. I have to be clever, outwit them at their own game.

As I run, I mentally calculate my options. My bound hands are still a hindrance, limiting my ability to defend myself if necessary. But I can't let that deter me. I have to stay nimble, swift, and focused.

With each passing moment, the forest seems to grow darker, and their laughter continues to echo around me, chasing my every step.

As I dash through the undergrowth, I spot a faint glimmer of moonlight reflecting off a small stream. It might offer a path to follow.

Without hesitation, I change my direction and follow the stream. The cool water soothes my skin through my clothes as I splash through it, the sound masking my footsteps. I know that I can't afford to be too loud or too careless.

I start to pick up on the patterns of the forest, the way the moonlight filters through the branches, and the subtle sounds of nocturnal creatures. I try to use this knowledge to my advantage, to stay one step ahead of them.

The darkness seems to be my ally now, concealing me as I continue to move through the forest. Every now and then, I get a glimpse of a figure in the shadows, but I refuse to let them know that I see them. Instead, I make quick detours, changing my path, keeping them guessing.

I stop again and crouch behind a tree when I see one of them ahead. The figure appears almost like he's taking a stroll, without a care in the world. I keep my eyes on him as he keeps walking, moving away from where I'm hidden.

"Boo, Little Darling."

The voice comes from my left, completely taking me by surprise, but I'm already moving. My feet take me quickly in the opposite direction of the voice.

My heart pounds in my chest as I try to suppress my ragged breaths. Every nerve in my body is on high alert and the adrenaline courses through me, urging me to keep moving, to keep running.

I can't see them, but I know they're out there; watching, waiting. Their voices and laughter continue to echo around me, taunting and tormenting me.

As I run, my mind races through possibilities. The forest seems to go on forever, and I'm lost in its labyrinth of trees and shadows. I don't know if I'm getting closer to the edge or deeper into its heart.

I spot a large rock formation in the distance, its dark silhouette contrasting against the pale moonlit sky. It could offer a vantage point, a place to gain a better sense of my surroundings.

I change course and head towards the rocks. Every step is careful and calculated, as I try to remain as silent as possible.

But just as I approach the rock formation, a shadow looms over me. My heart skips a beat, looking up to see one of them perched on top of the rocks, staring down at me.

"Hello, Little Darling."

I let out a startled yelp as I almost slide in the dead leaves. They scatter across the ground as I try to stop. Thankfully, I catch myself in time and change direction yet again.

The figure behind me laughs wickedly, his voice echoing through the forest. I curse myself for not being more cautious, for not paying closer attention to my surroundings.

I see one of their shadows ahead and I veer off into another direction, my breathing heavy, my heart pounding. Every sound seems amplified in the silence of the forest, and I can feel their eyes on me, their presence lurking just beyond my line of sight.

I stop again, trying to make sense of where I am. Suddenly a hand spins me and then closes around my throat, holding me against the tree at my back.

"Pretty Little Darling, are you having fun yet? Is this making you wet?" the voice growls at me.

He's right, it is turning me on, and when he grabs my pussy hard through my pants I can't stop the moan.

He squeezes harder and my body throbs in response.

"I'm going to fuck you so hard, Little Darling." His voice is a low, modulated groan.

As much as I want that, I am not going to give in that easily. I twist my body hard to the side and use my bound hands to knock his wrist aside. I'm shocked that it works, but I don't hesitate to take off running again.

I weave through the trees and their voices continue to taunt me from different directions. I change course every time their silhouettes appear.

I keep moving, my whole body burning. Need now pulses through me as I go.

Rounding another tree, I run solidly into something hard. The feeling of arms suddenly wrapping around me startles a scream from my lips.

The figure groans and I hear the familiar modulated voice. "That's it, Little Darling, scream for me."

I struggle as best I can in his arms until he releases me. I turn and race back in the opposite direction again only to run right into the arms of the other one.

Another startled sound comes from me as I'm lifted and walked backward until I'm pressed between them.

“Now, now, Little Darling, where do you think you're going?" He taunts, his voice dripping with amusement. “The fun is only just beginning.”

Chapter 26

Alex

Adrenaline is pumping through me and I'm panting. At this point I'm not sure if it's from running or simply from them.

I feel almost proud of myself for being able to tell that the one in front of me is Dare and the one behind me is Truth. I'm beginning to be able to pick up on the tiny tells, Dare is a little taller and the one who takes charge in all situations while Truth is wilder, a little more unhinged and less controlled in his actions.

A typical older brother and younger brother dynamic.

Truth wrapping his gloved hand around my throat from behind drags me from my thoughts. Dare loosens his arms from around me, bringing his hands to the front of my clothes and violently ripping the shirt and jacket open, buttons now lost to the forest floor. He shoves the material off my shoulders but my bound hands stop him from getting them off completely.

But it does draw my attention to my own hands, that are bound in front of me for once.

Making a split decision I dart my hands up toward his face.

My fingers just brush the silicone of his mask before my wrists are grabbed by Truth's other hand and pulled back to my chest.

"Still not able to control those hands I see," his voice chuckles in my ear.

"Obviously she doesn't want to use her arms either," comes the reply from Dare.

He reaches down toward his leg briefly before returning with another length of rope. He loops one end of the rope on my wrists before wrapping it twice around my neck and then tying the other end back to my wrists.

He pulls my hands forward and in that exact moment I realize exactly what he's done. The length around my neck tightens the further away my hands move.

The rope is just to the point of cutting my air when he speaks again. "I know how much you love being choked, Little Darling. Try to leave that to us though and keep your hands to yourself."

Air rushes back into my lungs as he lets go again and I pull my hands back to my chest. The message is clear, if I want to put my hands close to his face again I would choke myself to do it.

He tilts his head and then nods as though satisfied. "Now where was I, Little Darling, before you rudely interrupted?"

Truth chuckles from behind me, the rumble vibrating through my back.

I see the glint of a knife reflected in the light of the moon moments before he starts cutting into the material of my clothes. It's not long before they are hanging loosely from my arms and the bra I was wearing is now on the forest floor.

My heart is racing even faster now as he brings his hands to my now bare breasts, the knife dangerously close to one of my nipples. But he doesn't cut me, instead he takes both nipples between his gloved fingers and starts squeezing, applying pressure until it goes beyond the point of pain and I cry out as my clit throbs in response.

Truth uses his now free hand to rip the button and zipper on my pants and shove his hand into them. Two of his fingers shove hard and fast into my pussy.

There is no leather glove covering his hand, I can tell the difference immediately. I try to move my head, I'm not sure if I intended to look back at him or down at his hand, but his other hand is still around my throat and controlling my movement.

The pressure on my nipples increases as Dare starts to twist his fingers. The combination of pleasure and pain swirling inside of me has moans and whimpers escaping me.

"Please…" I breathe out past the tightening of Truth's hand. My whole body is arched as far as I can to push my breasts into Dare's hands at the same time as I rock my pussy onto Truth's fingers.

Dare steps closer to me again, applying even more pressure to my nipples. "Please what, Little Darling?"

I can't do anything but moan in response as Truth's hand squeezes hard enough to take my voice from me as his palm rubs firmly against my clit. My pussy is clenching down on his fingers as I get closer to the edge.

I'm almost there, my orgasm within reach when Truth speaks again, "I know what she wants." His fingers disappear and I'm whimpering in disappointment but then he shoves them deep into my mouth. "Suck," he growls into my ear as he releases his grip on my throat.

I do as I'm ordered, my mouth closing around his bare fingers. The taste of myself floods my mouth, but underneath is the taste of him, and it just makes me wetter.

He groans as I rock back into his hard cock and mumbles a curse from behind his mask. He pulls his fingers from my mouth and suddenly both of his hands move with him as he drops down and tears my pants all the way down my legs.

Dare releases my nipples and the rush of blood back to them has them throbbing hard as he suddenly picks me up by the back of my legs and stepping past Truth he slams my back against the closest tree. The bark digs into my bare back, scratching and pulling at my skin until I know it's not only reopened the cuts they already gave me, but creating new cuts.

He presses his chest against mine so he can use his hands to release his cock from his pants, and then he's thrusting deep inside my pussy. There is a feral quality to his actions, like he is past the point of control.

His thrusts are hard, his hips slapping solidly against mine with every thrust and making my ass slap painfully against the tree. And all I can do is moan and cry out with each movement of his pierced cock inside of me.

I can feel myself getting close to the edge again, my pussy tightening around the hard cock moving inside of me.

"Is this how you like it, Little Darling? Do you like being fucked hard and dirty?" his voice has a hard edge to it and I'm not sure how he wants me to respond, but my pussy tightens further around him, making him groan.

He pauses as he pulls me away from the tree, dropping to his knees and then slamming my back against the hard, unforgiving forest floor. I cry out as pain radiates from my back, but he starts thrusting his cock inside me again.

"That's it, Little Darling. Let me hear those pretty little screams." He growls as he adjusts his position, using his knees to anchor himself and gain more room to move. He presses his hands into the ground beside me, raising his body away from mine and watching me writhe beneath him.

My back arches and I can't stop my hands from reaching to grab the front of his hoodie. The rope around my neck flexes with each movement of his body.

I can see the silhouette of Truth leaning against a nearby tree watching us, his hand stroking his own hard cock as he watches Dare fuck me savagely into the dirt. The sight and the thrusts of Dare's cock have me flying off the cliff. My screams echo around the forest as I shatter underneath him.

Dare groans as his rhythm stutters and I feel him cum deep inside of me, the heat of him flooding me. He drops down against my chest and then digs his gloved fingers into my sides as he rolls us until I'm on top of him.

His cock is still hard and my pussy clenches around him automatically as my thighs tighten against his hips. I'm reminded of the previous night when he just kept fucking me without stopping until I passed out.

He groans at the movement. "Move those hips, Little Darling. Show us how much you love our cocks inside you."

I rotate my hips, rolling them slowly and feeling his hard cock with each movement. It feels strange to have any control at all, like it's some sort of miracle for him to allow me any free movement. I embrace it, rolling and rotating my hips until he groans beneath me, arching his own back and neck beneath me in the sexiest movement I've ever seen.

I choke myself slightly in order to get my hands to the zipper of his hoodie, pulling it down quickly and far enough to give me access to his chest, before burying my teeth into his muscular pec. His hands thread through my hair and tighten sharply as he holds my head there and starts slamming his cock up into my pussy and I feel his cum flooding me again.

But he doesn't let go as his hips stop and seconds later I know why. There is no preparation, no warning, nothing. Just the feeling of Truth's fingers thrusting hard into my ass, they are wet with what I assume is lube. He only thrusts and scissors his fingers for a few seconds before they disappear and his slick cock is pushing slowly into my ass, his piercings scraping hard against the inside of me as Dare holds me still and I whimper around the flesh that's still in my mouth.

He was too impatient, not preparing me enough so it burns, the pain bringing tears to my eyes as I bite down harder and make Dare grunt beneath me. Blood fills my mouth and I realize I broke his skin with my teeth. Dare flexes his hips and his own cock moves inside me, his own piercings rubbing the inside of my pussy, contrasting with the pain and mixing the signals going to my brain. The sounds coming from me are almost feral.

When Truth is buried completely inside me he stops, and he wraps a hand around the front of my throat and squeezes. I release Dare's chest from my teeth, allowing my head to be pulled up and back until I'm arched almost painfully between them.

My whole body is shaking, tremors completely taking over my body as the movement has both pleasure and pain merging inside of me until my whole body feels like a raw nerve. Truth rolls his hips, his cock moving inside of my ass slowly, retreating and then pushing forward. Then he does it again. The whimpers leaving my mouth are loud.

Dare still hasn't moved, just watching my face with each movement of Truth's hips. Watching the tears slide down my cheeks.

Something covers my eyes, everything going dark, and then a tongue slides up my cheek.

"Give us your pain, Little Darling, give us all your tears."

I know it's Dare that spoke, because I can still feel the wet glide of Truth's tongue on my cheek as he licks away my tears.

Suddenly Dare rears up also, his tongue slowly licking my other cheek as Truth continues to roll his hips. Dare then licks across my bottom lip and his groan tells me he can taste his own blood from my mouth, and then his mouth is on mine, his kiss almost as feral as the sounds leaving me.

They both move away from my face again before my eyes are uncovered, but they have their masks back in place. Dare's gloved hand reaches out and he brushes his thumb against my bottom lip, my whimpers are slowly changing to moans the more Truth moves.

It seems to be some sort of signal for him, because he starts moving inside me too. They both start thrusting inside me, alternating so that one thrusts as the other retreats. I have never felt anything like it before. There is still pain, from the stretch of both cocks inside me, from the cuts on my skin, the digging of the ropes in my wrists and neck. But the pleasure is sweeping me up in its grasp also.

They quickly set a savage rhythm, fucking me hard. Truth's hand tightens around my throat at the same time Dare wraps his hand around the ropes between my wrists and neck. He pulls tight, and my breath cuts off. My hands automatically go to my throat grabbing Truth's hand with one of my own as my other grabs at the rope. My body tightens around them.

Truth groans in my ear, his thrusts losing their rhythm until he's just pounding into me, his hips slapping hard against my ass with each thrust. "You like that, Little Darling, you like being fucked by killers?"

My mouth is open but no sound is coming out, no air is getting through at all. The already dim light of the forest is darkening further, my head feeling lighter as everything starts getting hazy.

I feel Dare lean up more than I see him move. "Do you ever think about it, Little Darling? Do you think about how it felt for us to thrust our knives into those women like we are thrusting our cocks inside you? To feel the hot blood hit our skin, covering us until we are red with it. Watching the life leave their eyes."

With each word my body tightens further around them, until all I can feel is them: their cocks, their hands, and their bodies. The darkness keeps taking over my vision second by second.

Suddenly air is rushing back into my lungs and my orgasm crashes into me with the force of a cyclone, catching me up in its whirlwind before smashing me back down to where I'm caught between these two men. My whole body convulses and shudders as I clamp down onto both of them, my whole body pulsing. My screams echo through the forest before turning to whimpers.

They have destroyed me. That's all I can think of as they still their movements. There is no part of me that is going to ever recover from my involvement with them. Their dark influence has been branded on my soul and there is no turning back.

Truth slowly pulls himself from inside me.I whimper again at the feeling. I can vaguely feel him move away, but he's back in only a few seconds, his hand brushing my sweaty hair aside as he crouches again and says, "Sorry, Little Darling, hopefully one day we won't have to do this."

The prick of the needle has a quick half protest falling from my lips before I'm dragged into unconsciousness again.

Chapter 27

Alex

When I wake up this time it's still dark, and I'm back on my couch as though the whole experience was a dream. Except I can feel every ache and pain in my body. I can tell that they spent time cleaning me and caring for my wounds, but the only sign of them is a glass of clear liquid on the coffee table next to what I'm assuming is pain medication.

Plus a small wrapped gift.

I eye all three items suspiciously as I sit up on the couch. But in the end, I pick up the tablets and swallow them down with the clear liquid. It has a mildly sweet flavor to it and reminds me of whatever Truth had me drink when I was tied to my wall. It soothes my throat and clears my foggy mind before the pain medication even has time to take effect.

Looking at the clock on the wall I'm surprised to see that it's only just about to pass midnight. I know that still means it has been hours since I first arrived at the house, but I thought with whatever they gave me, the run, and everything that came after, more time would have passed; they must have used something that only had me unconscious for a short time period.

They dressed me in one of my regular night shirts, even going so far as to put underwear on me. Looking down the neck of the shirt I can see that there aren't really any new dressings. If anything, they removed the one from the first cut I got on Dare's knife. I can't see my back clearly, but that too seems as though the older cuts have now been left to breathe while there are some smaller dressings in new places where my back was cut by the tree.

There is a small dressing on my leg and a vague recollection of a branch catching hard on my leg as I ran. One of them even brushed my hair.

My heart actually warms at the thought of these men taking such consideration and care.

Focussing back on the gift in front of me I look at the note tied to it.

Something small
for our
Little Darling Queen.

My lip twitches at the note even as a frown tugs at my forehead. Curiosity swirls within me, the last present they gave me was a USB with a wealth of information on it, everything I hadn't realized I needed. What could these men consider as something small?

Carefully, I unwrap the gift, revealing an intricately carved wooden box inside. It has an odd design but something about it seems familiar. It's only small, no bigger than the size of my fist. I push the thought aside and open it.

If I hadn't already been sitting down I would have fallen at the sight. Inside, nestled on a bed of velvet, is a delicate gold necklace with a pendant in the shape of a heart.

A memory tugs at me and I'm thrown into the past.

"Please mommy, just a little longer! We were playing hide and seek."

I was being carried in a woman's arms, my hand clutching at the necklace around her neck. A pretty pendant with a unique design. A large gold heart with different color stones at the top, reds and pinks and whites. Like a star shower, or at least that's what it looked like to me. And then a word written along one edge of the bottom. She told me it's our name but I can't read it yet.

"But sweet baby girl, it's time for dinner and bed."

Her voice is warm, like a soft blanket to wrap myself in.

I pouted. "But they will think I didn't want to find them, they will just keep hiding and they won't come out. They will be cold and hungry!"

She laughs softly and I can feel it through my whole body. "Baby girl, their mummy will let them know you went home, I'm sure she will be giving them dinner soon too."

I keep pouting, she doesn't understand. "No she won't. She's a mean mummy, she's not like you."

Suddenly the memory flashes to another moment in time and all I see is blood, and all I hear are screams.

The tears falling on my hand drag me back. I didn't even realize I was crying, but sobs shake my body as I slide off the couch and to the floor.

Even through my tears, I can see the engraving on the heart pendant that my five year old self couldn't read, *'Darling'*.

How did they even know about the pendant? How did they even find it? I couldn't remember if I even mentioned it to the police when they tried to get information out of me while my little body was in shock. And I wasn't about to look at the crime scene reports again to find out.

All I know is that I haven't seen this pendant for twenty years. And I searched for it, -extensively. Somehow in the few weeks since I arrived, they managed to delve into my past, my deepest darkest secrets. They found something that I had been looking for for most of my life.

I clutch it to my chest as sobs wrack my body.

As the floodgates of grief and confusion overwhelm me, I clutch the necklace tightly, feeling its weight against my chest. Memories of that fateful night try to resurface, vivid and painful, but I slam-the door on them.

I am not ready to relive that, no matter how much it influenced the path my life had taken. It was the whole reason behind why I became an FBI agent.

Allowing my body to fall sideways, I curl into myself as my tears continue to fall. I lose myself to my grief and time becomes irrelevant.

I'm not sure how much time passes before I feel myself being lifted from the ground. Blinking my eyes, I realize the light has been turned off. I should have protested or freaked out, but I am too caught up in my emotions mixed with exhaustion.

Whichever one of them is carrying me makes placating noises as they carry me toward my bedroom. I vaguely make out another figure in front of us, pulling down the blankets of my bed to allow the one carrying me to slide me into the bed and pull the blankets back over me.

The bed shifts, and I feel them curl around me, but my eyes are weighed down. The haze in my mind drags me deeper into the darkness of sleep. It's only moments later that I surrender to it.

In the depths of my slumber, my dreams are filled with fragments of memories and swirling emotions. The pendant's weight still presses against my chest, a constant reminder of the past that has been reawakened. Mixed with the weariness of my body, I surrender to the healing embrace of sleep, allowing it to sweep me away.

When I finally open my eyes, the soft early morning light is starting to filter through the curtains, casting a warm glow over the room. It takes a moment for my surroundings to register—my own bedroom, familiar yet tinged with an air of unfamiliarity. The events of the previous night come rushing back, and I sit up, searching for any sign of the men who strangely offered me comfort in my moment of despair.

It doesn't come as a surprise that the room is empty, devoid of any trace of them. I clutch the pendant, the chain now hanging around my neck. The unanswered questions gnaw at my mind, but I couldn't dwell on them now. I have a job to do.

I rise from the bed, pushing aside the heaviness that lingers within me. I know I can't let my grief consume me.

Pushing the stress of the past slowly from my shoulders, I decide to take a moment for myself—a chance to cleanse both my body and mind. A shower seems like the perfect opportunity to wash away the remnants of grief that cling to me, freeing myself from the heavy burden that had consumed me the night before.

I take a moment to appreciate the waterproof dressings before I step into the soothing embrace of the warm water. Letting it cascade over me, the droplets washing away the remnants of my tears. The gentle caress of the water feels like a tender touch against my skin. I close my eyes, allowing the sensation to envelop me, as if it could cleanse not only my body, but also the depths of my soul.

As I lather my skin with fragrant soap, I can almost feel the heaviness of the sadness being lifted, carried away by the gentle stream.

My fingers move over my skin, washing away the remnants of a sleepless night, as if they are subconsciously erasing the darkness and paving the way for a brighter day.

Reluctantly, I step out of the shower, wrapping myself in a soft towel, cocooned myself in warmth.

I look at the mirror and focus on the reflection staring back at me. My features look tired, etched with the remnants of the previous night's emotions. I know that I needed to regain my composure and put on a strong front, at least for the time being.

As an FBI agent, I had always been more comfortable embracing my natural appearance, relying on my skills and intuition rather than the façade of makeup. However, today feels different—I need a shield, a mask to armor myself against the world.

I carefully apply foundation, concealing any remnants of exhaustion that linger on my face. I outline my eyes with precision, enhancing their depth and intensity, intent on projecting an air of strength and determination. The lipstick I choose is a bold shade, a statement of resilience and defiance. With each stroke of the brush, I construct a new layer of armor, a shield that I hope will protect me from both external threats and internal vulnerabilities.

I slip into a new suit, complete with a dark blazer that adds a touch of authority to my appearance. The pendant now hangs prominently around my neck and between my breasts, a secret reminder of the past that I carry with me, concealed from the world.

As I briefly touch it, a thought occurs to me that has me rushing into my sanctuary. It feels like time drags, seconds feeling like hours, as my laptop starts and I open the USB onto the screen.

I know exactly what I'm looking for this time and it doesn't take long to navigate directly to it. The file that was so easy for me to disregard with everything else that I had been concentrating on, the one with the label Darling, Alexandra.

Clicking into it, file after file fills my screen. Everything that I saw in the victims' files and ignored, but now focused on. My heart races in my chest as I scroll through the folder and the files.

The files in the victims' folders were only a shadow compared to the files in my own folder. My whole life is there, everything.

Images flash across the screen dating as far back as there were images of me to be found. Images from the foster home I lived in, school records, my academy application, everything.

My heart feels like it wants to leave my chest completely. How long had they been watching me? Why? Had they been watching me or was this something someone else had done?

I am so confused.

Taking a deep breath, I know I need to think about what these revelations could mean. The necklace is a testament to them either spending far longer on me than I assumed or having more wide-reaching connections. Though my mind says that odds are it is the first option.

Promising myself to look more closely at it later, I temporarily decide on a different approach until I could make sense of this new and disturbing information.

Taking my phone out I type a new message to them.

Thank you, that wasn't something small.

Their response is almost instant but just as confusing as everything else.

It is small, Little Darling. We promised something big, and you will get that tonight.

I don't know if I should be happy they are honoring their promise, or worried about what they consider big.

Chapter 28

Alex

I couldn't let my emotions overwhelm me now; I needed to gather as much information as possible and figure out how to deal with this situation. After making sure I have everything I need, I step out of my house and head for my car. The drive-thru café is calling to me as I crave the comfort of caffeine.

At the café, I fleetingly think of James' comment from days before when I opt for a triple shot espresso. Yes, I am now at the three shot stage. He would be proud.

The drive to the office is filled with conflicting emotions. On one hand, I have a job to do, a job I'm trained to do, and part of that training is to focus on the immediate tasks ahead. On the other hand, the burden of the information I discovered gnaws at me, clouding my judgment. It feels like I am living a double life—one life as an FBI agent trying to solve a case and the other life where I know those who killed the victims intimately. But I also know there is a far bigger picture to the case that I can't share with anyone.

I am being torn in two directions, my emotions and my logic all over the place and not able to reconcile anything in my mind.

So for the moment, I would be the FBI agent, going through the motions until I could do something more.

I'm thankful not to run into anyone as I make my way to the parking garage and up the elevator to the office. I can only imagine what a sight I am, though I made sure there were no visible signs of anything that would raise questions, I also wasn’t one to wear makeup and that in itself might raise questions.

As I step into the office, I try to compose myself, adopting my usual professional demeanor. James is there, looking over the files that Derek and I have on the table, obviously looking for an update.

“Morning,” I say to him as I take a seat at the table.

"Morning," James replies, his voice tense with frustration. He finally glances up, and I can see the worry and concern in his eyes. "Any progress on the case? We need to find a break soon, or this investigation might be taken away from us."

I take a deep breath, trying to hide my own turmoil as I respond, "Derek and I are trying a different approach today. We'll keep you informed as we make headway."

James nods, but his frustration doesn't seem to subside. "I hope you're onto something because we're running out of time."

"I understand, James," I say, trying to reassure him. "We're doing everything we can. We just need a bit more time."

A noise behind me has me looking over my shoulder as Derek enters the office. His eyes land on me, and I see the slight widening of them and the almost misstep before he continues around the table. Yep, the makeup is definitely going to raise questions.

Everyone exchanges greetings before we go back to discussing the case with James. Until James suddenly changes the subject. "Have you heard from or seen Mark? I've been trying to get a hold of him, but he's not responding to calls or messages. It's unusual for him to be MIA like this."

Derek glances at me briefly before responding to James, "No, I haven't heard from him either. Maybe he's caught up with something and forgot to check his messages. You know how dedicated he is to his work."

James furrows his brow, clearly still concerned. "Yeah, I guess you're right. It's just unlike him to be so unresponsive. If you hear from him, let me know, okay?"

"Will do," Derek assures him with a nod.

James eventually takes his leave, reminding us once more about the urgency of the case. Once he's gone, Derek turns to me, his expression unreadable. "You look different today."

"I just felt like wearing a little makeup today. You know, to look more awake and less like a walking zombie." I respond, brushing it off.

Derek raises an eyebrow with a slight smirk, not entirely convinced by my explanation. "Or is there another reason for the sudden change? Are you trying to impress someone?"

I frown for a moment until I understand what he is implying, to which I throw the balled up garbage from my bagel at him. "No, I am not trying to impress anyone. I don't need to impress anyone. Except maybe whatever sleep gods are out there."

Derek scoffs but doesn't say anything further as we both get back to working through the available case information looking for new leads.

As we continue sifting through the case information, Derek glances at his watch and then looks at me with a knowing look. "It's almost time. We need to head to the café to meet Winters."

I frown down at the table for a moment before looking back at him. "Thank you for giving this approach a try, I know how much you dislike journalists and I appreciate you doing this."

He looks away from me for a moment and I can't tell what he is thinking. "We weren't making any progress. if there is the chance that he can provide some new insight or lead then my issue with the press shouldn't factor into it."

Tilting my head, I continue to look at him, "Are you going to tell me why you don't like them?"

"Maybe when this is over," he responds before looking at me with a grin. "Wouldn't want to affect our relationship with our new bestie."

We head out of the office together, making our way to the café where we agreed to meet Tristan. The streets are filled with the hustle and bustle of the morning rush hour, but my mind is preoccupied with the upcoming meeting.

When we arrive at the café, Tristan is already there, sitting at a corner table, waiting for us. He looks up as we approach, a half smirk on his face. "Well, well, fancy meeting you two here," he says, his tone playful.

I give Tristan a small smile, taking a seat across from him. "Good morning, Mr—

I mean Tristan. Thanks for meeting us."

Derek is more abrupt, nodding at Tristan. "Morning. Let's get to it. We're hoping you can help provide some new insights into the case."

Tristan seems unfazed by Derek's demeanor and instead, he leans forward, genuinely interested. "I'm all ears. Lay it out for me."

I proceed to give Tristan a brief overview of the case, careful not to reveal too much sensitive information. I share the basic details about the victims, the murders, and how nothing we have found connects them.

Tristan listens intently, occasionally asking questions to clarify certain points. When I finish, he leans back in his chair, deep in thought. "So you're looking for something more, something that ties all this together?"

"Yes," I confirm. "We believe there's a bigger picture, but we're missing crucial information to see it clearly."

Tristan drums his fingers on the table, pondering. "Hmm, interesting. Well, if you think there might be information hidden or deleted, my friend Max is pretty good with data recovery and digging up digital traces. He's a bit of a genius when it comes to technology."

Derek's skepticism is apparent, but he doesn't outright dismiss the idea. "And you trust this guy? We can't afford to leak any sensitive information."

Tristan nods. "Absolutely. He's trustworthy and discreet. Besides, he owes me a favor."

I glance at Derek, hoping he'll consider this option. "It's worth a shot, Derek. We're at a dead end, and this could be the breakthrough we need."

Derek looks thoughtful, then nods reluctantly. "Alright, fine. But I want to meet this Max and make sure he understands the importance of keeping this information secure. We can't risk compromising the case."

Tristan grins. "I'll call him and see if he can meet us here. He should be close by."

I watch as Tristan stands up and wanders away from the table, pulling out his phone and making a call. He speaks briefly and then hangs up before returning to the table. "He said he'll be here in a few minutes."

As we wait for Max, the anticipation builds. The cafe is bustling with customers, but our table feels like a little island of tension in the midst of it all.

A few minutes later, the café door chimes, and Max walks in. His eyes light up when he sees us, and a warm smile spreads across his face. "Hey, Agent Darling, it's nice to see you again," he greets me warmly.

I return the smile. "Hey, Max. Thanks for coming to help us out."

Derek observes Max cautiously, still assessing the situation. "So, you're the tech genius Tristan was raving about?"

Max chuckles, looking amused. "Genius might be a stretch, but I do know my way around computers and data. Tristan's just hyping me up."

Tristan playfully nudges Max. "Come on, don't be so modest. You're great at what you do."

Derek clears his throat, bringing the conversation back to the matter at hand. "We appreciate you offering your help, Max. We're dealing with sensitive information here, so confidentiality is crucial."

Max nods seriously. "I understand the importance of discretion. You can trust me to keep everything secure."

With Derek's concerns seemingly addressed, I decide to take the lead and brief Max on the case, providing him with a condensed version of the information we've gathered so far. Max listens attentively, his expression turning serious as he processes the details.

"Wow, this is a complicated one," Max remarks after I finish. "I can definitely see why you're looking for additional information. It may take some time to crack, but I'll do my best."

Tristan chimes in, sounding genuinely grateful. "We appreciate any help you can provide, Max. If anyone can find those hidden pieces of the puzzle, it's you."

Max shrugs. "Well, no promises, but I'll give it my best shot. I just need the names you want me to look into and if there's anything else I can do, just let me know."

I hand him the list of names he needs and he looks down at it with a frown. He looks deep in thought for a moment.

Derek leans forward, his expression stern. "Just remember, we're counting on you to keep this information secure."

Max nods, his demeanor serious. "Understood. I won't let you down."

With his promise of discretion we agree to stay in touch, and Max leaves the café to begin his work. The three of us remain at the table, deep in thought.

But Tristan can't resist teasing Derek a little. He smirks playfully and says, "You know, Derek, I never thought I'd see the day you'd be willingly working with a journalist. Guess desperate times call for desperate measures."

Derek rolls his eyes but can't help but crack a small smile. "Yeah, well, don't let it go to your head. This is purely business."

Tristan chuckles. "Sure, sure. Keep telling yourself that." Then he turns his attention to me. “And you, Agent Darling, first makeup and now you have my tech guy falling all over himself to help you… Who are you and what have you done with Agent Indifference?”

I roll my eyes at him before standing. “It was nice to see you again, Mr. Winters, let us know if you find anything.”

His laughter gets louder. “And there she is.”

I shake my head at Tristan's teasing, but I can't help but smile despite myself. "Goodbye, Mr. Winters. Thanks for your help."

As Tristan continues to laugh, Derek and I make our way out of the cafe and back to the office. Stopping briefly in the bathroom when we get back, I’m surprised when my phone buzzes with a message. Expecting it to be Tristan with another tease or even potentially Max with the first hint of the data I need uncovered, I open the message straight away. It's neither of them.

Do I need to make it a dare, Little Darling, or will you meet us tonight at the abandoned warehouse on Elm Street?

Chapter 29

Alex

Dare was right, I am too far down this rabbit hole. But that didn't mean I couldn't still play. Typing out a response I hit send and then wait.

I want a truth from you first. How long have you been watching me?

The response is immediate as I knew it would be and unsurprisingly cryptic.

Longer than a minute and less than a lifetime.

I can't stop the growl of frustration that escapes. The USB drive has been in my possession for days, so all the information that it contains was there almost straight after I arrived. There was information on there that wasn't available to the general public, sealed records, photographs that go back a long time.

I take a deep breath, trying to keep my emotions in check. Getting frustrated and lashing out isn't the answer. But then, it doesn't hurt to point out the obvious to them.

That isn't an answer.

Come to the warehouse at midnight and you will get your answer, Little Darling.

What did I really have to lose at this point, it's not like they are going to kill me, right? And judging by the files, they are more invested than I would ever have imagined.

Fine, deal.

Putting my phone away, I head back into the office. I can already tell I am going to be on edge for the rest of the day, my thoughts already half focused on my midnight meeting. But I need to continue trying to make headway in the investigation. I just hope that Tristan and Max have something to give me soon that I could actually use and work with.

Derek is on a phone call when I walk in but he hangs up moments later. "Still no Mark. It's a bit odd for him to disappear in the middle of an investigation."

I nod in agreement, my mind still preoccupied. "Yeah, it is odd. Maybe he's dealing with something personal or got caught up in another case."

Derek looks concerned, but he doesn't press the matter further. "I hope he's okay. We'll have to keep an eye out for any updates from him."

The rest of the day at the office feels like an eternity. I'm constantly glancing at the clock, counting down the hours. I find it challenging to focus on the case.

It's late afternoon when Derek leans back in his chair, running a hand through his hair. "Any updates from Tristan and Max?"

I check my phone but the screen is just as blank as it was when I checked not long before he asked. "Not yet. I'm sure they're still digging through the data."

He nods in response as though it's what he expected. “It's a lot of information to go through, so it might take some time. We'll have to be patient."

As much as I want to push for faster results, I know Derek is right. Rushing the process could lead to mistakes or overlooking crucial details.

Hours pass, and the afternoon turns into evening. The building seems quiet now, but Derek and I continue to work diligently, going over the case files yet again, trying to find any patterns or connections that we might have missed the previous times we looked at them.

Still, I press on, determined to make the most of the time I have.

As the clock inches closer to midnight, I decide to give Tristan a call to see if there have been any new developments. Dialing his number, I wait anxiously for him to pick up.

"Tristan Winters." Tristan's voice comes through the phone, sounding slightly tired but still attentive.

"Tristan, it's me," I say, trying to keep my voice steady.

“Are you calling to harass us already, Alex? I’m fast, but not that fast,” the humor in his voice manages to alleviate some of my tension.

“I wouldn’t go telling the whole world that fact,” I say to him with a grin.

He chuckles, “I certainly haven’t had any complaints.”

I laugh again, but my reason for calling has the laughter dying on my lips. "Any updates from Max on the data?"

There's a pause on the other end before Tristan replies, "I'm sorry, but there's nothing concrete yet. Max is still working on searching for information. The internet has a lot of data to sift through, and we want to be thorough."

I sigh, feeling a mix of frustration and disappointment. "I was hoping we'd have something by now. The clock is ticking, and we're running out of time."

"I understand, Alex," Tristan says reassuringly. "But we can't rush this. Max is doing his best, and we'll get back to you as soon as we have any leads."

"Okay," I reply, trying to sound more composed. "I'll trust in Max's abilities and your expertise. Just keep me informed of any progress."

"Of course," Tristan assures me. "We won't stop until we find something substantial. Stay safe, Alex."

"Thanks, Tristan. You too," I say before ending the call.

Turning my attention back to Derek, I find him deep in thought, his brow furrowed. "Any new leads?" he asks.

I shake my head, feeling the pressure of the situation. "Nothing concrete yet. Tristan and Max are still working on it. It's just a waiting game now."

Derek lets out a frustrated breath, but he knows as well as I do that we have to be patient. "Alright, let's keep going through the case files. Maybe we missed something."

We continue sifting through the information, searching for any connections or patterns that might have eluded us before. The hours pass, and the clock strikes 10pm before we know it.

Derek stretches and yawns. "I think we've done all we can for today. We should head home and get some rest. We can pick it up fresh tomorrow."

He's right, and I can feel the exhaustion settling in. But my mind is still preoccupied with the midnight meeting. I need answers, and I can't shake the feeling that tonight will be crucial in unraveling this web of mysteries.

"I'll check a few more reports before I head down," I tell Derek, trying not to let my anxiety show.

Derek eyes me for a moment, concern evident in his gaze. "Are you sure? I can walk you to your car. It's late, and I don't want you to go alone."

I appreciate Derek's protective nature, but I don't want him to worry even more. "It's okay, Derek. I'll be fine. I just need a little longer."

He studies me for a moment before reluctantly nodding. "Alright, but promise me you'll be careful."

"I promise," I assure him with a small smile, trying to ease his worries. "I won't be long."

Derek gives me a half-smile, still not entirely convinced, but he gathers his things and heads toward the elevator. "Okay, I'll see you tomorrow."

With that, Derek disappears into the elevator, leaving me alone in the office.

I work for another hour, but I know I'm not going to get anywhere with the files in front of me. There is nothing in them that will help, no new information is suddenly going to appear on the reports we have been over a million times.

At one point, my phone buzzes with a message, and my heart skips a beat. I see on the screen that it's Tristan and I open it straight away hoping it's a breakthrough. But it's not, it's just a simple update with no significant progress. They're still working on finding the information we need, but haven't found it yet. My frustration resurfaces, but I try to remind myself that finding the truth takes time, and Tristan and Max are doing their best.

I forward the update to Derek, who also seems disappointed, but understands the process.

With a sigh I go and freshen up so that I can head to the meeting. I thankfully don't look like a complete zombie and the makeup has held up well for the day.

As I walk through the quiet office, I can't help but feel a sense of unease. The place feels different at night, the shadows seem darker, and every sound echoes louder. I reach the elevator and press the button to go down to the parking garage.

The wait feels like an eternity as I stand there. It's already past 11pm and after looking at photographs of dead women and crime scenes, the building is now giving off an eerie feeling, as though the walls and windows themselves are screaming for answers and demanding I tell the world what I know.

I look around the hallway once more, trying to shake off the feeling, when the elevator finally arrives. When I look at the opening doors, however, I stop, my body not wanting to take the step forward.

The doors automatically start closing, but of course one of the occupants already inside does the courteous thing, holding them open for me.

"Hey, Darling," Agent Travis says to me with a smirk.

Agent Decker tilts his head as his eyes narrow at me. "Hop on, there's plenty of room in here for you too."

I hesitate still and Agent Travis chuckles in response. "We don't bite."

The words send a chill down my spine, but it would be beyond strange for me to not get into the elevator with them, no matter how much they set me on edge. I step into the elevator and they make room for me to stand at the back, while they stand to either side, their bodies turned toward me.

They both continue to look at me intently, not speaking for a moment, as I feel their eyes raking over me. My heart races as the elevator begins to descend, and the silence in the confined space feels suffocating.

Agent Decker breaks the silence first, his voice laced with amusement. "So, how's the investigation going, Agent Darling?"

I glance at him briefly before shifting my gaze to Agent Travis, who is studying me intently. "It's progressing, you know I'm not going to give you anything other than that," I reply, keeping my response vague.

Agent Travis smirks, his eyes gleaming with a hint of amusement. "You're looking very… lovely, considering the hour. Heading somewhere special, Agent Darling?"

He slides closer, raising an arm to lean against the wall beside me. He's trying to intimidate me, leaning over me to assert his dominance.

I swallow hard, trying to maintain my composure despite the uneasy feeling in the pit of my stomach. "Just some business to take care of," I reply, keeping my response vague.

Agent Decker's gaze remains fixed on me, watching my reactions like a hawk, and I can sense that there's more to this encounter than a chance meeting in the elevator.

Agent Travis leans in closer, a sly grin playing on his lips. "You know, it's not safe for a pretty little thing like you to be wandering around alone in the dark. There are all kinds of dangers out there."

I press my back further into the elevator wall, my unease growing. "I can take care of myself," I say firmly.

Agent Travis chuckles, his voice low and husky. "I'm sure you can, but wouldn't it be helpful to have us watching your back, maybe your front too."

His words send shivers down my spine, but I refuse to show any emotions. Instead, I meet his gaze with a firm look. "I don't need your help, especially not at midnight in an elevator."

Agent Decker smirks, seemingly amused by our exchange. "Feisty, Agent Darling. I like that."

Chapter 30

Alex

My heart is pounding, and I can feel the adrenaline coursing through my veins. “I don’t give a fuck what you like.” I grit out in response before looking back at Agent Travis.

Agent Travis leans even closer, his breath brushing against my ear, and I suppress a shiver. "You're a rare find, Agent Darling. Beautiful and strong-willed. Your talents are completely wasted where you are."

I narrow my eyes at him, trying to maintain a level of control despite my racing emotions. "I'm not wasting anything. This case is important, and I'm determined to see it through to the end."

Agent Decker chuckles, he’s also moved closer and his proximity to me is making me uncomfortable. "You're too serious, Darling. Relax a little. Life is short, you know."

"I'll relax when this case is solved," I reply firmly.

Agent Travis raises an eyebrow, seemingly amused by my response. "You've got fire in you, I'll give you that," he says, his voice filled with a mix of admiration and something else that I can't quite decipher.

I glance at the floor indicator, noticing that we're getting closer to the parking garage level. The thought of leaving this uncomfortable situation and facing the night outside brings a sense of relief.

"Well, it's been a pleasure chatting with you both, but I have places to be," I say, trying to keep my tone steady.

Agent Decker smirks. "Oh, we're not done with you, Darling. We'll be seeing each other again soon."

I suppress a sigh, not wanting to show any vulnerability in front of them. "I'll be looking forward to it," I say dryly.

Finally, the elevator doors open to the parking garage, and I step out quickly, not looking back at the two agents. I make my way to my car, my mind reeling from the encounter. They're up to something, and I can't shake the feeling that their interest in me goes beyond mere curiosity.

The tension doesn't ease up as I drive to the warehouse. The encounter with Agents Travis and Decker has put me on edge, and I can't shake the feeling that I'm being watched. I remain hyper-aware of my surroundings, constantly checking my rearview mirror, and taking evasive maneuvers to ensure I'm not being followed.

Finally, after what feels like an eternity, I arrive at the dimly lit, desolate area where the warehouse is located. I park my car a little distance away, not wanting to draw any attention. Taking a deep breath, I step out of the vehicle and walk toward the warehouse, my senses on high alert.

It's just as dilapidated and decayed as the last time I was here, just as dark and desolate. The memories of my last visit come back to me as I slowly make my way through the abandoned rooms. I know my ultimate destination is the heart of the building, just like last time.

To think about the events that have occurred in the time between that last visit and this visit has a slight flush coming to my cheeks. There is something about them that has gotten under my skin far quicker than I had anticipated. Something that spoke to a deep, dark part of myself and my very soul.

I'm in the hall leading to the center room when I feel the presence behind me. I don't even have time to reach for the gun in the concealed holster at my back before a body is pressed against me. My wrist is held tight in his gloved hand while his other wraps around my throat from behind.

I don't fight the hold though, there isn't any point; I already know who it is. The subtle spice that is all Dare. The scent tugs at a memory, but it is gone again like smoke.

"I was starting to worry, Little Darling. I expected you to be early in some attempt to catch us off guard," his modulated voice in my ear sends a shiver down my spine, that isn't altogether unpleasant now.

I can't hide the annoyance at my delay and the reason behind it. "I had an annoying delay on my way out of my office and then wanted to make sure I wasn't being followed."

He hums in response, "Is that so? I'm sure I will love hearing all about it some other time. In the meantime, you won't be needing this."

The hand he has wrapped around my wrist lets go and slides between our bodies, removing the gun. I don't see what he does with it, but when his hand returns to the front of my body it's gone. He presses against my stomach, drawing my body to close the gap between us, pressing me against the front of him.

My heart pounds in my chest as I feel the heat of his body against mine, his mask brushing against my ear. My mind is racing, torn between the situation I'm in and the strange allure of Dare's presence. There's something magnetic about him that I can't explain, and it's both unnerving and captivating.

He groans slightly, "I missed your body against mine, Little Darling."

Memories of them comforting me and their bodies pressed against mine the previous night flash through my mind. I had been too consumed by grief to protest and took all the comfort they had offered me, it had even tugged at something deep inside me that they had left before I woke this morning.

"What was last night?" I ask softly, expressing a portion of the confusion that has hounded me since I woke up.

His hand flexes against my throat. "You were upset. Nothing could have kept us away." His tone is so matter of fact, as though it is just a normal occurrence for them to be there for me.

The hand he has resting against my stomach moves up my chest, his gloved fingers undoing the top buttons of my shirt. Heat washes through me at the feel of his fingers moving against my chest, but I'm surprised by his next action. Instead of taking advantage of the moment, he hooks a finger under the chain of my necklace and draws it and the pendant out.

"I'm glad you are still wearing it. Don't hide it."

My heart races even faster as I feel Dare's gloved hand caress the pendant between my breasts.

"How did you find it?" I manage to ask, my voice trembling slightly. "What does this even mean to you?"

His fingers pause, "It means something to you and that's what matters."

I let out a frustrated growl, feeling like they are always speaking in riddles, never giving me a straight answer. "Can't you ever just be straightforward? What is it with all these cryptic answers?"

He chuckles, the sound reverberating through my body. "Little Darling, life is full of mysteries and secrets," he says.

I narrow my eyes, but I don't have the energy to argue further. Instead, I decide to bring up something that has been bothering me since this morning.

"You still haven't answered my question from earlier. How long have you been watching me?" I demand, trying to assert some control in this situation.

Dare's gloved fingers resume their gentle caress of the pendant, and he seems lost in thought for a moment. "Longer than you realize," he finally answers cryptically.

I grit my teeth, frustration building up inside me. "That doesn't tell me anything. I deserve to know the truth."

He tilts his head, brushing his head against the side of mine in an almost affectionate gesture. "Perhaps one day, you'll know everything you seek. But for now, focus on the present."

I huff in annoyance, feeling like I'm hitting a brick wall every time I try to get answers from him. "Fine. But just know that I won't stop until I uncover the truth about everything, including you."

Dare chuckles, the sound sending a shiver through me. "I wouldn't expect anything less from you, Little Darling."

He releases my throat and gently turns me around to face him, his hands sliding down my arms to take my wrists in his gloved hands. His grip is tight as he presses my wrists together in one of his hands. He brings his other hand up, rubbing a thumb against the lipstick on my bottom lip, my lips parting automatically.

“Do you want to know what I thought when I saw your lips like this?” he asks, his black eyes focussed completely on my lips.

“What?” I question him in response. He is affecting me more than normal this time, and I have to put it down to all the emotions I’ve been feeling lately starting to get to me.

He hums again, “That I can’t wait to see how that color looks smeared on my cock.”

Desire floods through me at his words and I can feel myself flush with arousal. I attempt to pull my hands free from his grasp, but he tightens his grip, keeping me in place.

"Let me go," I manage to say, my voice trembling slightly.

He leans in even closer, his mask brushing against my face. "We will never let you go, ever again."

I can’t stop the tremble that goes through my body at his words and I know he feels it. He straightens, moving back slightly.

“If I allow you to keep the use of these,” he raises my wrists up and I narrow my eyes at him, “Will you swear not to try to touch our masks tonight?”

I weigh his offer carefully, my mind racing with conflicting thoughts. On one hand, I want nothing more than to reach for their masks and uncover the secrets they hold. On the other hand, I realize that I will never accomplish that until they become complacent.

"I swear not to touch your masks tonight," I reply, hoping that my agreement will at least grant me some level of freedom.

Dare hums but seems satisfied with my response. He releases my wrists, allowing me the use of my hands again. I flex my fingers, feeling the tingling sensation of returning circulation.

"Good girl," he says, his fingers moving to brush briefly against my cheek.

“Where is your other half?” I ask, trying to think of anything apart from the feeling that washes over me at his praise.

“In the next room, we have another present for you,” comes his response. His tone is amused and I don’t know if he can see the effect he has had on me in the dim light or if something about the situation amuses him.

I raise an eyebrow at him. “The ‘something big’ you promised?”

He chuckles, his eyes glinting with mischief. "Oh, yes. Something big indeed. But you'll have to see for yourself."

I give him a suspicious look, my guard still up, but curiosity gets the better of me. Without waiting for my response, he steps away from me and heads towards the next room.

Taking a deep breath I follow after him, looking over the back of his body while I have the opportunity. It's still too dim to really make out any of the finer details, but I can see my gun tucked into the back of his pants, almost within reach.

But what would I really do with it? I have to admit to myself that even if I did have it in my hands, I wouldn’t shoot either of them. The knife I can see strapped to his thigh, though, might be a different matter.

We enter the larger room at the heart of the warehouse and I can see that there is a light set up toward the center of the room, but I can’t see around Dare’s broad shoulders as we walk. But then he stops and steps aside.

My eyes widen at the sight in front of me. “Mark?”

Chapter 31

Alex

My heart drops as I see Mark, hanging from the same hook they hung me from during my last visit to this warehouse. He's bound and gagged, his eyes wide with fear as he struggles against his restraints.

I can't get my mouth to form words, the shock of seeing him there has me frozen. "What is this?" I finally manage to get out, but I feel like I can barely hear my voice over the sound of my heart beating in my chest.

Mark's body suddenly swings from side to side like a pendulum. I look to see Truth standing next to Mark where he must have pushed him, his focus is completely on the swinging body in the center of the room.

"Oh, don't you know, Little Darling? Mark here likes to help evil people escape justice," he says.

The realization hits me like a ton of bricks, and I feel a mix of emotions surging through me – anger, betrayal, and a sense of disbelief. I would have trusted Mark with my life, he is part of our team, I never would have suspected him of that from the interactions I had with him.

"He's involved with them too?" I manage to say, my voice shaking with both anger and sorrow. "How deep does this corruption go?"

Dare steps closer to me, his presence both comforting and unnerving at the same time. "Deeper than you can imagine," he replies, his voice low and filled with an undercurrent of determination.

Truth leaves Mark to continue swinging as he saunters over to us, his own gloved hand coming up to brush my cheek. “Hey, Little Darling.”

I blink rapidly, focusing on his masked face in front of me instead of Mark. “Hi,” I breathe in response.

He chuckles, as he continues to brush gloved fingers against my skin. “You look beautiful. Well, you always do, but this color looks almost like blood, it's hot.”

There he goes, showing his psycho side again. Is it bad that it actually pulls a smile from me?

I shake my head at him and he drops his hand. “I think there is something else more important going on here than how hot you think I look.”

He leans closer to me and I still my movements. “Let me make something clear, Little Darling, nothing is ever more important than you.”

My heart skips a beat at his words, and I can feel my cheeks flush at the intensity of his gaze. It's both thrilling and unnerving to be the object of his attention, but I try to keep my focus on the gravity of the situation at hand.

"Thank you, but it’s a little hard to ignore the man hanging from the hook," I say firmly, trying to steer the conversation back to the urgent matter before us.

Truth leans back slightly, his eyes still fixed on mine. "Of course, you're right. We should deal with him."

He moves to stand on the other side of me next to Dare, turning so that we are now all facing a still swaying Mark.

I narrow my eyes at Mark, my anger bubbling inside of me, “So is he the person in charge of the corruption?”

Dare shakes his head, his dark eyes never leaving Mark's form. "No, Little Darling. Mark is not the mastermind behind the corruption. He’s just a pawn, albeit a willing one, but he doesn’t hold the reins of power."

Truth chimes in, "Mark's role is to assist in covering up crimes and destroying evidence whenever he can. He doesn’t call the shots, but he is complicit in the evil deeds."

I clench my fists, my anger now directed not only at Mark, but at the entire organization. "So he willingly chose to be a part of this? To protect those monsters and let them continue their atrocities?"

Dare finally turns toward me, his eyes taking in my anger. “Yes, he did, Little Darling.”

I walk slowly over to the hanging man, my anger burning inside me. They follow closely behind me until we get a few feet from him and Truth touches my arm, stopping me from getting closer. He steps past me and rips the tape covering his mouth.

Pain flashes across Mark's features but his voice is already rushing out. “Run Alex, they’re psychos! Look at them! Too many movies fucked with their heads, they’re delusional!”

Truth laughs loudly, his modulated voice making it even more eerie in the decaying room. “Oh, wait! I’ve seen this one. Scream right?”

Dare chuckles as he steps up to my side. “What is it that Billy Lumos says? ‘Movies don’t create psychos, movies make psychos more creative.’”

I have to roll my lips between my teeth and bite them so I don’t join in on their humor.

The humor disappears from Truth's face like a switch and suddenly he's holding his knife pointed at Mark's face. "Honestly though, I don't even think Wes Craven could predict the level of your depravity."

The glint of the blade catches my eye as Truth moves it down to Mark's chest, pressing it against his skin and drawing it down. The fabric of Mark's shirt parts, and blood wells up in its wake, accompanied by haunting whimpers.

Dare's eyes follow the path of the knife, and he smirks maliciously. "Hell, I'm even surprised our Little Darling caught your attention. After all, she's a little old for you, right?"

I blink in disbelief at Dare's words, struggling to comprehend the twisted revelation.

"That's why you're really here. You shouldn't have tried to go after what's ours." Truth's modulated voice is a low growl.

"I didn't know! I'll leave her alone, I swear," Mark cries out, his voice reflecting the pain he is experiencing.

"Whoa, wait, back up!" I say loudly, interrupting everyone.

Truth turns toward me, dismissing the man he has bleeding and whimpering. "You are ours, Little Darling."

My heart is racing in my chest, my emotions feeling all over the place. That wasn't what I was protesting about, that is a conversation for another time.

My mind is reeling, trying to process everything that's happening. Amidst the chaos, I struggle to focus on the strange revelation they've just made. I'm looking back and forth between Truth and Dare as I try to get my mind to catch up with what they said.

"That's not what I meant," I manage to say, my voice shaky but firm. "We can talk about that later. What did you mean, I'm a little old?"

Dare steps toward Mark, I can see his hands clenching as though he would love nothing more than to tear him apart with his bare hands. He glances at me before responding. “Ah yes, Mark here has a taste for young girls.”

Shock grips me, my mouth agape as I try to comprehend the sickening truth. "What?" I manage to utter, disbelief and revulsion overwhelming me.

Dare’s focus is back on Mark, his voice is pure rage, and I don’t blame him. “The younger the better right? It’s how they pay him.”

Disgust and anger flood me as I look at Mark’s wide, fearful eyes. But mixed in with his fear, the look of guilt. I feel like the world is crumbling around me, the weight of the darkness and horror too much to bear. “Excuse me?”

Truth growls, his attention also now focused completely on Mark. “In exchange for him doing their cleanup and making evidence disappear, they pay him by giving him young girls to do with as he wants.”

My heart feels like it's lodged in my throat, and my whole body trembles as I take in the horrifying truth about Mark's depravity. The dim light of the warehouse seems to dim even further, casting haunting shadows on the walls, adding to the sinister atmosphere of the room.

Dare reaches out and grabs Mark’s jaw, and I can see him digging his gloved fingers in, “And with his skills and connections, those girls are never seen again.”

Dare's grip on Mark's jaw tightens, and I can see the anger in his eyes, mirroring the fury I feel within myself. My mind struggles to process the heinous revelations about Mark's actions.

I feel sick, there is a faint buzzing, like a swarm of bees coming toward me. “He kills little girls?” I ask. I feel like the air is freezing in my lungs. It is a struggle to get air past the feeling of my heart pounding in my chest.

Dare glances back before returning his gaze to the bleeding and whimpering man in front of him. “Yes, Little Darling.”

My mind is a whirlwind of emotions as I try to comprehend the gravity of Mark's horrifying actions. The room seems to close in around me, suffocating me with its darkness. My heart races, and the buzzing in my ears intensifies, drowning out all other sounds.

Truth crosses his arms over his chest, the knife still in his hand. I could see the gleam of the blade flashing a reflection of the dim light illuminating the room. There is blood coating the blade. Mark’s blood. “He does much more than that, don’t you Mark? You call us psychos, but even we wouldn’t do what you do to the bodies of children.”

There is a ringing in my ears, loud and drowning out all other sounds. My vision goes black.

Chapter 32

Alex

I don't remember moving.

I don't remember somehow taking the knife from Truth.

I don't even remember stabbing that knife into Mark.

Mark's pained screams snap me back to the present, and I find myself standing before him, my hand gripping the knife buried in his chest. The sight of blood spreading around the blade sends a shiver down my spine, but I can't bring myself to let go. There isn't much blood, so it doesn't seem like I've hit anything important.

Everything feels foggy, my mind not feeling like it wants to register anything that is happening. It's as if a dark part of me has taken over, a part that is fueled by rage and vengeance. I should let go of the knife and step away, but I can't find it in me to release my grip on the weapon that is now embedded in this monster's chest.

This monster hurt little girls. He killed little girls. And he was allowed to get away with it. How long had he been getting away with it? How many little girls had he killed? Did I really want to know what else he did to them?

My breathing is surprisingly steady for the thoughts going through my mind and the fact that I stabbed a man.

Truth hums behind me moments before he presses his body into my back. "That was so fucking hot. You have no idea how much it turned me on to watch you stab him."

Actually, I did, I could feel his hard cock pressed against me. My whole body flushes with arousal.

He slowly slides his gloved hand along my arm, wrapping it around mine on the handle of the blade. “When you stab someone, Little Darling, you need to mean it. If you want to cause the most damage, twist the blade.” He uses his grip on my hand to turn the blade in Mark’s chest.

Blood starts coming faster from the wound around where the blade is buried and my heart starts pumping faster in response. The screams leaving Mark’s mouth and the sight of the blood now pouring from him tugs at a memory but I push it aside. I can’t let myself be distracted right now.

Truth groans and suddenly pulls my hand and the knife out of Mark’s chest. The spray of blood as the blade is pulled out hits me in a hot wet spray of crimson. I can feel flecks of it all over the bare skin of my hands and face.

“And if you want them to die slowly and painfully, aim right about… here.” He uses my hand and thrusts the knife into Mark’s stomach. There isn’t even any resistance, the blade just slides into his flesh like a hot knife through butter. He twists my hand again, turning the blade inside of Mark. It’s hard to tell how much blood is coming from the new wound with so much of it already covering the front of his body.

Mark just continues to scream.

Truth’s other hand comes around the front of my body and within seconds he has my pants undone and a gloved hand inside them, his fingers gliding along my pussy before he pulls out his hand again.

He groans, his masked face brushing the side of mine as he speaks, his voice dripping with arousal. “Is this making you wet, Little Darling? Is listening to his screams and watching the blood seep from his body turning you on?"

I can't deny the evidence shining on his hand that he holds up in front of my face. Something has to be very wrong with me to feel the way I'm feeling right now. My mind is trying to rebel against the feelings coursing through me.

His words send a flare of heat through me, and I can't tear my eyes away from the sight before me. Mark's pained screams intensify as Truth twists the blade again, causing more blood to spurt from the wound.

I should be repulsed, sickened by the violence, but there's a strange fascination that keeps me rooted to the spot.

My mind is a chaotic mess, torn between the desire to turn away and the perverse allure of the violence in front of me. My heart pounds loudly in my ears, and I can't seem to shake off the arousal that courses through my veins.

Truth's hand leaves mine wrapped around the blade and he tears at my clothes, ripping my shirt and jacket open and shoving my pants down my legs. I vaguely have a fleeting thought about my diminishing wardrobe, but then Truth's now bare hands are on my pussy again, and despite everything that is unfolding, my body reacts to his touch.

I don't know when he removed his gloves, but the feel of his bare hands on my bare skin shoots my arousal through the roof. He groans again as he thrusts two fingers inside of me. My whole body throbs at the sound, and yet I still can't let go of the knife in my hand, the blade still buried inside Mark's stomach.

"That's it, Little Darling. Embrace what you're feeling, dance in the darkness with us."

Truth's other hand trails upward and cups one of my breasts, his fingers starting to pinch and pull at my nipple and my pussy tightens around his fingers in response. A moan escapes me and he twists my nipple sharply, his thumb moving to circle my clit. Pleasure and pain swirl within me and my body is climbing toward a climax rapidly.

Mark is still screaming and blood continues to flow from the wounds in his body.

A gloved hand wraps around the hand holding the knife inside of Mark, dragging the knife out slowly. Dare is beside us now, one hand squeezing mine on the knife as his other reaches up to grip my jaw.

He tilts my head to look into my eyes, his black eyes filled with heat as he watches me panting and moaning from what Truth is doing to me. His fingers move on the skin of my face and I can only imagine the blood being smeared across it.

My hips rock onto Truth's fingers, my body right on the edge as he continues to thrust them inside me, pushing my hips backward to rub against his hard cock.

Dare tilts my head again so that I'm looking back at the still screaming man in front of me. "And if the screams become too much, and you are done with them, then you do this." He moves my hand for me, like Truth did, and drags the blade hard across Mark's throat.

There is no avoiding the blood.

I'm surprised there is still so much of it left in him with how much has already made it to the floor beneath his body, but I still manage to get hit by some of the blood spray across my chest.

Truth's fingers in my pussy push me over the edge to the sound of Mark's last gurgling breaths, the wave of my orgasm washing over me and dragging me under. My body is awash with pleasure and my cries replace Mark's to echo around the decaying room.

Dare's fingers dig into my jaw as he watches my face with an intensity that should frighten me, taking in every twitch of pleasure and moan as my orgasm pulses through me. He pulls the knife from my hand and tosses it to the side. Finally when my moans die down and Truth stops moving his hands, Dare says, "On your knees, Little Darling. I want to see those blood red lips wrapped around my cock."

Even the amount of blood coating the floor doesn't stop me from dropping to my knees. For a moment the strangeness of having the use of my hands hits me, but then I'm using them to tear open Dare's pants, pulling his hard cock out and wrapping my lips around it. The groan he releases as he buries his hand in my hair and twists is obscene.

My tongue swirls around the head of him, sliding along his piercings before I take him into my mouth again. His hand tightens on my hair and he starts to control my movements, pushing me down onto him as he thrusts into my throat. I gag around him but he doesn't stop. He forces my head all the way down, holding me there and I make myself breathe through my nose.

Words start tumbling from him between his groans as his hips flex beneath my hands. "Fuck, you feel so good choking on my cock, Little Darling. You need my cum don't you? Hmm? You need me to fuck your throat to make you feel like you're being punished for killing a monster? He deserved it though, and you look like a Queen with his blood on you."

He still keeps my head there as he drops down to his own knees on the warehouse floor. I'm surprised by the action, but then Truth is there, lifting my hips and repositioning me, to thrust his cock deep inside my pussy. I'm whimpering as he stretches me, his piercings scraping on my sensitive walls. It pushes me further onto Dare and I gag around him again, choking on him.

Truth groans as his fingers dig deep into my hips and my pussy tightens on his cock. "Our Little Darling Queen," he growls as he pulls back and thrusts hard into me. I moan, my eyes fluttering shut as the sensations rage within me. "You're so fucking wet, did it feel good thrusting that knife inside him like I'm thrusting my cock inside your greedy little pussy?"

Seriously, if they don't shut up I'm going to cum just from their dirty fucking mouths.

Dare twists his other hand into my hair, pulling my head further back and I'm forced to put my hands down on the ground to keep my balance. Straight into the cooling blood, but my mind and body don't even really register it as Dare starts thrusting hard into my mouth. "Open your eyes, Little Darling, I want to watch them as we both fuck you."

I obey immediately, looking up at his masked face as he thrusts into my throat. They set a hard, brutal rhythm between them; they aren't gentle, they are rough and vicious with their movements. Truth's hips slap hard against my ass as Dare continues to make me choke on his cock. It feels like the adrenaline from what we did is propelling us into the darkness and we are reveling in it.

The sound of our moans and the slapping of our skin echoes through the room and creates a soundtrack to the pure raw depravity of the moment. My pussy is tightening around Truth's cock as he thrusts into me until I'm teetering on the edge of my climax.

Dare thrusts hard into my throat, holding my face against his skin as he groans, his own orgasm hitting him. I desperately try to swallow around him as my airways are cut off by his flesh, but I can't do much more than choke on him.

My whole body is throbbing, my pussy clamping down so hard on Truth that he groans low and his pace stutters until all he's doing is pounding into me. He reaches around under my body and his fingers find my clit, swirling around it once before pinching it hard, at the same time as Dare pulls me off his cock and air rushes into my lungs.

I shatter beneath him, my body feeling like it's exploding into a million different directions. Truth follows me over the cliff, his shout all I can hear over the rush of blood drowning out the world. The power of my orgasm hits me like a freight train, my body shuddering and pulsing from the intensity. As it ebbs away I become aware of the tears streaming down my face and Dare watching every one of them fall like they mean everything to him.

Chapter 33

Alex

I can't stop the moan as Truth withdraws from my pussy. They help me stand and rearrange my clothes, though it's a bit of a lost cause. They are destroyed, but there is still enough there to cover the important bits.

Tremors start taking over my body as I start to come down from the adrenaline that had been pumping through me. I wince slightly at the soreness making itself known in my muscles.

I try to steady my breathing as the tremors gradually subside, my mind struggling to process everything that just happened. Dare's gloved hand cups my face, and I find some comfort in his touch, even amidst the chaos and darkness. His thumb brushes gently across my cheek, and I lean into his touch, seeking solace in his presence. "Truth will take you home and clean you up while I deal with Mark."

I nod, wrapping my arms around myself for comfort as I glance over at Mark's lifeless body hanging from the chain. The sight is chilling, and the weight of everything that has transpired weighs heavily on my mind. "What are you going to do with him?"

He just chuckles in response and nods to Truth.

As usual I'm not going to simply get a straightforward answer. It's not like I wasn't used to it by now.

Truth steps forward and he wraps an arm around my waist, supporting me. "Come on, Little Darling. Let's get you home and cleaned up," he says, his voice soft and reassuring.

I lean into him, letting myself momentarily feel his warmth and strength, and allow him to guide me toward the exit of the warehouse.

As we step out into the cool night air, the world outside the warehouse seems oddly unchanged. It's a stark contrast to what unfolded inside those walls, a reminder that evil often lurks where we least expect it.

Truth leads me to my parked car, taking my keys, and helps me slide into the passenger seat. He takes the driver's seat and starts the engine, the low rumble providing a semblance of normalcy amidst the chaos that now resides in my mind.

During the car ride, we exchange few words. I'm lost in my thoughts, trying to process everything I've learned and experienced. The events of tonight have shaken me, and I can't help but wonder about the true depths of darkness that exist in the world.

The car ride is not a long one, but every minute feels like an eternity. When we arrive at my rental house, Truth helps me out of the car and guides me inside. His presence offers comfort, but I can't help but feel a mix of emotions. The events of the night have left their mark on me, and I know I'll never be the same.

Once inside, Truth leads me to the bathroom. I catch a glimpse of myself in the mirror, and the reflection staring back at me seems like a stranger. My clothes are tattered, my hair disheveled, and I'm covered in blood. My eyes hold a weariness that goes beyond physical exhaustion.

Truth's demeanor is gentle as he helps me undress and step into the shower. The warm water cascades over my body, washing away the grime and the remnants of the night's horrors. I try to let the water cleanse not only my body but also my mind, to wash away the darkness that threatens to consume me.

As I continue to stand under the soothing stream of water, I can feel the heaviness of the night's events slowly starting to lift. The warmth of the water calms my nerves, providing a brief respite. Truth stands nearby, his watchful gaze never leaving me, and I find a strange sense of comfort in his silent presence.

"What Mark did... It's unimaginable," I manage to say.

Truth nods. "Yes, he was a monster in his own right, Little Darling. The things he did were beyond comprehension. But we have now ensured that he can never hurt anyone else."

As I continue to let the water wash over me, I can't help but wonder how deep this corruption goes. The revelation of Mark's involvement with the dark forces he was supposed to fight against has shattered my trust in people I once considered allies.

"Is there no one I can trust?" I ask, my voice laced with despair.

Truth steps closer to me, his intense gaze locking with mine. "You can trust us, Little Darling," he says firmly. "We may be dark, and we may be dangerous, but we're on your side. We'll protect you, no matter what."

With the water finally washing away the last traces of blood, I step out of the shower.

Truth is waiting for me with a soft, fluffy towel in hand. However, instead of handing it to me, he takes a step closer, his black eyes locked onto mine. There's an intensity in his gaze that sends a shiver down my spine, a mix of desire and concern. He gently takes the towel and starts to dry me off, his touch deliberate and meticulous.

The sensation of the towel against my skin is both soothing and arousing. I can feel my body responding to his touch, my heart rate quickening, and a flush of warmth spreading through me. It's as if the adrenaline from the night's events has awakened a primal response within me, one that I can't fully comprehend.

Truth's hands move with care, trailing over every curve of my body. I can't help but moan softly as his touch lingers in certain places, teasing and igniting a fire within me.

Truth's gaze never wavers, and it's as if he can see every emotion playing out across my face. He seems to understand the impact of his actions, yet he continues to dry me with careful attention to detail. His fingers trail along my skin, sending shivers of pleasure through me.

I bite my lip, trying to suppress the moans that threaten to escape my lips. The intimacy of the moment is both unexpected and undeniable.

He moves the towel lower, focusing on my thighs, and I can feel the tension building within me. It's like a magnetic pull, drawing me closer to him, craving his touch in a way I've never experienced before.

"Truth..." I breathe out his name, my voice a mix of need and uncertainty.

Truth's gaze remains locked with mine, his eyes burning with a mix of desire and a need to comfort me. "Shh, Little Darling," he whispers, his voice soothing. "Let go of everything for now. Just focus on this moment."

As he continues to dry me with gentle precision, my mind begins to drift away from the darkness of the night, replaced by the warmth of his touch. The soreness in my muscles starts to fade into the background, replaced by a growing arousal that I can't ignore.

Truth's fingertips brush against my skin, tracing delicate patterns that send pleasure through me. I find myself surrendering to it, the turmoil inside me momentarily forgotten. It's a strange contradiction - finding solace in the arms of someone who is as dark and dangerous as he is. Someone who is normally so rough and savage.

His hands move up my body, caressing my curves with an almost reverent touch. Every stroke, every brush of his fingers, ignites a fire within me, and I feel myself growing wet with desire.

I reach out, gripping the edge of the bathroom counter for support as my legs start to feel weak under the onslaught of sensations. Truth's gaze never falters, his focus solely on me, as if he can see through my soul.

"You're beautiful," he whispers.

A blush rises to my cheeks, but I don't look away. There's something about the way he sees me, as if he sees the parts of me that I try to hide.

His touch becomes more intimate, more sensual, and I find myself leaning into him, seeking more of his caress. The towel slips from his hands, forgotten on the bathroom floor, as he wraps his arms around me, pulling me close.

I let out a soft gasp as he lifts me effortlessly into his arms, and I instinctively wrap my legs around his waist.

He carries me with ease, his strength and grace evident in every movement. I feel a sense of vulnerability being in his arms like this, but there's also an undeniable thrill coursing through me. His touch has awakened a primal need within me, and I can't resist the magnetic pull between us.

As Truth walks us towards the bedroom, I can feel my heart pounding in my chest. The anticipation and arousal grow with every step, and I find myself yearning for more of him. My body responds to his proximity, and I know he can feel how wet and ready I am for him.

Once inside the dimly lit bedroom, Truth gently lays me down on the bed, his dark eyes never leaving mine. I can see the desire and hunger in his gaze, mirrored by my own. There's a raw intensity between us, and it's both exhilarating and terrifying.

"Little Darling," he murmurs, his voice low and husky, "I want to make you feel good, to take your mind off what happened."

His hands roam over my body, igniting sparks of pleasure everywhere they touch. The gentleness he displayed earlier is now mixed with possessiveness, and I find it intoxicating. His fingers find their way to my breasts, teasing and squeezing, sending waves of arousal through me.

I moan, my body arching into his touch, craving more. "Truth," I gasp, my voice trembling with need.

His fingers trail down my body, teasingly skimming over my sensitive skin. The anticipation builds, and I bite my lip. He slips two fingers inside my pussy, and I gasp, the pleasure surging through me. His touch is both firm and gentle, and he takes his time, pushing me to the edge and pulling back, teasing me with each stroke.

He lifts his head, his gaze locking with mine. "Tell me what you want, Little Darling," he says, his voice a dark whisper.

"I want you," I reply without hesitation, "I want you inside me."

He lays down beside me, pulling his cock out of the confines of his pants. "Ride me, Little Darling," he commands, his voice low and commanding. "Show me how much you want this."

Without hesitation, I position myself over him, lowering myself onto his hard cock. A gasp escapes my lips as he fills me, and I'm overcome with a wave of pleasure. I begin to move, slowly at first, finding a rhythm that has us both moaning.

Truth's hands roam over my body, his touch turning hard and demanding, guiding me in my movements. I let myself be carried away by the pleasure, giving in to the raw desire that flows between us.

His hands grip my hips firmly, urging me to ride him harder, and I comply willingly, losing myself in the sensations that consume me. The connection between us intensifies, and it's as if we're bound by something more profound than physical pleasure—there's an unspoken understanding between us, a shared darkness that brings us closer.

As I arch my back, surrendering to the pleasure, I catch a glimpse of Truth's face contorted in pleasure. His neck arches, and for a brief moment, his eyes close.

It's at that moment that I see an opportunity. I reach up and grab hold of his mask and in one swift motion, I pull it down, revealing the face underneath.

Before I can say or do anything, he snarls. In a swift movement, he grabs my throat, his grip tight but not suffocating. He rolls us over, pinning me down onto the mattress with an intensity that leaves me breathless.

His face is now mere inches from mine, and I can feel his warm breath against my skin. The air between us crackles with tension, and a part of me wonders if I've gone too far.

His voice is a low growl when he speaks, "Oh, you are in so much trouble, Little Darling."

Chapter 34

Alex

The shift of his hips reminds me of how deep he's still buried inside of me, but it's his hand tightening around my throat that makes me whimper. His grip is firm as he keeps me pressed against the mattress.

"My brother is going to be so disappointed in you. I thought I heard you swear to him you wouldn't touch the masks tonight," he says as he uses his other hand to undo his hoodie and remove the mask fully.

"Technically, it's now morning," I manage in response as my eyes flick to the clock beside the bed that reads only 2:40 am.

He chuckles, leaning back down over me until his lips are just brushing mine. He shifts his hips again and I can't stop my moan from escaping. "Do you want me to stop?"

I growl in response, my hands coming up to grab and pull on his hair. "No, don't stop."

He moves his hips back and thrusts his cock hard inside of me. He's buried so deeply it feels like he is wanting to make us one body and soul. When he repeats the motion my back arches in pleasure, my pussy tightening around him.

"Tristan…" his name escapes my lips in a breathless moan.

"Fuck, I love the sound of my name on your lips," he groans as he continues to move. "Say it again."

A smile tugs at my lips and I narrow my eyes at him, I'm not going to just roll over and make it easy for him when he didn't for me. "Fuck me, Mr. Winters, or I won't say your name ever again."

He chuckles again, the grin on his face almost joyous. "There she is."

He closes the distance to capture my lips with his own, kissing me passionately as he starts to thrust harder inside of me. His grip on my throat tightens slightly, adding that edge that I have become so familiar with when being with them. The sensation only fuels my desire for him, making me feel alive in a way I never thought possible.

His lips curl into a grin, the intensity of his thrusts sending waves of pleasure through me. The room is filled with the sounds of our pleasure—moans, gasps, and the rhythmic slapping of skin on skin.

I manage to utter between moans, "You... need to… earn... it."

The challenge seems to ignite something in him, and he responds with even more intensity. His movements become faster and more forceful, driving me closer to the edge.

"Is this what you want, Little Darling?" he breathes.

I moan, my words caught in my throat as pleasure overwhelms me. He tightens his grip on my throat, and I feel myself surrendering completely to him.

His other hand goes to my leg, lifting it and changing the angle. I arch my back, giving in to the feelings he's igniting in me. We move together in a rhythm that feels almost primal.

I can't get enough of his touch and the way he fills me so completely.

He gazes into my eyes, and there's a hunger there, a craving for more than just physical pleasure. "You want to cum, Little Darling?"

I moan, my body trembling. "Please," I whimper, my voice barely audible.

He smirks, his eyes dark with lust. "Then say my name," he demands, his voice low and commanding.

I bite my lip. "Make me cum first," I challenge him defiantly.

He thrusts harder inside me, hitting that perfect spot that sends waves of pleasure coursing through me. "Say it, Little Darling," he whispers, the huskiness in his voice affecting me on a deep level. "Say my name, and I'll make you cum so hard you'll scream it."

I meet his gaze. "Make me scream it then," I respond breathlessly.

His grin widens, and he takes that as the green light to unleash everything he has. He thrusts harder and faster, hitting all the right places inside me, pushing me closer to the brink.

I feel myself teetering on the edge of an orgasm, pleasure building like a tidal wave. He continues to move, my pussy tightening on his cock with each thrust. My moans become louder, mixing with his growls of pleasure, filling the room with the sounds of our passion. I'm so close, and I know he can feel it too.

His breath is hot against my ear as he breathes, "Cum for me, and scream my name."

The words are all I need, the final trigger that pushes me over the edge. My back arches, and I scream out his name as waves of pleasure crash over me, consuming me entirely.

He doesn't let up, keeping his pace relentless as I ride out my climax. He groans as my body convulses with ecstasy, eventually pulling him over the cliff after me. We lose ourselves in the sensations that wash over us and my body shakes as I cling to him.

Finally, as the waves of pleasure subside, he releases his grip on my throat, and I'm left panting and gasping for breath.

He takes a hold of my wrists, restraining them in one of his own and I'm reminded of the late night visit from Dare only days ago. "Now where was I? That's right, my brother is going to be so disappointed in you. You realize that he's really quite attached to you, right?" He moves to sit up as he rambles, then fishes around in his pants until he pulls out a phone. "I mean I'm pretty obsessed with you myself, but he's on a whole other level. But then he always knew you were ours, even when we were children."

I'm so confused at this point and with the haze of pleasure still clouding my mind it's taking a little longer for his words to register. "What?"

He grins down at me with a tilt of his head. "Don't you remember? Little Darling girl."

The memory is almost a slap in the face.

"Come out and play, Little Darling girl!"

I creep to the door, opening and peeking out at my friend. "I can't. Momma said I have to stay home while Uncle Jimmy visits. But she said I can play after."

"Not fair. She can't stop us from playing together."

Him being sad makes me sad but I promised Momma. "I'm sorry, Dare."

He pouts. "After?"

I nod in response.

He shrugs, turning away to go back to his place, I can see his brother hovering at the end of the hall waiting. He has a sad look too when I don't follow. "Okay, see you after, Little Darling girl."

My heart feels like it's actually stopped in my chest. Tristan seems to know something is wrong as he is looking at me with concern clouding his eyes. But when I don't say anything he brings his phone to his ear. I don't hear what he mumbles, but the flinch on his face tells me all I need to know about who he is speaking to.

He hangs up and tucks his phone back away, pulling me up from the bed completely until we are both standing beside it. He lets go to put himself away and straighten his clothes before he pulls out one of my night shirts from the drawer and throws it to me.

I look down at myself and then back at him with a frown and a raised eyebrow. I have his cum still dripping from my pussy. When I only get a grin in response I roll my eyes and pull on the shirt, grumbling to myself about never saying his name ever again.

He just chuckles in response and grabs my wrist, pulling me behind him out of the bedroom. I almost stumble when he moves too fast for me, but it doesn't take me long to figure out where he is taking me. My office, the sanctuary I set up with its walls lined with images of the crimes that brought me here.

Stopping just past the doorway, he propels me further into the room. Dare is there, his masked face looking around at the photographs covering almost every inch of space.

Tristan lets go of me and when I glance over my shoulder I see him slowly backing out of the room. "I'll, uhh, be out here." With that he is gone, like smoke.

Turning back around I can see Dare looking at me from under his hood, his black eyes piercing mine with an intensity that has my heart racing in my chest again. But then he looks back at the photographs, almost as though he is lost in his own thoughts.

We stand in silence for a few minutes until he speaks, his modulated voice almost soft. "When we started this I knew they would call you. We had tried to reach out to you before, but for a while there I thought maybe you had found a normal life, away from the darkness that I knew lived inside us. We kept an eye on you, but nothing indicated to us that you remembered."

He turns to look at me directly. "But then I saw you one day in the newspaper. The FBI agent who had an affinity with death and murderers. You can't escape it any more than we can. It's in our very souls, the connection we feel to the evil in the world. I knew it was only a matter of time before the people, like the ones who controlled all of these, would sink their claws into you." He indicates to the dead women on my walls.

I narrow my eyes at the images. "So you figured you would just kill them and hope for the best?"

Dare sighs, shaking his head as he takes a step closer to me. "No, we couldn't stand by and let them get to you, we couldn't let them hurt you or anyone else anymore for that matter. You were in danger, and we had to do something."

I cross my arms, trying to ignore the fact that I'm still wearing nothing but a shirt. "And what about me? Did you think about how this would affect me? How I would feel, knowing that you're the ones behind all of this? I still have a case to solve, I have a job to do, and I need to give them someone to hold responsible."

My heart skips a beat when he pulls my gun from the back of his pants. With everything that happened I completely forgot he took it from me. But he doesn't aim it at me.

Moving to stand in front of me, he uncrosses my arms and places my gun in my hand, moving it so that it's aimed directly at his chest. "Then shoot me. You want to end this? You want to close this case? Shoot me."

I feel like I can't breathe, my mouth is hanging open in shock. I can't comprehend what he is even saying. "What??"

"Shoot me!" he growls loudly and forcefully, letting go of my hands so I'm just standing there aiming my gun at his chest.

My heart is pounding in my chest and it feels like the whole room is closing in on me. The gun hits the floor moments before my hand reaches up to yank the mask down from his face, my eyes widening at the face revealed underneath.

"My god," I breathe out, my heart squeezing painfully.

He narrows his black eyes at me. "I told you before, Little Darling, god isn't here."

Chapter 35

Alex

My hands are moving before I even think about it, shoving at his chest. But instead of moving backward he moves into me, picking me up and continuing until my back hits the wall behind me.

Going on what I feel when I shoved at his chest I rip open the hoodie he's wearing from the neck down. "You asshole," I snarl but his lips are already on mine, biting and moving in a way that I have no choice but to surrender to him.

My lips part and his tongue sweeps into my mouth to tangle with mine. I wrap my legs around his waist, and he uses the leverage to reach down to open his pants. I moan into his mouth when he thrusts his cock deep inside me, his brothers cum making the slide of him easier.

Letting my head fall back against the wall, I narrow my eyes at him, my hands moving between us to yank at what was revealed when I opened the hoodie. "I should remove this and shoot you just on principle."

He laughs, thrusting hard inside me again before he carries me toward the center of the room. He lowers my back to the desk while he stays standing between my legs, his cock still buried inside of me.

His hands pull off the hoodie, then the mask, and then the goddamn bulletproof vest underneath before he leans back over me. He braces his hands on the desk to either side of my head. “You really want to shoot me, Little Darling?”

I growl at him in response, my hands moving to pull at his hair to bring his face closer to mine as I raise my head toward his. “Shut up and fuck me, Derek, or I just might.”

My words only seem to fuel Derek's desire. "Mmm, I love how feisty you’ve become," he purrs, “Are you going to scream my name like you did Tristan’s?” I let my head drop back to the desk with a groan, knowing now that he listened to his brother fucking me. But I see nothing but heat in his eyes.

"You'll have to earn it just like he did," I challenge.

He chuckles, but he seems all too eager to take on that challenge. Without hesitation, he starts moving inside me, his thrusts deliberate and powerful.

His lips find mine again, kissing me hungrily as our bodies move in perfect sync. He isn’t gentle. His thrusts are hard, his skin slapping sharply against mine, and I cling to him, lost in the ecstasy of the moment.

I moan into his mouth, unable to hold back the sounds of pleasure he's drawing from me. His hands find their way to my hips, holding me firmly as he drives into me with a force that leaves me breathless.

He pulls back slightly, his dark eyes locking with mine. "You feel so good," he groans, his voice husky.

I arch my back, meeting his every thrust, the sensation of him filling me completely driving me wild. "More, harder," I gasp, my fingers digging into his skin as I grip his waist.

Derek complies willingly, increasing his pace, pushing me closer and closer to the edge. I can feel the tension building inside me, my pussy tightening around his cock, and I know I won't be able to hold back much longer.

"I'm going to make you scream my name, Little Darling. I want to hear you say it over and over again." His lips brush against my lips, and I find myself unable to resist his command.

I wrap my legs around him tighter, pulling him deeper inside me. The sensations are almost overwhelming, and I feel myself teetering on the edge of release.

With each thrust, the pleasure builds, ready to crash over me. I feel myself losing control. It's as if the world around us fades away, and there's only him, me, and the ecstasy we share.

I let out a breathless moan, my body trembling. "Derek," I whisper, my voice filled with need.

His grin widens, sensing that he's got me right where he wants me. "That's it, Little Darling," he murmurs. "Say it again, louder."

I gasp as he hits just the right spot inside me, and my words become a desperate plea. "Derek!" I cry out, unable to contain myself any longer.

He picks up the pace, driving me toward my orgasm. I feel the pleasure building, spiraling out of control. I'm so close, and he knows it.

His growl fills my ears, his voice filled with possessiveness. "You're ours, Little Darling," he says, punctuating his words with deep and deliberate movements. "No one else can touch you like this but us."

His possessive claim only fans the flames burning out of control inside of me, the primal desire to belong to him completely. "Scream for me, Little Darling," he commands. The world explodes in a burst of pleasure, and I scream his name as waves of ecstasy crash over me.

Derek's own release follows shortly after with a groan, and he holds himself above me as we ride out the orgasm together. His eyes burning into mine as he watches every second of my climax cross my face.

He chuckles again after a moment. "We really need to do something about those wandering hands," he says, his voice filled with humor.

I raise an eyebrow at him and move my hands to the skin of his back. "I wouldn't suggest cutting them off, otherwise I can't do this."

I rake my nails down his back and he groans loudly, thrusting into me again. I shouldn't tempt him, since I know he can just keep going until I pass out. He has done it before after all.

"Awww, you already know his love language, how sweet," comes Tristan's voice from behind Derek as he saunters in to perch himself on the desk beside our sweaty and spent bodies.

Derek pulls himself from me slowly, fixing his clothes before helping me sit up on the desk. Guess we aren't having a repeat of last time.

A strange memory hits me, more a knowledge than a visual memory this time. "I remember now, I couldn't say your names when I was little, so I started calling you Truth and Dare," I recollect with a smile.

They both smile softly at me and Derek moves to lean against the desk on my other side.

He brushes a hand down my arm in an almost comforting gesture. "What do you remember?"

I shake my head in response with a wince, "Until the other day, nothing, but a few memories have come back since you gave me this." My hand reaches up to briefly touch the pendant hanging between my breasts. "The doctor said it's dissociative amnesia."

Derek brushes a thumb against my cheek and he frowns deeply, his gaze full of concern. "We will have to sit and talk about it when all of this is sorted and we can just be us together."

I nod in response and then try to brush down my hair with my hand but at this point it's a lost cause. "What now?"

They glance at each other before Derek turns back to me. "We have a few more loose ends to tie up, that's all you need to know for now."

"Really? More cryptic answers?" I scowl, I should be used to it but that still doesn't lessen the annoyance.

They both chuckle and it's in that moment that the fact they are siblings becomes more obvious.

"I would never have pegged you as brothers," I huff.

Tristan grins. "Can't you see the family resemblance?"

Derek scoffs at him, but I can see the fondness in his eyes that I didn't see previously.

"Wait, does that mean you're digging up information for me that you already gave me?" I asked Tristan with a frown.

His grin gets wider, his hand reaching out to brush his thumb across my cheek. "Not really digging, no. Obviously you know we already have the information. Max was the one that retrieved it in the first place for us."

I'm so thoroughly confused now. "So why am I waiting for him to dig up the information for me?"

Derek growls at that. "Well, you weren't meant to connect the pieces just yet. Or remove our masks when you swore not to. You definitely have some punishment coming in the near future, Little Darling."

My heart skips a beat at Derek's threat, but I refuse to back down. "Punishment? You're going to punish me for wanting to know the truth?" I retort.

Tristan leans in, his lips brushing against my ear as he whispers, "Don't worry, Little Darling. We'll make sure your punishment is... enjoyable."

I feel a rush of desire course through me. It is both exhilarating and terrifying how they can command my body and mind so effortlessly.

Derek smirks, clearly aware of the effect their words have on me. "But first, we need to deal with those loose ends," he says, bringing the focus back to the task at hand.

"Do I get to know what these loose ends are at some point and what you plan to do?" I ask him, but I already know what the answer is going to be.

Derek chuckles, running his fingers through his disheveled hair. "You'll know in due time," he replies cryptically, not giving away any details. "For now, you need to get cleaned up and ready to go to work."

I raise an eyebrow at him. "Work? Are you kidding me?" I say, incredulous. "After all that just happened, you expect me to go to work today?"

Tristan smirks, crossing his arms over his chest. "You're an FBI agent tasked with an important case, remember? Crimes don't stop just because you had a wild night with us," he says, his tone teasing.

Derek grins also. "Besides, I have a feeling you might have a new crime scene to deal with today from your mysterious murderers."

I sigh, rubbing hands down my face when I realize what he's implying. "I'm going to need lots of coffee," I say, trying to lighten the mood.

Derek leans in, brushing his lips against mine. "I'll make sure you're well-caffeinated," he says with a wink. "How about you go get cleaned up and ready, Tristan can stay with you. I'll go do the same and come back with your caffeine, since I know you still have nothing in this house."

I scowl at him. "A little less judgy please, I had two stalkers to deal with."

He just laughs in response before straightening and pulling me up from the desk. He pushes me out the door of the office with Tristan following us. He pushes me in the direction of the bedroom with a light smack on my ass while he continues toward the front door.

As I make my way to the bedroom, Tristan follows close behind. "You heard the man," he says, grinning. "Time for us to shower to get cleaned up and ready for the day."

I stop and look at him with a smirk. "And what makes you think you're joining me in the shower?" I tease.

He chuckles, raising an eyebrow. "Well, I wouldn't mind seeing if I can make you scream my name again," he says, his voice low.

I roll my eyes playfully. "You're insatiable," I say, though I can't deny the appeal of the idea.

He smirks, stepping closer until he's only inches away from me. "Can you blame me? You're irresistible," he whispers, his fingers gently tracing along my jawline.

Before things can escalate further, I playfully push him away. "As tempting as that sounds, I really need to get cleaned up," I say with a grin.

Tristan chuckles, taking a step back. "Alright, I'll behave for now," he says, though the mischief in his eyes remains.

I head into the bathroom, and after exchanging a teasing grin with Tristan, I close the door behind me. The hot water soothes my body.

As I lather up with soap, I can't help but smile at the unexpected turn the night has taken and the ridiculousness of needing two showers because of it.

Once I finish and step out, I dry myself and wrap the towel around me. The mirror reflects a happier and still slightly flushed version of myself. I shake my head, amused at how my life has changed.

Putting on fresh clothes I head back into the bedroom, where Tristan is waiting for me, a playful smile on his lips. "Feeling refreshed?" he asks, raising an eyebrow.

I nod with a grin, "Definitely."

As I open the drawer where I keep my birth control pills, I hear Tristan's voice, stopping me in my tracks. "I wouldn't bother with those."

I turn to look at him, puzzled. "What do you mean?" I ask, a sinking feeling taking over.

He looks serious now, his playful demeanor gone. "They, uhh, haven't worked since the first night we fucked you."

Chapter 36

Alex

My heart skips a beat, and my mind races to process what he just said. "What the fuck did you do?" I demand angrily.

Tristan takes a step closer to me, but he doesn't look guilty or contrite, he just looks possessive. "You are ours, and you are never leaving us again, even if we have to make you stay."

I growl as anger flares within me. I hear a faint sound from the living area and storm out of the bedroom in that direction.

Derek has returned and placed a coffee and a bag of what I assume is food on the coffee table. All I can do is narrow my eyes at it and him.

"If you give me that right now I may just throw it in both of your faces." I growl pointing at it.

Derek, having not been a part of the conversation, frowns and then looks toward his brother. "I wasn't even gone an hour, how did you piss her off?" I turn in time to catch the end of Tristan's wince.

"So, who's idea was it exactly that I needed to be knocked up in order to stay?" I say into the momentary silence and this time it's Derek's turn to wince.

But then he gets the same possessive look that Tristan had. Derek strides straight over to me, grabs the back of my neck with one of his big hands and tilts my head so I'm looking directly at him and only him. "We will never apologize for things we do in our efforts to show you that you belong with us."

My heart speeds up at the tone of his voice, there is a dark edge to it that reminds me very clearly that he is also Dare, the controlling psycho that kills people.

His other hand comes up to close around my throat as he brings his face closer to mine and I whimper. "Don't mistake us for good men, Little Darling, there is no line we won't cross to keep you by our sides."

I let my eyes close briefly before looking back into his eyes, only now noticing he has removed the contact lenses that turned them black. Looking into his piercing blue eyes at that moment is almost too much. "Don't talk like that."

He frowns in response, "Why?"

"Because as much as my pussy wants it, I don't think I have the energy for you to fuck me again. And now I can't even have coffee in case your psycho plan actually worked." I wanted to pout, really I did, but something about what they did just made a part of me want them more.

He chuckles and brushes his lips against mine before releasing me and pointing at the coffee. "That's only a single shot. You're allowed up to two each day."

Tristan comes up behind me and kisses my cheek. "If we see you have more, I will tie you up and bleed it out of you."

That draws a startled laugh from me, "Somehow I think the blood loss would have a worse effect than the coffee."

He shrugs as though his craziness makes sense to him before moving to sit on my couch and prop his feet up on the coffee table. It is the strangest thing to note that while Derek had changed into his work attire and shed the appearance of Dare, Tristan still had most of his outfit on since he had barely left my side.

I rub my hands down my face in frustration before sighing and moving to pick up the coffee. Exactly how I liked it. And peeking in the bag it is also my regular bagel order.

The creepy stalker.

They're infuriating, possessive, and controlling, yet somehow, a part of me enjoys their attention and affection. As much as I try to resist, there's a magnetic pull they have on me that's hard to deny.

Looking at Tristan, I raise my eyebrow as I take a seat next to him on the couch. “Don’t you have a job you need to go get ready for as well?”

Tristan smirks at me, settling in comfortably. “I’ll leave when you both do. Technically, I’m very deep into some research for this amazing FBI duo that I know, so my absence won’t be too out of place.” He shrugs again. “But then, not everyone keeps to stupid hours like you two. Though it did make watching you easy when you only really went between here and your office.”

I chuckle at Tristan's teasing, unable to completely suppress the amusement despite the situation. "You're unbelievable," I remark, taking a bite of my bagel and letting out a moan as I taste the familiar flavors. "Mmm, at least you got the bagel right."

A flash of heat and hunger enters Derek’s eyes as he watches me, his tongue swiping at his bottom lip as though he is trying to still taste me there. “Careful with those moans, or we will be checking just how tired you really are. You have no idea how hard it was restraining myself when you ate breakfast at the office.”

I smirk, savoring the bagel even more, partly enjoying the effect my actions seem to have on him. "Oh, is that so?" I tease, taking another deliberate bite of my bagel and letting out another soft moan, just to see their reactions. "I guess you'll just have to restrain yourself a little while longer then."

Tristan's eyes darken, and he leans in closer, a low growl escaping his throat. "You're pushing your luck, Little Darling," he warns.

Derek's gaze intensifies, and he leans in as well, his lips grazing my ear. "You have no idea what you do to us," he murmurs, his breath hot against my skin.

I can feel the heat rising between us, the tension thick in the air. But I also know that we have other priorities this morning and we can't afford to be distracted.

I roll my eyes, trying to ignore the impact of their words. "So, how did you two end up hating each other in public, but yet you're brothers, and you obviously don't hate each other?"

Derek and Tristan exchange glances, and there's a combination of hesitation and something else unidentifiable in their eyes. Derek finally speaks up. "It's a long story, and we will tell you every tiny detail, some day."

Tristan sighs. "Do you really think two men working together to kill people are going to act all cutesy family friendly in public?"

I nod, now understanding the gravity of what they were doing and the need for secrecy. "I get it. You had to maintain a facade to protect your covers. But it must have been tough, pretending to hate each other all the time."

Derek's expression softens. "It was, but we knew it was necessary. We had to make some sacrifices for the greater good."

A frown crosses my face as another thought occurs to me. "You will still need to maintain that until you sort those loose ends won't you?"

Tristan chuckles in response. “Just think of us as your own messed up personal love triangle, like something out of those smutty romance novels.”

Derek chuckles, reaching for his own coffee and taking a sip. "Well, it's not exactly your average love story, that's for sure."

I smirk, leaning back against the couch, emotions bubbling inside me. "No, definitely not your average love story. But I guess I've never been one for mundane and ordinary. That’s what they say about me after all, I’m the profiler with the penchant for the macabre and an affinity for murderers."

Tristan tilts his head, his gaze lingering on me with an intensity. "Good," he says, his voice low and husky. "We wouldn't want average. We want extraordinary. And you have always been that to us."

Derek nods in agreement, a serious look in his eyes. "We want you, all of you, just as you are. And we'll do whatever it takes to keep you. We were always destined to be together."

I take a deep breath. It's overwhelming, this connection I have with them. But it's also undeniably intoxicating.

I look into their eyes, realizing that despite their controlling and dangerous sides, they are also offering me something that I've secretly yearned for — a deep connection, an unconventional love that defies societal norms. And in a way, I've always been drawn to the darker aspects of life, to the enigmatic and complex personalities of those I've studied and profiled.

"I've always been drawn to the darkness," I admit, my voice softer now. "But with you two, it's different. You're the darkness I'm not afraid to embrace."

Tristan's hand finds mine, his grip gentle yet firm. "Then embrace it, Little Darling. Embrace all of us, like you were always meant to."

Derek leans down, his lips brushing against mine in a tender kiss. "We're not just random killers without an agenda, we're more than that. And so are you."

I close my eyes, savoring their touch and the emotions swirling inside me. It's complicated, messy, and uncertain, but at this moment, it feels right. I can't deny the pull they have on me, nor can I ignore the connection we share.

"So, what now?" I ask, my heart beating faster.

As if on cue, mine and Derek's phones buzz. He just smiles at me, "That would be our signal. We have a new crime scene to look at and evil people to catch." He reaches down and pulls me up from the couch so I'm standing in front of him.

I sigh and pick up the rest of my coffee to take with me. "This is going to be a long ass day."

Tristan stays where he is, but gives me a little finger wave. "See you around, Little Darling."

Derek leads me to his sleek black car parked outside, and as I slide into the passenger seat, I can't help but turn sideways to look at him all over. The intensity in his eyes sends a thrill down my spine, and a rush of desire and adrenaline courses through my veins. I know we have work to do, but I also can't deny the attraction between us.

He smirks, catching my gaze. "Like what you see?" he teases, his voice low and seductive.

I raise an eyebrow, a playful glint in my eyes. "Maybe I do," I reply, not bothering to hide my curiosity.

His hand reaches out, gently tracing the outline of my jaw, sending shivers down my spine. "You're quite distracting, you know," he says, his voice husky. "But we have work to do. Can't let ourselves get too distracted."

I nod, turning to face the front, trying to regain my composure. "Right, the crime scene."

Derek starts the engine and begins driving us to our destination. The atmosphere in the car is tense, and I find myself unable to resist stealing glances at Derek whenever I get the chance.

He notices my looks and smirks, "Something on your mind, Little Darling?" he asks.

I bite my lip, unable to hide my curiosity. "Just wondering how you can be both Derek, the FBI agent, and Dare, the ruthless killer. It's like you're two different people."

Derek's expression softens, and he reaches out to gently thread his fingers through mine and draw my hand to his lips. "I am two different people, but they're both parts of who I am. Derek protects and serves justice, while Dare deals with those who think they can escape it. It's a balancing act, but somehow, it works."

I listen to Derek's explanation. It's hard to wrap my head around the duality of it, but I've seen enough to know that it's not a facade or just a game they're playing. Derek and Tristan are both genuine in their own ways.

"You must have to compartmentalize a lot," I say, still trying to process the complexity of it. "It's like leading two separate lives."

Derek nods, his eyes fixed on the road. "It can be challenging at times, but I've been doing it for a long time. It's a necessary part of it, and we've become skilled at it."

I lean back in my seat, my mind wandering to the crime scene ahead. "How do you manage to stand at a crime scene knowing that you're the one who committed the act?"

Derek's grip on the steering wheel tightens momentarily before he takes a deep breath. "It's not easy," he admits. "There's a level of detachment that comes with what we do. We may have done terrible things, but we also eliminated dangerous criminals who were a threat to innocent lives."

I nod slowly, trying to comprehend the weight of his choices he had to make. "So, you believe the end justifies the means?"

"In a way, yes," Derek says. "I believe that sometimes, to protect the innocent and ensure justice, you have to step into the shadows and confront evil head-on. Sometimes it's necessary. Sometimes there is no other option. Take Mark for example, even you knew that there was no other option for someone like him. He would never have been stopped and made to pay for his crimes any other way."

I fall silent, contemplating his words. It's a morally complex situation, one that challenges my understanding of right and wrong. But I can't deny that I completely understood the reasoning behind it, especially given my own past experiences of injustice.

As we arrive at the crime scene, the atmosphere is somber and tense. The flashing lights of police cars illuminate the area, and the familiar sight of the crime scene tape reminds me of the gravity of the situation. Because I know this time, it's different. This time, it's closer to me than any others before.

The body in the center of the police officers and forensic technicians swarming the area is Mark.

Chapter 37

Alex

I am glad that I hadn't known Mark for long. It is easier to hide my lack of emotional response under a layer of indifference, since I barely knew him. But looking down at his body I can now see how Derek is able to separate his reactions and responses to his own handiwork.

Looking at that lifeless body, all I can see is a man who committed unspeakable acts, but now, because of my actions, would never harm another innocent life again.

I can see James, Emily and Michael in the distance. Michael appears to be consoling an upset Emily, while James is staring into the distance with a devastated look on his face.

I can't fully imagine the pain they are going through, but I can empathize with the burden of loss and grief.

Derek crouches down on the other side of the body, his back to the rest of our team. His eyes aren't on the body though, they are on me, watching my reactions as I look at Mark's body. I'm sure he has some plan to be able to extract me from the situation if necessary, but it won't be. "How are you doing?"

I hum softly, my eyes flicking around and then over to the rest of the team. "We should go talk to them. They may think it's strange if we spend too much time here."

He nods and stands, sliding his hands into the pockets of his dress pants, “Just wanted to make sure you’re all good first.”

Standing, I move around the body and then walk beside him as we make our way over toward James, Emily, and Michael.

As we approach, the gravity of the situation hangs heavily in the air. Derek remains composed, while I do my best to maintain a neutral expression, not wanting to betray any lingering emotions from witnessing Mark's lifeless body.

"Hey," I say softly as we reach them, my voice steady but sympathetic.

Emily looks up, her eyes red from crying, “Why would they do this?”

James, who has been staring into the distance, turns his attention to us, his face still showing the strain of his stress. "It's just so hard to believe. Mark was part of our team. How could this happen?"

"We're going to do everything we can to find out," Derek assures him. "We'll leave no stone unturned."

James blinks and looks at Derek. “Should we pass the case to another team?”

I reach out and put my hand on his arm, trying for some semblance of comfort. “He worked with many of the teams, not just us, it would be the same for whoever the case went to.”

James nods, taking a deep breath to steady himself. "You're right. I just... I can't wrap my head around it."

"I understand," I say softly. "We'll do our best to find justice and bring closure to the case."

Emily steps forward, her eyes filling with tears, as she wraps her arms around me in a tight hug. I hesitate for a moment, unsure if it is appropriate, but then I realize that this is about comforting a grieving friend.

"It's okay," I whisper, returning the embrace. "We'll get through this together."

As she steps back, she notices that our necklaces have gotten tangled during the hug. "Oh, I'm sorry," Emily says, her embarrassment evident as she gently untangles the necklaces.

I smile softly as I smooth a hand down the chain and pendant, assuring her, "It's all right. No need to apologize."

Emily offers me a grateful smile as she continues to untangle the necklaces. "Thank you," she says softly, her voice still laden with emotion.

Derek, James, and Michael move away, giving us some privacy. As Emily finishes untangling the necklaces, she steps back, wiping away a tear. I can see Michael looking at Emily as though her pain is affecting him also. "Is there something going on with Michael?"

She looks startled and glances at him. I can sense a subtle change in the atmosphere as Emily's eyes meet Michael's concerned gaze.

Emily takes a deep breath, appearing hesitant yet determined to share her feelings. "Yes," she admits softly. "We've been seeing each other in secret for a while now."

I offer Emily a supportive smile, knowing that revealing their relationship is a significant step. "I'm glad you found someone who can bring you comfort and happiness, especially given the current circumstances."

She nods, her eyes glistening with emotion. "It's been hard to keep it a secret, but we didn't want to cause any additional complications for the team. That's why I was upset that day in the office."

"It's understandable," I say, trying to reassure her. "Sometimes, life throws unexpected challenges our way, and we find solace in unexpected places."

Emily glances back at Michael, who is still watching her with a tender expression. "Yes, exactly. We didn't plan for this, but it happened, and we're navigating it together."

"Take all the time you need," I say, giving her a comforting pat on the shoulder. "I'm sure the rest of the team will understand when the time is right."

Emily nods gratefully, and we move to rejoin the rest of the team in silence. James finally breaks it, his voice determined.

"Are we all okay to proceed with collecting evidence and working on the case like normal?" he asks, looking at each of us.

"I'm ready," Derek replies, his tone steady and resolute.

I nod in agreement. "Yes, let's focus on closing the case."

"We owe it to Mark, and we owe it to ourselves. We can't let this stop us from doing our jobs," Michael chimes in.

Emily wipes away another tear and nods. "You're right. Mark would want us to keep going."

James gives a small nod of approval. "Then let's get to work. We have crimes to solve and murderers to catch."

With a collective nod of agreement, we set everything else aside for the moment and get back to work. The investigation requires our undivided attention, and we are, of course, committed to finding the truth behind Mark's murder. Or at least the truth that Derek, Tristan and I want them to believe.

As a team, we go about our normal routines, collecting evidence, interviewing witnesses, and analyzing data meticulously. And all the while the reality and truth of the situation is constantly at the back of my mind.

At the end of the day, Derek drives me back home and drops me off, stating he would be back but had something he needed to do. Which of course he isn't going to tell me any details about.

As Derek drives away, I step into my rental house, exhaustion starting to weigh down on me. The events of the day, coupled with the pressure of keeping my true involvement in Mark's death a secret, are taking their toll on me. Not to mention that I have officially been awake now for 36 hours straight.

I know Derek has a plan to handle the situation, but it is difficult not to feel slightly anxious about the potential consequences of our actions.

I decide to take another shower to clear my mind and wash away the weariness that is settling into my bones. The hot water feels soothing against my skin, and for a brief moment, I allow myself to forget about the case and the secrets we are keeping.

As I rub the body wash into my skin, my hand brushes my abdomen and my mind drifts to the other matter lingering in the back of my mind. They tampered with my birth control. They have been fucking me for days, knowing that I was ignorant to the fact that I wasn't covered, because they wanted it that way.

Dare's words when he came to me in the middle of the night come back to me, that they they will keep fucking me and filling me with their cum until I am round with their babies. They knew what they were doing and what they wanted.

At the time, I had dismissed his words, thinking there wasn't a chance of it actually happening. But I was wrong. And as I think about the possibility of it, it doesn't upset me as much as I thought it would.

I know it is too early to take a pregnancy test, but the mere thought that I might be carrying their child makes me excited. As I mentally calculate the days of my cycle, I realize that the creepy psychos may have timed it exactly right.

With a shake of my head, I turn off the shower. That's a problem for later. I put on a clean night shirt and grab my laptop, making my way to the living room. I need to distract myself until Derek and Tristan return, no matter how long that is.

A sudden knock on the door interrupts my thoughts, making me jump slightly. I frown, finding it strange that someone is actually knocking on my door. I don't really know anyone here, and Derek and Tristan wouldn't bother with such formalities; they would have their ways of letting themselves in.

I peer through the peephole and see a familiar face – James. My heart sinks at the thought of having to face him again so soon after the emotionally charged day we just experienced.

I take a deep breath, trying to compose myself, before opening the door. James stands there with a weary expression.

"Hey, Alex," he says softly, offering a small smile that doesn't quite reach his eyes. "I'm sorry to bother you so late, but I was just wondering if we could talk."

"It's okay," I reply, trying to be understanding. "Come on in."

James steps inside, and I close the door behind him. He looks like he has a lot on his mind. "I'm sorry to drop by unannounced," James continues as he steps into the living room, his eyes flicking to the laptop and then back to me.

"It's alright, James," I say again, "Would you like some water? It's the only thing I have in the house at the moment. I still haven't had the chance to go shopping yet."

He chuckles softly. "Somehow I'm not surprised."

I shrug, unashamed, chuckling to myself. "You know how it is when I am deep into a case, I will always forget about everything else. I would probably forget to eat unless someone else makes me."

He smiles at me but I can see the strain in it. "I can relate to that. Sometimes, when we're so focused on the job, everything else just falls to the wayside." He wanders away toward the curtained window, looking out briefly before rubbing his palms across his face. He looks frustrated.

"Is everything alright?" I ask, concerned.

James turns back to me and hesitates for a moment, as if trying to find the right words. "I was going to ask you the same thing. At the crime scene today, you seemed different."

I frown, I had thought I had kept it hidden well enough not to raise any suspicions, but James has known me a long time. “Different?”

James nods and then starts pacing the living room floor, "I know we all deal with things differently, but it almost felt like you were detached from the whole situation," he snaps.

"I assure you, James, I care about Mark's death just as much as anyone else," I reply.

He doesn’t respond, just keeps pacing the floor of the living room. I can see him still looking at me narrowly every time he is facing my direction. My anxiety only increases, I have to be careful not to give anything away, but something seems to have set him off. He isn’t acting like the man I know now.

His hands rake through his hair, clenching the strands and then letting them go. “You were meant to have found these assholes by now!”

I’ve never heard him speak to me like that before, but the tone he uses seems to tug at a memory for a second before it disappears. “We are trying, James. There is no evidence to find. Nothing is there to tell us who is doing this.” I try to keep my voice as calm as possible but my heart is starting to race in my chest.

He stops pacing and turns to face me, his face filling with rage. “You aren’t trying hard enough! I’m the one who trained you Alex, I know you can do better than this pathetic excuse of an effort.”

My heart drops at his words. I suddenly feel so torn. He’s right, he did train me from the moment I left the academy. I have known him for years, I have a loyalty to him.

Then, his eyes land on the pendant I’m wearing. He narrows his eyes as he takes a step toward me. "That's a very pretty necklace. Where did you get it?" His tone hasn’t lost any of the aggression, if anything it's now worse.

I glance down at the pendant, my heart skipping a beat, my hand touching it automatically. “Oh, it was my mothers. It was in her belongings.”

He takes more steps toward me and I can see the frustration and anger on his face more visibly now, surprising me. “You’re lying to me! How did you get that necklace, Alex?”

I take a step back from his advancing form, confused, my hand now closing around the necklace in question. “I don’t understand why you're asking me that, it was my mothers, why wouldn’t I have it?”

James is now so much closer, his hand reaching out to grab me, but suddenly he stills in mid motion, his whole body freezing with his hand halfway toward my throat. I’m so focused on his face I can barely see anything but his angry eyes bearing down on me. But in that moment of utter stillness, a glint of light catches my attention and my eyes are drawn to the knife pressed to the front of his throat, a small drop of blood starting to trail down his skin from where it must have cut in when he was still moving.

“Yes, James, why wouldn’t she have it? It wouldn’t have anything to do with how you had it hidden in your safe would it?” comes a familiar voice from behind James. I know that voice. I don't even need to look to know that Tristan is behind James and that it's his knife.

I take another couple of steps backward, moving further out of James' reach. I'm momentarily startled when my back makes contact with a hard body, but then the familiar scent of Derek hits me. His hands slowly grip the sides of my waist and he squeezes me in a comforting gesture as he presses himself to my back. "Silly fucking place to hide something you took from a dead body, Jimmy."

Chapter 38
Alex

(8 Years Old)

"Please Momma, I wanna go play with Truth and Dare."

She laughs at me, I love the sound of her laugh, it makes me happy. "Sweet baby girl, their names are Tristan and Derek, but you know Uncle Jimmy is coming over. You can go play after that."

I pout at her. "But Momma, Truth and Dare are so much fun! I like playing with them! We swore we would always play together."

She smiles and bends down to my level, ruffling my hair affectionately. "I know, sweetheart, but Uncle Jimmy is coming over for something important. After he leaves, you can go play with Tristan and Derek, okay?"

I nod, still a little sulky, but the promise of playing with Truth and Dare later cheers me up a bit. "Okay, Momma, but make sure Uncle Jimmy doesn't take too long!"

She chuckles and gives me a gentle hug. "Don't worry, my darling girl. He won't stay long. Now, why don't you go pick out your favorite toys, and we'll get ready for when he arrives? You remember what to do?"

I eagerly nod, rushing off to my room to fetch my favorite dolls and games. I hope Momma is right and he doesn't stay long. But I know what I need to do when he visits. Keep out of sight and don't make a sound.

I don't know why I even have to keep doing this every visit, why I can't be playing with Truth and Dare. Uncle Jimmy knows I'm here, he has been visiting since before I can even remember. But Momma is always making sure I'm home and hidden whenever he visits. Always making sure I remember not to come out when the adults talk. No matter what.

While I'm busy playing with my toys, I can hear the soft murmur of voices as Momma and Uncle Jimmy talk in the living room. I can't make out their words, but the tone tells me it's a grown-up conversation.

The serious murmur of voices gets louder and the sound of Uncle Jimmy's voice growing angrier. I can feel his anger in the air, and it makes me uncomfortable. I want to go and hide, but I also want to know what's happening.

Curiosity gets the better of me, and even though I know I'm not meant to I cautiously make my way toward the living room, trying to stay hidden. I peek from behind a corner and see Momma and Uncle Jimmy standing face to face, their expressions angry.

"You can't back out now!" Uncle Jimmy's voice is loud and furious. "You knew what you signed up for!"

Momma looks worried, and scared. I don't like seeing Momma scared. "I know, but I can't do this anymore. It's wrong, Jimmy. I can't keep going down this path."

"Wrong?" Uncle Jimmy's voice is so angry. "You're in too deep now! You can't just walk away! You think you can just quit? That's not how it works!"

Momma takes a step back, her hand covering her mouth as tears appear in her eyes. "I never wanted any of this to happen! I never wanted to hurt anyone, and I definitely never wanted my daughter anywhere near this!"

Uncle Jimmy growls at her; he reminds me of a wild dog I saw once. His hand grabs Momma's hair and twists. I know it would hurt because it hurts when Momma brushes my tangles, so I'm not surprised when she cries out. I want to go to her, but I'm so scared. "I dragged your pathetic fucking ass from the gutter with that baby in your arms. I gave you a place to raise that brat, I'm the one that gave you food and clothes for both of you and all you had to do was work for me and not complain."

Momma is crying and making the same noises I make when she pulls on my tangles. I can see her hands trying to make Uncle Jimmy let go of her hair. Why won't he let go of her and go away? Momma is upset and I just want her to stop crying. I want it to be a good day again so I can play with Truth and Dare.

She must know he isn't going to let go because she tries to scratch at him. "You just wanted me to deal your drugs and manage your whores and bend over for you on command."

I didn't understand what Momma was saying. I wish I knew what to do, I'm so scared.

Uncle Jimmy grabbed Momma's neck and shook her again, he needs to stop that, she isn't a doll. Please someone make him stop. "And now you don't want to, you pathetic bitch, you don't have another option. You will do what you're told, darling, or you and that brat will be out on the street again. That means sucking my cock and letting me fuck that cunt when I want, as well as making sure those other whores are working for the drugs they put in their veins."

He lets Momma go and she falls down. I want to run to her, but I can't get myself to move from my hiding spot. She has told me so many times to stay hidden. I'm trying so hard to be quiet so he doesn't hear me and get mean and angry with me like he is with Momma.

I can see she is getting up and I'm happier now. But she looks upset, and that makes me upset. "No, I won't. I watched Beth almost overdose on those drugs while those men did terrible things to her, all while my little girl played with her sons. I won't do it anymore. I'm taking her and our kids out of this hell you have us in."

She is so brave to stand up to mean Uncle Jimmy. I want to be brave like her when I'm older. I can't bear to watch Momma get hurt like this, and I want to run to her, but my feet feel glued to the floor. My body doesn't want to disobey her. I can't move, I can't make a sound. I just want this nightmare to end. Can't I wake up now, please.

Uncle Jimmy's face twists with rage, and he grabs Momma by the hair again, pulling her close to him. "You ungrateful bitch!" he hisses. "After everything I've done for you, this is how you repay me?"

Momma is in pain, I can see it on her face, but her voice is so strong. "I never asked for any of this, Jimmy. You forced me into it, and I won't let you ruin my daughter's life too. We're leaving, and there's nothing you can do to stop us! Being a cop doesn't mean you own us."

Uncle Jimmy slaps Momma hard across the face, making her stumble backwards. Tears are streaming down my cheeks now, and all I can feel is fear shaking my whole body.

"I should have known better than to trust a worthless whore like you!" Uncle Jimmy snarls. "You think you can just leave? You aren't going anywhere. You will be here till I say otherwise, and when that happens, that little brat will take your place. I can already see her and that junkie whore's brats are going to make a good team for me, they even call her their Little Darling."

I feel sick to my stomach, my heart is going so fast in my chest as Uncle Jimmy's cruel words echo in my ears. I don't know how someone could be so evil. I don't want to hear any more, I just want to go far away from here.

But I can't leave my Momma. I can't leave her alone with this monster. I need to be strong, just like she's always been for me. I can't let him hurt her anymore.

My body won't move though, and it's getting harder to see through my tears.

I do see when Momma jumps at Uncle Jimmy though and I almost cheer for her being so brave. "Don't you dare fucking touch her."

I wish I understood what they were saying. I wish I could just tell Uncle Jimmy to go away. I just want to cuddle my Momma and make her happy again.

Uncle Jimmy seems surprised by Momma's sudden movement. He shoves her away roughly, and she stumbles backwards, trying to regain her balance. Her eyes lock onto mine for a brief moment, and in that look, I see love and a fierceness like she is a warrior. Momma won't give up, not for herself, and certainly not for me.

Momma reaches for the nearby kitchen counter and grabs a knife. Her hands are shaking, but she holds it out at Uncle Jimmy. "Stay away from us!" she warns, her voice trembling like my body.

But Uncle Jimmy's face twists with rage, and he moves faster than I thought possible. He hits Momma hard across the face again, making her drop the knife, which clatters to the floor. My heart sinks to my stomach, and I wish I could find the strength to run to her and protect her.

"You think you can fight back?" he snarls. His eyes look so evil. "You're nothing without me, you hear? You're just a worthless piece of

trash, and your daughter is no different. You're both mine to do with as I please."

I can't bear to hear the mean words, but I can't block them out of my ears. Momma is trying so hard to protect me, to keep me safe, and all I can do is stand here and watch. I feel so small and weak, like a tiny leaf being tossed around in a storm.

I feel anger, fear, and sadness inside me as I watch my Momma being hurt by this monster. I want to run to her, to stand between her and any harm, but my body still won't cooperate. My voice and my feet are stuck.

Momma tries to stand tall, even though she's in pain, I can see it in her face. She wipes the blood from her lip with the back of her hand, and her eyes meet mine again. It's like she's trying to reassure me, to let me know that she's strong and brave, that she won't let anything happen to us.

Tears blur my vision, but I can still see Momma trying to fight back.

She charges at Uncle Jimmy again, but he steps to the side, and I watch in horror as he raises his hand, clutching something shiny and sharp. The knife in his hand goes into Momma's side, and she gasps in pain. My heart feels like it's being ripped apart as I watch the redness staining her clothes, her hand pressed against where the knife hit, trying to stop the blood.

He does it again and again. I don't want to watch, but I can't look away. I'm curled up on the ground and I don't know how I got there, but all I can see is Momma laying on the ground. And there is blood all over her pretty dress, it's on the floor moving like water. Like when I overflowed the bath, but this is so red.

Uncle Jimmy leans over Momma and grabs her necklace. He pulls it hard until it snaps. I want to scream at him to give it back to her, it's her necklace, not his, but he just leaves the apartment.

He needs to get help. Momma is hurt!

Time stands still as I crawl to her side, my tears falling onto her face. "Momma, Momma, please, get up. We need to go before he comes back. Please get up Momma," I sob, shaking her arm.

She looks at me and all I can see is the love and strength in her eyes, her voice is so soft as she whispers, "I love you, my darling girl. Be brave, be strong, and remember that I will always be with you."

I can't bear to hear her weak voice, and I cling to her hand tightly, feeling so helpless. "Please, Momma! I need you. Please, get up. We have to go," I plead, my voice cracking.

But Momma's arm feels limp and she isn't moving. Her eyes are closing. Why is she going to sleep now? We need to run away.

Please, Momma, wake up.

Chapter 39

Alex

"That's it, breathe with me. In and out." The voice is soft and directly in my ear.

I'm not sure when I started crying, but I can feel the tears on my face and the tremble shaking my body. I can also feel Derek's arms wrapped around me, grounding me as he whispers in my ear. He keeps murmuring to me, but my mind is now focused on the man in front of me.

I remember. I hadn't before now. At some point, after the ambulance and police came to the apartment, I completely blocked it all out and forced myself to forget everything. Including the boys who had been my best friends.

I barely even remembered my own name. The only memory I ever really held onto was her necklace, and even then it was just a concept and not an actual image, and now I knew why.

No one listened to me when I tried to tell them who killed her. They just said that my mother didn't have any siblings called Jimmy. But I knew now, he wasn't her sibling at all.

She worked for him. The 8 year old me hadn't understood what she did for him, but I did. The man that I came to know as James Bennett was nothing but a monster who killed my mother.

He currently has his cold, hard eyes fixed on me and his lips pressing together in a thin line. Tristan has a hand gripping his salt and pepper hair while his knife stays steady at his throat. The extra blood now there is a testament to one or both of them moving while I was lost in the fog of my memories.

His voice is sharp when he finally breaks his silence. "Alexandra? I don't know what lies they are telling you but you need to listen to me right now."

Derek has a knife in his hand and is pointing it straight at James a moment later. "Do. Not. Fucking. Speak. To. Her."

The movement of the knife draws his attention and his eyes narrow on it. "So you're the ones killing my employees?"

I cling tightly to Derek, feeling the weight of the memories crashing over me. My mind is reeling, trying to process the truth I buried deep inside for so long. I finally remember everything – the darkness of my past, the horrors I witnessed, and the man who took my mother away from me.

Tristan's grip tightens on James, and I can see the anger in his eyes. "Your employees?" Tristan scoffs. "They were criminals and monsters, just like you. They hurt innocent people and destroyed innocent lives!"

James is still focused on Derek though. "You had known Mark for years. You killed your own team mate."

I'm almost startled when Derek laughs, but the mention of Mark has a wave of calm washing over me. It's as though I am moving past the memory of the trauma and sliding into the darkness that my men love so much.

Derek moves the knife in his hand from side to side, almost in an imitation of a head shake. "Oh, I would love to claim that one myself, but that wasn't me. That was our Little Darling." He brushes a kiss against my temple and I nudge my head against his to let him know I'm okay.

James narrows his eyes and after a moment I see it dawn on him. “Little Darling? You’re those junkie whore’s brats?”

Tristan snickers, but jerks hard on James’ hair. “I wouldn’t recommend using the term brat, we aren’t exactly fond of it. Unlike our Little Darling, we do remember you calling us that.”

James winces in pain as Tristan tightens his grip on his hair. "You remember too, don't you?" Tristan says, his voice cold and filled with anger. "You remember how you used to use our mother, how you made her do unspeakable things just to survive."

Derek's hand tightens around the knife as he points it at James. "We almost felt lucky you stopped coming around when Alex’s mother died, but you still pushed your drugs, you still let your men use our mother. She didn’t even last another 12 months before we found her dead," he says, his voice steady. "They separated us, sent us to different families, so not only had we lost our soulmate when our Little Darling disappeared, but we lost each other too. But then we found each other again, and we found a purpose – to protect the innocent, to bring death to those who deserve it, and to make sure people like you pay for your crimes."

James sneers, trying to put on a facade of bravado. "You think you're heroes, huh? You're nothing but a couple of deluded vigilantes."

Tristan's grip on James' hair tightens even more, causing him to wince in pain again. "We may be a little psychotic, but we're not deluded," he says, his voice low and dangerous. "We've seen the worst humanity has to offer, and we've made it our mission to make sure those monsters get what they deserve. Just like you will."

James’ eyes find mine again. “Alex, are you really going to let them do this? We have known each other for years. I thought the legal system meant something to you?”

I can't stop the growl that comes out of my mouth and Derek rubs a hand against my skin in response. "I can only assume that it was some weird sense of guilt that kept you from doing anything before now. You're lucky I don't have a knife in my hands or you would already be dead."

Derek chuckles and kisses my temple again before looking back at James and resting his head against mine. "I suppose you do only have yourself to blame for how this all turned out though. If you hadn't turned our mother into a junkie whore we would have been together and started doing much more depraved things from a much younger age. But being separated, we learned to be patient, to watch and collect information and plan our moves."

I let the smile curve my lips, I did reap the benefits of those skills after all. "I really don't want to say thank you for how they learnt to stalk me, or how much I love it. But you did get something right in what you said to my mother. Me and them, we make an amazing team." I slide a hand along Derek's arm and slowly take the knife into my own hand to point it at James.

Derek seems to take that as the assurance he needs to move away from me, walking over to get a dining chair from my unused table and bringing it back to where Tristan is holding James. Tristan pushes him into it and James must realize then what the future holds for him as his eyes widen, and a look of resignation crosses his face. "You won't get away with this."

Tristan laughs at that as Derek starts tying James to the chair by his arms and legs. Judging from the look of pain on James' face, the bindings are tight. "Yes, we will. You even made it so easy for us."

These men and their secret plans. We are definitely going to be having words about letting me in on them in advance.

Derek finishes tying James to the chair and turns to me with a mischievous grin. "There are two names that keep appearing in those files that we haven't allowed you time to explore. Two more people in James' evil little empire that are perfectly placed to take the blame."

Well, it is good to know that they have kept distracting me on purpose. So I really can't blame myself for drawing a blank on what he is talking about. "What do you mean? What two names?"

Tristan chuckles and moves around to stand in front of the chair with James tied to it, his fingers deftly twirling the blade in his hand. James' eyes don't leave the knife. I can't blame him, it is a pretty sight, but somehow I don't think he appreciates it in the same way that I do. "Has it not rang any alarm bells that certain people are a little too close to this investigation when they shouldn't be?" Tristan asks.

Derek comes to stand in front of me, raising a hand to brush against my cheek. "If we didn't need someone to take the blame for all this, I would have killed them myself anyway. Like I said before, Little Darling, no one is ever to touch you or come near you again but us. I would have happily fucked you in their blood like we did with Mark's."

Realization dawns on me. "Decker and Travis."

A wicked smile crosses his lips, as though he's proud of me for putting the pieces together. "Yes, James knew you were his best bet at figuring out who was behind it all, but of course, they wanted to deal with the killers themselves outside of the law. So he sent Decker and Travis to sniff around your investigation in the hopes of not only finding out the culprits, but recruiting you as a side benefit. They planned to seduce it out of you. But none of them could have predicted what was truly going on."

I look back toward James, hatred burning through me. "You used them as pawns in your sick game, just like you used our mothers. You deserve every bit of what's coming to you."

Tristan twirls the knife again, and James gulps audibly. Derek looks back to James, his voice is cold and unforgiving as he continues, "Decker and Travis were nothing more than your lackeys, following your orders, while you hid in the shadows, thinking you were untouchable. Do you still feel untouchable, James?"

I barely see Tristan move but suddenly there is a trickle of blood sliding down one of James' cheeks from a cut just under his eye. James remains silent, no shout or screams to even indicate that he felt it, but I can see the strain on his face.

Tristan leans in closer, his voice low and dangerous. "That's for the life you stole from me. You see, James, we're not just going to kill you and be done with it. No, that would be too easy. We want you to feel every ounce of pain and suffering that you inflicted on us. We want you to understand what it's like to be at the mercy of someone else."

I take a step forward, holding Derek's knife in my hand, my anger now burning like a white-hot flame. "You ruined so many lives, including ours. You didn't even spare a thought for how it would affect us."

James scoffs, and I can see that he has now fully shed the good guy exterior, the evil look in his eyes only reminding me more of the day he took my mother from me. "How exactly was I meant to predict it would make you all crazy."

Derek steps forward, another knife in his hand that he must have hidden somewhere else on him. He moves the blade just as quickly as Tristan and draws another thin line in the skin of his other cheek. "I think we already established that we prefer the term psychotic. That's for the life you stole from me."

I step closer, my heart pounding in my chest, but there's a strange calmness in me now. The darkness that once haunted me is now becoming my strength. Tristan and Derek step back, giving me the space I need to confront James directly. They move to stand beside me, their presence silent but powerful, showing their unwavering support.

I lean in close to James, the anger and pain in me burning. "You took everything from me. My mother, my childhood, and the chance to grow up with my Kings, the other pieces of my soul. It's impossible to inflict enough pain on you in a thousand lifetimes to be enough for what you did."

James almost physically relaxes as my words register, a slight look of relief entering his eyes.

Foolish. He obviously has not been paying enough attention.

"That doesn't mean I'm not going to try."

Chapter 40

Alex

I silently observe James for a moment as I collect my thoughts. Playing with the blade of the knife in my hand, I use the tip of it to carefully clean under one of my nails before pointing it back at him. "So, if creep one and creep two had failed to seduce me, because let's face it, they were going to, what would you have done? Would you have tried to do it yourself?"

Derek growls slightly, but doesn't interfere, letting me take the lead for now. James' eyes bore into mine, but I can no longer see the man that I came to admire anymore, all I can see is the monster he truly is underneath the polished facade of a FBI Agent.

I tilt my head in contemplation, bringing the tip of the knife to my chin as I take a moment to think. "I remember what you said to my mother that night. That she was to keep sucking your cock and letting you fuck her cunt until you said so, and then I was to take her place."

The whole room is still, as though the room itself is holding its breath. The atmosphere in that moment is so tense it becomes stifling. But James still doesn't look like he is ashamed of what he has said or done. I lean forward so that my face is now closer to his, letting the knife fall forward, the tip pressing very slightly into the suit shirt he has on. I look down at it as I trail it down his chest, a slow scrape against the fabric there.

Peeking up at him from under my lashes, I give him a look, almost as though I would have seriously contemplated the thought. As though the very thought doesn't make me sick to my stomach. "I'm sorry that I don't have a Daddy kink, but I am now very fond of the concept of thrusting things inside of others."

I push the knife inside of his abdomen to the hilt and watch his eyes widen and his jaw flex as he clenches it. I sigh to myself, happy to have gotten a reaction, even a small one. The wound won't kill him, it isn't placed to kill, there is nothing of importance there. Well, not that I am aware of anyway. But the red of his blood starts spreading across the material in a pretty color anyway.

Derek steps up to my back, molding himself to my body and bringing his hand over mine on the knife, wrapping the fingers of his other hand against the side of my neck. He brings his face close to mine and I can feel his hot breath against the side of my face. The combination of that and the feel of his hardening cock against my ass has a heat going straight to my pussy. "Do we need another lesson, Little Darling? If you mean it, twist it."

He turns my hand slowly. At the same time, he licks upward along my jaw toward my mouth at the same speed he's turning my hand. I turn my head toward him and let him flick his tongue through my parted lips as I pant slightly. I touch my tongue to his as I continue turning the knife and then his hand trails back up my arm before he pulls away and steps back.

I return my attention to James again to see the hatred and rage on his face from watching us together, and blood pouring in a slow and steady stream from his wound. "Was that your intention, 'Uncle Jimmy'?" my voice is caustic as I ask him the question, pulling the knife out of him. "Did you get hard thinking about using me like you used my mother? Did you imagine thrusting your cock into my cunt as you worded it?"

The knife in my hand gets buried in another part of his abdomen and this time he hisses out a breath as he flinches and jerks slightly from the pain. A new pattern of red blood starts to spread, almost like a liquid material dye.

Tristan chuckles from almost directly behind me, his hand smoothing up the skin of my leg revealed by my nightshirt until his hand is cupping my pussy. "I know I'm hard, and definitely not from thinking about his cock." He removes his hand, but then his hand smacks hard against where it had cupped only a moment before. I moan softly and push backward as my pussy throbs, but my eyes remain fixed on James.

"I suppose we could end you right here, right now, they do have me feeling all sorts of impatient now," I say to James, my voice steady and cold. "You'd prefer a quick death, right? But what was that other thing you said that night? That's not how this works."

Pulling the knife back out, I then slowly push it back into him just below one of his shoulders, stopping and shifting when it hits bone. He grunts, his whole face twisting in pain as the knife continues to scrape against the bone as it slides past and deeper into him.

"Hmmm, what information do we need from you?" I glance back toward Derek in question and see the hot look in his eyes as he watches me. "Do you need me to get anything from him while I have my fun?"

The low rumbling chuckle from Derek just turns me on even more. "No, Little Darling. We have everything we need about his whole organization. The wheels are already in motion to tear it all apart. We just wanted you to be able to have your moment and get your revenge."

My heart gives a squeeze at his words. They may be psychos, but they are my psychos. They did everything for me and I love them for it.

Turning my attention back to the man tied to the chair in front of me, James tries to speak. All that comes out is a strained groan as the pain from the knife intensifies when I turn the knife again and pull it out slowly. More blood pours from the new wound.

"No, you don't get to talk anymore," I say, cutting him off. "You had your chance, you had years of chances, but you chose evil instead."

I move the knife downward, until I reach his stomach and then start pushing the knife in again, this time slowly twisting it like a corkscrew as it enters his flesh. He groans through a tightly clenched jaw.

“I’m getting impatient too, Little Darling. End it or I’ll fuck you while he’s still watching and bleeding out,” Derek growls from behind me.

I laugh in response, but he smacks a hand against my ass cheek and the movement just pushes the knife deeper into James’ stomach. James cries out from the pain this time. The pleasure just has my whole body throbbing.

James is looking at me as though I’m something from one of his nightmares. “Were you always this twisted? Who are you?” he manages to slur out. Okay so that last one may have been a bit too deep, obviously my play time is up.

I reluctantly pull the knife back out, watching the blood start pumping out of the new wound. “If you asked me that a week ago I would have said I don’t know. But now I do. I’m their Little Darling. Their goddamn Queen.”

With that, I bury the knife in the center of his chest and twist it and then yanking it out. His shirt is now completely red with blood. If it wasn't for the gaping holes in the material, it may have looked like it was bought in that color. James' head lolls forward and his breathing takes on a shallow wet gurgling sound.

Oops, must have hit a lung.

A hand grips my hair and jerks me upright, twisting me around until I'm looking directly into Tristan's burning green eyes. "Enough, I need to bury my cock inside your pretty pussy, Little Darling." His other hand grips my throat and pulls my mouth to his.

The kiss is impatient and aggressive, full of lips and teeth and tongue. I moan into it, heat pulsing through me.

My hands grab at his shirt trying to tear it from his body, but my hand is still gripping the knife in my hand. I use the knife to cut down the center of the shirt. Tristan doesn't have the same issue, the ripping sound barely registers in my ears before the cool air is against my bare breasts.

Derek presses his already naked body against my back, his hand through my hair and wrapping it around his hand. At the same time Tristan drops to his knees in front of me, his mouth closing over a nipple as his hand squeezes my other breast.

My heart is racing and the adrenaline is pumping through me. Derek wrenches my head to the side as his teeth nip and bite at my neck, moving progressively toward my jaw.

Tristan bites into the flesh of my breast hard enough to bruise, and I gasp loudly. Derek takes advantage, thrusting his tongue into my open mouth, tugging my head back further by my hair. Pain and pleasure swirls through me and collides together, trying to overwhelm my senses.

There's another flash of pain as my underwear is ripped from my body before fingers are being thrust inside my pussy. I don't even know whose fingers are inside of me, all I know is they feel so good as they push in and out, while another is pressed against my clit.

I moan and whimper against Derek's mouth. They already have me racing toward an orgasm, my pussy tightening around the fingers inside me before they curl and hit that perfect spot. My orgasm crashes over me, my body trembling as Derek swallows my cries with his lips and tongue.

Tristan releases my breasts and I feel his tongue lick over the tender flesh of his bite mark, the slight sting telling me he broke the skin with his teeth. The fingers leave my pussy and Derek releases my head in time for me to see Tristan licking his fingers clean. The sight makes me burn hotter for them.

Tristan drops further back on the ground, pulling me with him by my hand. "Ride my face, Little Darling. I want to worship my Queen on my back, drown me with your cum."

Derek releases me and I obey, kneeling on either side of Tristan's head and lowering myself to him. He grows impatient again and wraps his hands around my thighs, pulling me down onto his face. The first swipe of his tongue has a loud moan escaping me.

Then Tristan starts to devour my pussy with an enthusiasm that has me shaking and moaning. I roll my hips in a rhythm that has another orgasm building.

I barely notice Derek until he is standing beside me, his hard cock moving through his hand as he brings it to my face. I open my mouth eagerly for him, groaning at the taste of him heavy on my tongue, as he pushes straight to the back of my throat.

He grabs a fistful of my hair as he holds me down on his cock and I gag around him, the flexing of my throat letting him push even further down. "That's it, Little Darling, choke on my cock."

Pulling back, he starts thrusting hard into my mouth, pushing into my throat each time. Very quickly the only sounds echoing around the room are our moans, my whimpers and the wet sounds of me sucking Derek's cock as I grind down on Tristan's face.

The second orgasm hits me quickly, my whole body convulsing as the pleasure washes through me. Derek groans, and I feel the pulse of his cock seconds before the taste of his cum slides down my throat.

I scrape my teeth against him as he pulls himself from my mouth and he growls at me. I smirk in response.

My world tilts suddenly and then I'm looking up at a grinning Tristan as he drags my legs up before thrusting his cock hard into my pussy. My back arches off the floor as a stunning combination of pleasure and pain hits me. The feeling of Tristan's piercings scraping the sensitive walls of my pussy adding to the whirlwind inside of me.

My hands move across the ground beneath me trying to find something to hang on to, but my arms just slide through the wetness. Looking at my arms as I hold them up, all I can see is blood and I can't bring myself to feel any sympathy or remorse.

He pulls back and thrusts hard again, his hips slapping against mine painfully. "You feel so fucking good, Little Darling." He thrusts again and sets a rough, hard rhythm.

Tristan's hand wraps around my throat and my pussy tightens around him in response, dragging another groan from him. He suddenly rolls us so that I'm back on top, I rock my hips, the feeling of his cock moving inside of me has me clenching and a desperate moan escaping me.

Tristan stills my movements with a grip on my hip while he uses the grip of his other hand on my throat to drag my lips back down and onto his. We both moan into the kiss, but it turns into a whimper as a finger circles my ass before pushing slowly into it.

Tristan keeps shifting his hips as the finger moves in and out of me, then another finger pushes in. "Please," I whimper, the sensations overwhelming my body until all I can feel is pleasure.

"Please what, Little Darling? Are you going to let me fuck your ass while my brother fucks that pretty little pussy?" Derek growls in my ear before adding another finger and scissoring them, stretching me deliciously.

"Yes, Please." I've never agreed to do anything so fast. My hips are rocking onto Tristan's cock and then back onto Derek's fingers as the sounds tumble from me.

The fingers disappear and Derek's hand firmly presses to my back to push me further against Tristan's chest. The fingers around my throat tighten as Tristan pulls my lips back to his, licking and nipping at them.

Derek starts pushing inside of me and my body is drowning in the sensations. The pain of him stretching my ass to the limits while Tristan's cock stretches my pussy has my body shaking between them.

The time seems to stretch as he pushes his pierced cock deeper until he is completely buried. Derek groans as he pauses for a moment. "You're so fucking tight."

He drags his cock back before thrusting in again, and I cry out. The pain is starting to give way to the pleasure as he repeats the movement. All the while Tristan stays still to allow me time to adjust.

He must see something in my face or Derek must give him a signal because he starts to move, slowly and in contrast to the movement of the other cock inside me.

"Hold on tight, Little Darling, we're going to fuck you until you scream our names again."

I barely have time to even think about that statement before they are setting a savage pace. It all feels too much. Too much pain, too much pleasure.

It is a growing storm inside of me as they thrust their cocks into me, one pulling out as the other pushes in. The slap of skin against skin, the wet slide of our bodies, the groans are a secondary soundtrack to the cries spilling from my mouth.

My whole body feels like it's on fire. I don't ever want them to stop. I want them to tear me apart, shatter me into dust and then put me back together.

And that's exactly what it feels like they are doing. Their grips feel bruising on my skin as they dig their fingers into me.

It doesn't take long for them to get what they want, my screams echoing around the house as they fuck me hard. Their cocks are rubbing and stretching me and hitting all the right spots so that I dangle off the edge of a powerful orgasm.

Tristan slides his hand between us and his fingers find my clit and twist. I shatter on a scream. Ecstasy rushing in to overwhelm all of my senses until I feel like I've become detached from my reality.

I must have passed out because when reality returns to me we are all lying, panting hard, on the floor of the living room in the pool of blood.

My attention takes a weird turn as I lift my head and look around. "This is going to be impossible to clean up, I'm definitely going to lose my deposit," I pant out as I try to regulate my breathing.

They chuckle and Derek sits up to look down at me. "You'll be fine, not like you aren't already fucking the owners."

I let my head fall back against the floor with a groan. I really should have seen that coming.

Chapter 41

Alex

Derek and Tristan are taking the body away. According to them they have everything all planned out. They just want me to relax and get some sleep.

I vent my frustrations for a good ten minutes before Derek threatens to knock me out again just to make me go to sleep. So in the end, I do as I am told and go to bed. Sleep pulls me under before they even leave the house.

I never feel them return, nor do I feel them cuddle up to me in bed. As the morning light peeks through the curtains, I find myself sandwiched between Derek and Tristan in bed. They hold me close, and I can feel the beat of their hearts against my back and chest. It is a feeling of safety and love that I haven't felt since I was a child, and I never wanted to let go.

"Good morning, Little Darling," Derek says with a smile, his eyes slowly opening before brushing his lips against my forehead.

"Morning," Tristan mumbles also as he brushes a kiss against the sensitive spot just behind my ear.

"Mmm, good morning," I reply, feeling a rush of affection for them both. I snuggle closer, basking in their warmth.

"We will need to get up soon," I say reluctantly. "For James. There's bound to be a crime scene they will want us to investigate."

Derek shakes his head, his expression serious. "They won't call us in for his murder. It would be a conflict of interest since he was our Agent in Charge, they'll assign another team to handle it."

I feel a twinge of worry creeping into my mind at Derek's words. "But what about Decker and Travis?" I ask, concerned. "They were working with James. We don't want them to be called in to investigate."

Tristan tightens his arms around me. "Don't worry, Little Darling. We made sure the call wouldn't go to them. We took extra precautions to keep them out of this investigation. At least from an agent standpoint."

I start to ask more questions but Derek takes a hold of my chin, focusing my attention on him. "Hey, we just need to go about our day like any other day. We will head into the office and you will have that meeting you need to have with a certain tech genius that Tristan works with," he says calmly. "Don't stress… it's not good for the baby."

I roll my eyes and playfully push at his chest to move him away from me. "We don't even know if your crazy plan worked. Chances are pretty slim, so there may not even be any baby. Which means I can then have my coffee the way I like it."

Tristan chuckles, his fingers gently stroking my hair. "There will be. But we still want you to take care of yourself, whether there's a baby or not. I went ahead and got you some vitamins, just in case," he said, a hint of mischief in his tone.

I turn to look at him with a frown, not sure if I should feel annoyed or touched by his gesture. "You got me vitamins?"

He nods, a cheeky smile spreading across his face. "Yeah, I figured it wouldn't hurt to be prepared. They're in your bathroom cupboard."

Derek leans in, planting a soft kiss on my lips. "And I'll make sure you have your coffee just the way you like it," he says, his voice soft.

I sigh in mock exasperation, unable to resist their thoughtful gestures. "Fine, I'll take the vitamins and let you pamper me a little," I say, giving in with a smile. "But only because you're both stubborn stalkerish psychos."

Tristan grins, planting another kiss on my forehead. "That's our Little Darling, always putting up a fight," he says, his eyes twinkling with affection.

We get up and prepare for the day, Derek and I heading to the office together. As we drive, we make a stop at my favorite drive-through for coffee and a bagel. Derek knows exactly how I like my coffee and made sure it was perfect before handing it to me with a smile.

Entering the office, I find Max already there leaning against the table with the pile of paper evidence and digital copies that he prepared for me. He greets me with a grin, reminding me that he is already aware of our secrets. Derek stands nearby, watchful as ever. Max hands me the evidence, and I give him a grateful smile, knowing that he has gone above and beyond.

"I hope this helps," Max says, a hint of mischief in his eyes. "And remember, if you need anything else, you know where to find me."

"Thanks, Max," I reply, trying to suppress a smile.

Derek clears his throat, giving Max a stern look. "We appreciate your help, but let's keep this professional, shall we?" he says, subtly reminding Max of the need for discretion.

Max chuckles, raising his hands in mock surrender. "Of course, Agent Matthews. All business," he says with a wink before turning to leave.

As I start to look at the information that Max left, I find a lot of it is what I had already seen, but with the corresponding paper trail and evidence of it being manipulated by Mark.

Derek steps up beside me to look down at the information. “You will find that everything is there, plus some extra carefully created items that all lead to Decker and Travis.”

It isn’t long after that when news reaches us that they found James’ body and assigned it to a different team. The most surprising piece of information is that there is evidence left at this scene while before there had been none.

With our Agent in Charge being brutally murdered by the same murderers we were chasing, the whole case is handed over to the new team that has been called in for James. Including all of the new evidence and paper trails that lead to Decker and Travis below the initial layers of corruption.

Derek assures me that the physical evidence found with James will also lead to Decker and Travis.

For handsome damaged psychos, they sure are organized.

Barely any time passes before we are watching from the sidelines as Decker and Travis are arrested. I have a smile on my face as their eyes meet mine while they are led past.

The look of pure hatred when they look at me might have scared most people. I just smile wider, giving them a little finger wave.

As Decker and Travis are taken away, Derek stands by my side and I know Tristan is watching from the shadows, their presence providing comfort and strength. It is a bittersweet victory, knowing that justice was served to who truly deserved it but also acknowledging the dark path that led us here.

I request to be permanently reassigned to this field office, and Derek and I move to a new team together, which according to Max is completely corruption free.

It doesn't come as a surprise either when Derek and Tristan talk me into moving in with them either. They have a large older Victorian style home near the abandoned warehouse they love to use. But it also backs onto a very familiar looking forest.

Emily and Michael are reassigned to a different team as well, but Emily and I soon become close friends outside of the office. Michael finally stops wanting everything to stay a secret, and they take their relationship public. Though, apparently, I am the only one who has been too caught up in other things and didn't already know.

Amidst the chaos of everything, I can't help but notice the changes in my body. The pregnancy symptoms had become more apparent, and soon, it is time to find out if Tristan's sneakiness has paid off. Because I know it was him, it screams his brand of craziness.

Nervousness buzzing inside of me, I take the pregnancy test Tristan secretly got for me and left in the bathroom. Derek and Tristan stand by my side the whole wait, while my heart pounds in my chest.

Moments later, the test shows the two pink lines, confirming their crazy plans worked. I am indeed pregnant.

"We did it! Told you there would be a baby," Tristan exclaims, a grin taking over most of his face.

Derek pulls me into a tight embrace. "We're going to be parents," he says, "you're going to have our Prince. I'm never letting you leave my side again."

Clearly someone still isn't over everything.

A mixture of emotions wash over me, and I can't help but feel overwhelmed. "I'm going to be a momma," I say, my voice trembling.

Tristan kisses my forehead, his touch gentle and reassuring. "And we're going to be with you every tiny step of the way," he says softly. “Every second of every day we will be there.”

Yeah, that sounds exactly like the crazy psychos I’ve come to love.

Epilogue

2 Years Later

"Fancy a game of Truth or Dare?"

Looking over my shoulder I grin at Derek as he slides his hands around my waist and gives me a soft kiss. Then I return my attention back in the direction of the forest behind our home.

Well, more specifically the playset that is set up on the grass in front of it, where Tristan is sitting, his face lit up as he makes weird noises at our twin daughters. If I thought that they would be disappointed to not get the prince they originally wanted, I was severely mistaken. Those two beautiful little girls have both of them wrapped around their little tiny fingers.

Hydessa and Seanna Darling made their entry into the world in such an over the top, dramatic fashion that seemed fitting for us. My body started shutting down from blood loss and my heart stopped in the delivery room. When I woke up the following day, I was told all about how both Derek and Tristan threatened several of the hospital staff with a violent death if I didn't survive.

They all passed it off as an emotional response that wouldn't have happened… but I know differently. In the end, we all recovered and we were discharged to go home and we were glad to part ways with the hospital staff. However, it did end up making them that much more obsessive about mine and the girl's health.

"Hmmm, I want to choose Dare, but I'm not sure I'm up for another run in that forest at the moment," I reply to him, laughter creeping into my voice.

He chuckles and kisses my temple. "Truth then, are you happy?"

My smile gets wider at the question. He is always asking me that, always so conscious of making sure he does everything he can to make sure I am happy. "Nothing could make me happier."

He hums for a moment, the vibration of the noise moving through his chest and into me. "I'm sure I could make you happier."

Laughing, I turn in his arms, forcing myself to move my attention completely to him instead of Tristan and our girls. "We are not having sex right now, it's the start of red week."

He pulls me closer and presses my back against the railing behind me. "I think we have already well and truly established blood turns me on and not off. If you really didn't want sex, you are going about it the wrong way."

I laugh even louder at him and smack a hand against his back. "I mean I'm feeling off right now, you know how I get at the start."

He reluctantly nods and gives me a soft kiss. "I know, but that wasn't actually what I was meaning before. That team we had Max looking into, he came back with the information."

I grin in excitement. "And?"

A slow smile spreads across his face. "And you were right... there is definitely something there. They haven't been as discrete or as good at covering their tracks as we were, but I'm sure they can be trained."

I want to jump up and down with excitement. Over the past two years, since we took care of James, we have expanded our focus to the more wide reaching corruption and evil both inside and outside of law enforcement. We have gradually been adding people to our own organization that sought true justice and protection for the innocent by any means necessary. I had recently come across the work of a team of 'vigilantes' as they were called in the official reports and had my suspicions about who they were, so I had Max look into it.

I suppress my excitement for the moment, knowing that there is still a bit of work to do in recruiting them. "I will get Emily and Michael to start testing the waters."

We recruited Emily and Michael after a year of being friends with them. They were already enlightened to some of the information on the circumstances around Mark and James from the case against Decker and Travis. When we explained the history and how it had all actually gone down, Emily stated quite loudly and vehemently to us that she wished she had been there for both of the deaths to get her own knife into them.

She became my best friend at that moment and they both started helping us expand our organization.

I give Derek another quick kiss before asking him, "Truth or Dare?"

His smile gets wider, "Truth."

I glance back behind me, "Do you think the girls will eventually want to kill you both for naming them after another game?"

He flashes me a wicked grin as we both turn our attention back to Tristan and the girls. "I mean, who doesn't like a game of Hide and Seek."

Author's Note

I hope that you enjoyed hunt me darling!

As usual, thank you to my husband and my mum for always supporting me and putting up with my random obsessive personality that gets me totally lost in my writing etc. My husband was amazing during the writing of this book when I needed answers to questions that would otherwise have the federal police knocking on my door… And whoever monitors my searches for those he couldn't answer… I'm so so sorry, really I'm a totally normal person, I don't have any plans to strangle or kill anyone.

I want to also say a huge massive thanks my 'secret society' (Amanda, Danielle, Ellie, Kayla & Jenny) for being my own personal cheerleaders and Alpha readers. I'm so happy and thankful to have you as my friends and constant supporters.

To my amazing Beta readers Anaceli, Lauren and Chelsi (my unofficial editor), you are amazing, thank you so much for helping me!

Thank you to my ARC team, for helping a mostly unknown author.

And lastly thank you to you, my readers, for picking up this book and taking a chance on a me out of all the amazing authors out there, I completely appreciate it and you.

xx

Maree Rose

About the Author

Maree is a baby author who although she has been writing most of her life, never thought she would ever get something published, which is now why she published this herself. She has always been an avid reader since a young age after roaming through book exchanges with her mum when she was just starting to read serious big girl books.

Maree lives on the East Coast of Australia with her wonderful husband, her son and her two gorgeous squishy british bulldogs.

When she is not writing she is working in a financial career (for something completely different to the creative side) or she is working on her photography (which is just as hot as her books).

Stalk Me

Please feel free to stalk me.

Like metaphorically, not literally of course!

Facebook:

Follow My Page

Join My Readers Group

Make sure you join my Reader Group for bonus scenes and extra content!

Amazon:

Follow My Author Page

Goodreads:

Follow My Profile

Made in the USA
Monee, IL
13 March 2024

55023232R00193